ROGU

By John

BRAVESHIP BOOKS

Table of Contents

CHAPTER 1

The commando lieutenant colonel entered the penthouse suite and caught his senior sergeant snacking on caviar and truffles. He pointed at the extravagant spread. "What's this?"

The sergeant powered through chews like an angry bulldog and swallowed. "I'm having something nice before risking my life."

"You're too crude to appreciate the finer things."

"You may have a point. I'd prefer a hamburger, to be honest, but I figure that rich people order the expensive stuff for room service."

"And the steward didn't notice your ugly face drooling when he brought the food?"

"I left instructions to enter our room while it was empty, and then I hid in the bathroom."

"You were giggling like a little girl, I'm sure."

The bulldog sergeant shrugged. "Not too loudly, since I didn't get caught."

"It was an unnecessary risk."

"It's part of our cover. People who rent rooms like this need to splurge to avoid attracting attention."

The colonel clenched his jaw. "Fine. I disagree, but let's not argue it. I don't care how much you spend, but watch what you eat. You're in the water in an hour."

As the sergeant bit off another mouthful, the colonel walked towards the window. His Louis Vuitton loafers sank into the Berber carpet as he grabbed binoculars from his partner and draped them around the collar of his Tom Ford blazer.

At the frame's edge, he leaned forward, pushed the curtain aside, and beheld Muscat, Oman's evening shoreline. His eyes found the whitewash of gentle beaching waves and then tracked the water southeast into the darkness of the Gulf of Oman.

A lone party craft approached the city pier, casting the luminescence of its leisure deck over the wake it drew pointing towards the anchored deep-draft vessels. Farther out, he saw dual white navigation lights stacked atop ships that swung in their prescribed circles while tethered to the seafloor.

When he spied his target, he held his breath, lifted the optics from his chest, and studied the magnified vessel.

The sergeant verbalized the view of their victim. "You should see up to four guards, two on each side of the ship."

The colonel exhaled and accepted the gravity of watching men he would kill. "You said there were six."

"Two are over the side."

The colonel lifted the binoculars' neck strap over his head and then handed it to the sergeant. Letting the curtain slide closed, he leaned back. "You're certain?"

"I saw them enter after their shift change. Rebreathers, fins, underwater rifles. They look professional like you predicted, but we can handle them."

"How's the target's position holding?"

The sergeant turned and stooped over a coffee table that a laminated chart covered. He grabbed a grease pencil and darkened an existing dot. "Its anchor landed here, about two hundred yards northeast of the center of the circle. It's holding with its chain pointing west by northwest, and its position will hold as we approach."

"Good. Everything's ready."

The sergeant stared at him during a disquieting silence.

"You're looking at me strangely. What's wrong?"

"I'm impressed with how nicely you clean up."

While the sergeant stuffed a huge caviar-covered cracker into his face and chewed, the colonel studied his partner.

Though wearing a tailored Prada sports jacket and Ferragamo slacks, the elder warrior resembled a muscular, compact canine. His barrel chest tugged the fine threads in unintended directions, and his bulging thighs strained and lifted his pants.

"I can't return the compliment. You're built too much like a bulldog for those overpriced clothes."

The bulldog jammed truffles into his mouth and mumbled a muffled response. "I prefer combat gear anyway."

"That's it then. The point of no return. I'm making the call." The colonel lifted a global satellite phone from his blazer and called his liaison. He heard a hint of sadness in the remote voice.

"Hello."

The colonel pressed the phone against his cheek. "All is ready, my distant friend. It's happening."

"So many years you've been preparing for this day, and it comes so quickly. You're sure you want to go through with this?"

The colonel strangled his rising doubts. "I couldn't live with myself if I turned back."

"This may be the last time we'll talk."

"You're probably right, but you never know what the future holds."

"Right. A man of your skill. You might somehow..."

Grateful for the friendly stranger's support, the colonel expected to survive his mission, but survival meant beginning his life anew. "Don't dwell on it. I can't thank you enough. This wouldn't be possible without you."

"It's the least I could do after all the selfless service you've provided."

"Good bye, my distant friend."

"Good bye and good luck. I'll be watching and rooting for you."

After he hung up, the bulldog mocked him between chews of foie gras. "That was touching."

"Shut up. Swallow that and let's go."

A rapid elevator descent brought the duo to the lobby, and the colonel marched behind his squatty companion. After passing from the hotel's dry interior into the sultry evening air, he leaned into the sergeant's ear as the bulldog handed a card to a valet. "What vehicle did you rent?"

"A Range Rover."

Minutes later, the colonel saw a silver supercharged model arrive and stop at the curb. "I see that you spared no expense."

"I thought you'd be impressed. It also has the five-liter engine, in case performance becomes an issue."

The colonel scoffed. "It won't. But good thinking anyway."

The valet sprang from the driver's door and extended the keys towards the sergeant, who queried his leader. "Do you want to drive?"

"No, I want to think."

"I prefer to use my instincts. Thinking is exhausting."

The colonel stepped around the grill, reached the SUV's far side, and climbed into the passenger seat. "I also prefer that you work on instincts. They'll serve you well. But I can't afford the luxury." Thoughts consumed him as his bulldog sergeant took the Range Rover southerly towards the Almouj Marina.

He questioned a mission for which a rapid window of opportunity had precluded extensive preparations for the logistics of the raid. He questioned the resolve of the technical men who lacked combat experience. He questioned his own sanity in leading an improbable mission.

At the entrance to the marine port, the automobile swung left and opened a view to the basin. The colonel gazed upon upscale boats. "Which one is it?"

"The fifth vessel on the right."

The forty-eight-foot Fairline Targa oozed extravagance, but it blended into the marina's moored masses like a single pearl on a long necklace.

The Range Rover stopped, and the colonel walked onto the dock. His heels hit hard wood and echoed on the water. As his yacht came into view, it appeared flawless in its design for performance and luxury. "It's beautiful. I trust you rented it."

"Yes, it's a rental."

"I'd hate to waste the money of a purchase."

Aboard the vessel, the colonel found the environs quiet.

"Everyone's below?"

"Yes. It's comfortable enough for them, including space for their equipment. I didn't want them to feel cramped while waiting. The upgrade for the larger size vessel was worth it."

"Good decision. Make sure they're ready."

As the bulldog ducked into the cabin, the colonel recalled the skills of his sixteen-man team—nine warriors, including himself, and seven technical experts. He wanted more combatants for stealing the ship and more technicians for operating it, but he accepted the limits of his funding and the circle of men he could trust.

And when he'd reflected upon the final numbers during moments of brutal honesty, he'd admitted the perfection of his staff's size. Anything larger would have implied a need for contingencies, which the speed and decisiveness of his strike would preclude.

The sergeant's heavy steps thudded on the fantail. "They're ready, sir."

"The keys are in the ignition?"

"Yes, sir."

"Take in the lines and head below to suit up."

Alone on the weather deck, the colonel nudged the throttle into reverse and backed he yacht from its mooring. A few gentle rudder and engine movements placed the vessel in the marina's exit channel.

He turned northeast and accelerated to the channel's permissible limit. Turning, he saw Muscat's graceful nighttime skyline, including his former vantage atop the hotel, which a backdrop of mountains humbled.

With satellite navigation guidance, he ignored landmarks and focused on his electronic display. The icon of the target's anchor awaited him seven miles away. Angling the yacht out of the channel, he shoved the throttle forward until the speed gauge indicated fourteen knots. The gulf became choppy, and he steeled his grip on the boat's wheel.

The bulldog's voice overcame the wind. "How's it going, sir?"

The colonel glanced behind him at a wetsuit's hood poking from the cabin's door. Wind whipping his cheeks, he screamed over his shoulder. "I want you in the water in twenty minutes."

The bulldog sergeant nodded and disappeared.

His heart racing with anticipation, the colonel pushed the vessel toward the target. A white mast light signaled its forward orientation, and its silhouette began to form.

With his yacht's lights illuminated to prevent suspicion, he knew the sentries saw him. He kept his radio silent and drove.

Two miles from the target, beacons of white light shot from the target, and the colonel turned to see his sergeant awaiting his order. "Get over the side!"

Like bullets, seven dark figures shot from the cabin and hurled themselves over the yacht's far flank. The eighth fighter, the sergeant, hesitated until the colonel locked eyes with him. In a moment of understanding, the bulldog offered a thumbs-up before jumping overboard.

To appease the sentries and keep pace with his submerged swimmers, the colonel slowed the boat to a crawl. As the sentries' forms became visible, one barked commands and waved him away.

The colonel kept his craft pointed at his target.

As a sentry raised a rifle, the colonel started his charade.

From the adjacent seat, he grabbed a bottle of premium vodka that he'd emptied and refilled with water. He waved it over his head and screamed a feigned crazed yelp while turning the vessel's broadside to his audience.

Keeping his distance, he turned away while reversing course to reveal the yacht's other side. He cut in front of his target to see the sentries on both sides. Feeling like an idiot, he continued his performance as a drunken buffoon, guzzling from the bottle and then spitting water into the wind.

He glanced at his phone hoping for readiness messages from his swimmers, who he expected had separated into two groups. The first team had broken the water's surface and had sent him a note, but he awaited communication from the second.

He steered away again for another broadside pass, and the sentries appeared irked but tolerating of the yacht-driving fool. The tardiness of his second team's signal undermined his theatrical performance, and he remained muted during his third run.

Twisting the wheel away again for a fourth broadside pass, he cursed the inactive phone. "Damn it. Where are you?"

With his first team expecting an order, he lifted his phone and dictated a text message for them to hold while he awaited his second team's report. Then he verified and sent the message.

Realizing his charade had stalled, he turned, stopped the yacht, and sat in silence. Deciding his unanimated presence presented adequate distraction to the topside guards, he waited.

And he waited.

Five minutes later, his receipt of the second team's report calmed him, and he dictated a request for verification, asking both teams to confirm their readiness.

They did, and he dictated his final text–a single word ordering them to 'shoot'.

With his finger over his phone's 'send' button, he nudged the throttle. As the yacht accelerated, he turned to the sentries and howled. When they looked to him, he lowered his finger and held his breath.

Silenced subsonic rounds ripped through the sentries, and their silhouettes collapsed.

Killing the guards allowed boarding, but it also started a race against a clock. Whether his victims had raised an alarm or not, the ship's owner would react.

The colonel turned the yacht towards the target to board it.

Wanting his swimmers to scout ahead before sending his technicians, he willed them forward. As if fate heard his quiet prayer, four forms climbed one side of the vessel, and two forms mounted the other.

Questioning the numerical disparity, he noticed a clue. A rebreather appeared on the water's surface atop the protruding hump of a motionless body, and he tallied a rising death toll.

He stamped his heel on the floor three times to signal the

team below, and a technician's head emerged from the cabin. "Is it safe?"

"Yes. Get ready to throw the lines over."

Recognizing the squat shape of his sergeant on the target's deck, the colonel aimed the yacht at him. He then veered his vessel alongside the anchored ship and ordered his technician to toss a rope to the waiting warrior.

As the ships became mated, the colonel yelled. "Where are–"

The bulldog interrupted him. "Gone, sir. We lost two guys."

The colonel settled his eyes on the bulldog's body in the weak lighting, and he noticed a foot-long cut down his wetsuit. From his vantage, the bleeding appeared nonfatal. "You've got a gash on your side."

"Oh this? I may have picked up a scratch helping out our guys a bit. I think our guys surprised the sentries, but whatever happened, it happened fast. By the time I could get involved, it was too late to save our men."

"But the swimming sentries are taken care of?"

"Our guys got one. I took care of the other."

"Then this is still a successful insertion, if we can get inside."

The bulldog craned his neck to a nearby swimmer who had removed keys from a deceased sentry and stooped over a hatch. After the swimmer rotated a latch back and forth, withdrew the key, and nodded, the sergeant affirmed the good news. "We'll get in, sir. Should I bring a man over from the other team?"

"No. There's no time. I'll go with you." He backed to the yacht's far end and then broke into a sprint. After accelerating across the deck, he leapt off the edge and reached for the targeted ship. Landing on all fours, he regained his balance and gathered himself to his feet. "Give me your pistol."

The bulldog obeyed.

"Now a concussion grenade."

The sergeant extended the second requested object.

The nonlethal weapon weighed upon the colonel's hand as he walked to the hatch and knelt. "Get ready."

The sergeant squatted behind the hatch, took the key from

the other swimmer, and jammed it into its latch. He twisted it, and a click signaled the unlocking. "I'm ready, sir. How about a countdown?"

"On three. One, two, three!"

The sergeant yanked open the portal, the colonel tossed in the grenade, and the two men slammed the steel circle shut. After the exploding thud, the bulldog opened the hatch, and the colonel jumped into the hole.

His feet smacked the deck, and he stepped forward with his pistol up. In the dim light, he felt isolated until the dense mass of his partner landed behind him. In tense moments of silence, the colonel scanned his surroundings. "We're alone."

"As expected."

"That's the good news."

"What's the bad?"

The colonel lowered his weapon. "Do you think a ship of this value has only six guards?"

"On board? Yeah. We just killed them all."

"It's not those on board who concern me anymore. It's those from beyond. The owner of this ship will come for it."

"I know that, sir. What are you getting at?"

The colonel reflected upon the vessel's owner. "I've studied him. I know him. When I say he'll come for this ship, I mean he'll do so like his life depends upon it. And he'll bring a fury like you can't imagine."

The bulldog guffawed. "You're not scared, are you, sir?"

"If you knew what I know about him, you'd be scared, too. Get the men onboard and to their stations. We need to get out of here. Now."

CHAPTER 2

As Jake Slate swallowed a tasty mouthful of medium-rare filet mignon, he realized he'd chewed the first bite with an open mouth. He scanned the head table's other faces to assure himself nobody had seen him.

While celebrating the recent success of diverting Israel from a war, his mercenary fleet's leadership ignored him during the silent exploration of their main courses. Fatigue and relief consumed his colleagues.

On his right, his French mechanical systems expert, Henri Lanier, sported his usual head of impeccable silver hair. But under the strands of perfection, the skin around the mechanic's eyes sagged.

Next, Jake reviewed Terrance Cahill, former commanding officer of the Australian submarine *Rankin* and present commander of the mercenary fleet's flagship *Goliath*. Though his cheeks flushed with the satisfaction of a deserved feast, the Australian slumped tired shoulders over his planked salmon.

To Cahill's right, Liam Walker, a lean officer who had learned naval surface warfare aboard an *Anzac*-class frigate and served as the *Goliath's* second-in-command, appeared consumed in slow reflection while chewing on shrimp and scallops.

Beside Walker, Dmitry Volkov, former commanding officer of the Russian submarine *Krasnodar* and present commander of the *Wraith* submarine, wiped gravy from his short, graying beard. To the Russian's right, a translator leaned into his ear, uttered an inaudible phrase, and then accepted a cellar of salt from his comrade.

Between the translator and Jake's left arm sat the table's final occupant, French arms dealer and the fleet's patriarch, Pierre

Renard. Though he'd managed the naval combat off the Israeli coast remotely, Jake's leader's recovery from the mission
seemed the slowest.

Renard owned the fleet of two *Scorpène* submarines and the
mammoth submersible combat-transport ship, *Goliath*, exposing him to more than a billion dollars' worth of worry. Worse,
Jake knew his mentor felt responsible for each person's life
within the hundred-man fleet. The burden of profit, mission ac-
complishment, and preservation of life and property was his.

The Frenchman sipped from his imported Rhône Valley Mer-
lot, lowered the glass, and then gazed at it with pensive eyes.
As some unknown spark within him catalyzed his energy, color
rose to his cheeks, and he cleared his throat. "Gentlemen, I propose a toast."

As the table's occupants reached for their glasses and waited,
a moment of understanding revealed to Jake the orchestrated
order governing the seating geometry.

Seeing himself as Renard's first among commanders, he sat by
his patriarch's right. To their leader's left, the newest and rising
hero, Volkov. Farthest from the king sat his diametric opposite,
the one from across the globe who commanded the chameleon
Goliath–a vessel which could labor as a beast of burden or rise to
the pinnacle of the fleet's firepower.

Next to each commander sat his primary confidant, shaping a
perfect arrangement reflecting Renard's worldview. Jake forgot
if the Frenchman had guided the men to their seats or if each
minion had obeyed a subconscious order from their boss' in-
escapable will.

Beyond the dining leaders, sailors from the fleet's three vessels filled tables in the private banquet hall. Encircling the
crews, personnel from a private security group Renard had
formed from former legionnaires and French national veterans
patrolled a perimeter.

The room's murmur fell as the Frenchman stood and cast his
voice towards the far wall. "Forgive me if I wax poetic. And forgive me if I embellish a bit."

Men chuckled in anticipation.

"We navigated the delicacies of our first civil affair flawlessly, and I thank you all for a job well done. I could ask for no better staffing of my ships, and I consider each of you a valuable member of an elite team."

The Frenchman sipped, and a hundred men raised their glasses and drank, but Jake protested. "You already kissed our asses in Port Said."

"Yes, I did. But with the staggering amount of alcohol consumed then, I'd wager that only a dozen men can remember it. I'd like to express myself to this somewhat coherent audience."

"Fine. I'll shut up now."

"Now, lest I become too nostalgic, let me give credit where it's due to someone outside this room. Let me thank a great woman who predicted the former Israeli prime minister's missteps almost as easily as she defeated Terry Cahill's throbbing heart."

As laughs and catcalls billowed, Cahill blushed from the reference to the Israeli military intelligence major whom Jake predicted would become his fiancée. The Australian then shot a glance at the Russian. "Should I say it, Dmitry?"

Despite a lingering language barrier, the Russian displayed his understanding of the inside joke. "*Da!* Say it!"

"Bite me bare hairy arse, Pierre."

"I will not, but I'll drink to the audacity of your request. Enjoy your feast gents!"

As the Frenchman sipped and sat, a room of men returned to their seats.

Addressing the leadership at the head table, Renard continued expressing his gratitude. "Now, where was I? Yes, five weeks ago, we finished a mission in which we sent a formidable navy back into its port and stopped an invading army from begetting unacceptable hostilities. I salute you for a lucrative and noble job."

Jake continued harassing his boss. "Then how come you never give bonuses?"

"The one thing I never hear complaints about is the pay."

"I'm just messing with you."

"But as long as you've broached the subject, I've decided to share a significant percentage of my profit from our Israel campaign with the entire crew, pro-rated proportionally to each man's pay."

"Can you dumb that down please?"

"Bonuses. Can you drink to that?"

Though Jake had given up alcohol, he would drink to it. "Sure. Thanks, Pierre." After a tiny sip as a gesture of camaraderie, Jake lowered his glass and reached for his fork in anticipation of another meaty bite. But then his leader's face turned ashen while reading a text message, and he leaned into the elder Frenchman. "What's wrong?"

"The sentries aboard the *Specter* and *Wraith* have lost contact with the *Goliath's* sentries."

"It could just be a radio problem." Jake felt like an idiot for voicing a foolish hope. He knew better than to allow the luxury of optimism.

"Perhaps. But I'm taking precautions."

"Like what?"

"Weighing anchors, for starters."

Jake's stomach became a pit as he grasped his friend's fear. "Shit. You're getting the submarines underway?"

"All the ships, including the *Goliath*, if I can hail it. Excuse me." The Frenchman stood, turned his back, and walked away with his shoulders hunched over his phone.

To allay suspicion by the table's onlookers, Jake returned his attention to his steak and took several bites. Though the taste was savory, his thoughts remained on his boss.

Moments later, the Frenchman returned and addressed his fleet's leadership with a stern but calm voice. "Gentlemen, the security teams aboard the submarines have lost radio contact with the *Goliath*. I'm assuming the worst. I fear the *Goliath* has been compromised."

The Australian commander sounded mortified. "That's me

ship. How the bloody hell did it become compromised?"

"I'm not sure, but I'm afraid this is what it feels like."

The Frenchman pursed his lips and looked downward.

Cahill shook his head. "Like what feels like?"

"Being the victim. I believe we're under attack."

Jake returned the team's focus to the task. "Are the submarines okay?"

"For the moment, but they need to get underway."

After running the security staffing through his mind, Jake questioned the possibility. "With just six-man commando teams?"

The Frenchman remained confident in his staff's reaction. "They know enough to drive away on the surface. You know the contingency plans. I've briefed you on this. Switch your mind into crisis mode, man, and keep your wits about you. All of you."

Cahill gravitated towards his ship. "What's going on with the *Goliath*?"

Raising his voice, the Frenchman revealed the first blemish in his composure. "Damn it, man, it just happened! I've told you all I know."

"I don't mean to be an arse, but me ship is at risk, and we need to act."

"We will. I called our Omani contact. He's making assets available to us."

The Australian remained agitated. "What assets? Nothing can outrun me ship."

Renard showed coolness under stress. "Helicopters can."

"Right. Sorry. I was losing me head."

"A helicopter will land outside to pick up our initial response team. It can take only ten men."

"You mean us? None of us knows how to properly storm me ship."

"You're not going to the *Goliath*. You're going to the submarines. Four men to each submarine plus you and Liam split between each crew to serve as onboard advisers."

Acceptance seemed to calm the Australian. "Right. Who's with Jake?"

"You are. Liam will go with Dmitry."

Jake found himself lagging in understanding. "Wait. What are we doing?"

"The first order of business is saving the submarines. That's why I'm sending you to them."

Jake nodded as the tactic of manning the submarines landed in his mind as the proper action. "Yeah. Ships are safer at sea."

"Gather your three most important crewmen outside."

Minutes later, Jake huddled with his team in the warm humidity. In the small circle stood his mechanic, Henri, his toad-headed sonar ace, Antoine Remy, his wire-framed engineering expert, Claude LaFontaine, and Cahill.

The group stared at each other in dumbfounded silence until Renard joined them. "That's your ride." The Frenchman pointed at lights that floated over the city's low skyline. "The helicopter will drop off Dmitry's crew first since the *Wraith* is closer. Then you'll be dropped on the *Specter*. The security teams already have your submarines moving to sea."

Jake wanted to avoid sounding ignorant, and he was relieved when the Australian posed the question. "What do we do when we get aboard?"

For the first time Jake could remember, he observed the friend, boss, and mentor he idolized operating beyond the bounds of his planning.

But like a warrior, the Frenchman adapted. "We're reacting. That's all we can do. Get your submarines to sea to keep them safe from whatever force took the *Goliath*, and standby for further orders. The security teams are already taking them toward sea, but each submarine should have its experts aboard. God knows if there are submarines waiting in ambush. God knows what other dangers await, and I want the submarines staffed and ready to run."

Cahill smirked. "For a moment there, I thought you were going to say 'ready to fight'."

The Frenchman raised his voice as the Omani helicopter's blades became audible. "I was thinking it."

"Sink me ship?"

"I consider that an unacceptable loss. But I fear we're likely to be battling someone. Sentries on the submarines can see the *Goliath's* anchor chain being hoisted."

As the somberness of victimhood weighed upon him, Jake likened the experience to a terrorist attack. "They mean business."

But his pain paled against that which he saw in Renard's tight eyes and heard in his melancholy voice. "Indeed. And they're moving with impressive speed through our complex ship. Someone's done their homework."

"But we can stop me ship without destroying it. Crippling ships is our specialty."

Renard waved his palm. "You're getting ahead of yourself. Let's first turn the tide of this disaster before I decide future steps." A warm wind arose as the Lynx touched down on the restaurant's lawn. "Dmitry's crew will be last in, first out. Get the ships rigged for submergence and get them to snorkel depth. I don't know what else is coming, if anything, but it's best if you're ready to hide. Now go!"

Leading his small reaction team, Jake ducked and trotted towards the helicopter. A crew chief extended his hand and helped him climb into the cabin's stale air. Realizing he'd boarded an Arab-speaking nation's war craft, he offered a probing salutation. "Do you speak English?"

The chief shook his head, but a crewman stepped forward. "I do. I handle translations for exercises with English-speaking navies."

As his crew boarded, Jake sat amidst them and slipped on a helmet. While Volkov and his crew stepped into the aircraft, the Omani translator's voice became crisp in speakers by his ears. "I am Chief Petty Officer Dawood. Raise your hand if you can hear me."

Seven out of ten hands rose, and Jake spoke into his boom

microphone. "Three of our team don't speak English. Give our translator a moment please."

Volkov's translator nodded at Jake and repeated the instructions. A second order from the Omani with a subsequent Russian translation assured the strapping in of each passenger. Then the twin engines whined as the Lynx ascended.

Jake's mind went numb as altitude offered him a bird's-eye view of the harbor. With the aircraft beelining towards Volkov's anchored submarine, the helicopter's flight deck obscured his view of the crime scene.

The Omani's voice crackled in Jake's headset. "I will now hand you each your rappel harnesses. Please put them on. You'll be at low altitude when you descend, but you still need to follow the procedure to avoid possible injury."

Jake accepted his harness from the crew chief, contorted himself into it, and then felt it pinching him.

Like a flight attendant, the Omani stood and pantomimed the operation of the harness. "The most important tool is the brake. The crew chief will hook you in one at a time before you rappel." He turned full circle and demonstrated how to slow the descent. "You'll want to squeeze it liberally. It's better to drop slowly and safely than to hurry. This is harder than it looks. We'll be dropping you from approximately three to four meters. Keep the harnesses when you're done. We brought extras."

Minutes later, the cabin dipped and steadied as the helicopter hovered.

"We're above the first submarine." The Omani extended his arm. "Have the first crew form a single line."

Jake watched Volkov's team stand and disappear out the aircraft. The Lynx then climbed and veered towards his ship.

Hovering above his *Specter*, Jake stood first and met the Omani crew chief at the door. Below, his submarine carved solid blackness in the water's reflection of the shimmering moonlight. He noticed a thin wake aside his vessel.

Unsure if he trusted the rope, he leapt. Judging the distance tolerable if he entered freefall, he took the risk, but the harness performed as promised and allowed him a controlled descent.

His shoes hit hard steel, and a lone sentry greeted him with a thick French accent. "I help you."

As the guard freed him of the rope, Jake remembered that Renard staffed his security teams from former French fighters. He responded in the sentry's native language. "We all speak French except one of us. Let's speak French."

"Good. I'm the only one who speaks English."

Jake walked to the open hatch and descended the ladder. As the submarine's interior became his new but familiar universe, he walked to the control room's elevated conning platform.

The mechanic, Henri, joined him, followed by his sonar ace, Antoine Remy. He'd assigned his engineer, Claude LaFontaine, and the Australian to the propulsion spaces.

Henri joined a commando by the ship's control station and examined the status of the *Specter's* hydraulics, pneumatic, water, and air systems. Remy sat at a console of the Subtics tactical system and turned his toad-like head. "It's all turned off. I need a few minutes to warm it up."

Jake gave his first order of the crisis. "Get it up and running so you can start listening. I want you to split your time between listening to the *Goliath* and listening towards the sea for submerged threats."

The toad-head nodded in compliance.

But from his control station, the French mechanic protested. "I'll need at least fifteen minutes to verify we're rigged to submerge. I need to walk the ship."

Jake knew the silver-haired veteran could verify the location of each air, water, and hydraulic valve in half that time. "Get it done in ten. Go!"

The loudspeaker above Jake's head squawked with LaFontaine's voice. "The engine room is ready to answer all bells on the surface."

Jake angled his jaw upward to aim his response at a microphone. "Already?"

"The sentries followed an abridged procedure to warm up the propulsion machinery. Everything's online and running fine at three knots. Terry and a couple of sentries are helping me latch the anchor into its stowed position and prepare the lubrication oil cooling water for high-speed running."

"Very well. Make turns for five knots." Pausing for a moment of reflection, Jake tried to let the shock of a celebration-turned-crisis settle. He placed his hands on a polished rail that circled his conning platform, and he lowered his head between his shoulders.

Turning his toad-head, his sonar ace interrupted him. "What do you think's going on?"

"We're being ambushed. And I think it's someone doing a damned good impersonation of us."

"You'll have to be more specific. We do a lot of things well. We fight, we cripple, we destroy, we steal."

"Good point. I think someone's trying to steal the *Goliath* to do something only the *Goliath* can do."

"So, it's a theft?"

"Why not? It's as good a guess as any. If they wanted to sink the *Goliath*, they'd have done it already. This is something more elaborate."

The tactical system flittered to life in front of the sonar guru, and the toad-head rotated towards a monitor. Remy lifted a headset over his ears, curled forward, and listened. "You're right, Jake."

"About what?"

"About this being a theft."

"How can you tell?"

"I hear the steam ring of one of the *Goliath's* MESMA systems. It's up and running."

"Shit. That means our thieves have a MESMA technician, and they intend to operate submerged."

"Do you want to tag them with limpets?"

"Yeah, I do."

"Or you could use a slow-kill weapon."

Jake pondered the modified torpedo that used magnetic submunitions to blow holes in a target's hull. He considered the weapon humane, as it had proven effective in giving time for submarines to surface before sinking. "No. Not yet. My second shot will be a slow-kill." Resolved to prevent the flagship's escape, Jake looked to the room's solitary commando. "Do you have Pierre Renard's phone number?"

"Yes."

"Head topside and call him. Tell him we hear a MESMA system running and that I'm going to shoot a limpet torpedo at the *Goliath*. Got it?"

"MESMA system running. Limpet torpedo. Got it."

Jake reached into his pocket for his key to unlock the use of torpedoes, stepped forward to a command console, and slid the metallic teeth into a keyhole. "Antoine, assign tube five to the *Goliath*, and get ready to support my first command decision in this mess."

CHAPTER 3

The colonel hovered behind his engine room expert, who craned his neck and aimed a flashlight through a maze of piping. Since the stocky man knew the *Scorpène*-class equipment that inspired the *Goliath's* design, he found the expert's animation unsettling.

"What's wrong?"

"I can't find the inlet valve to the main cooling water pump."

"What the hell?"

"The gas turbine on this ship isn't an exact three-dimensional replacement of the diesel generator on *Scorpène* submarines. So, many components are moved from their proper place."

"What if you can't find it?"

"Then I can't check if it's open, which means I can't use the cooling water pump. and everything in the engine room that creates heat will eventually overheat and break down."

"How do you know that it's not already open?"

The stocky man paused before answering. "I don't."

"If you can't run the pump, how long until something overheats and breaks?"

"I don't know. It would depend on how fast we're going."

"Five knots."

"That's with just one engine room, though. One propeller. So, it's a strain of more like seven knots."

"Fine. How long, then?"

"Maybe ten, fifteen minutes. But I'm just guessing."

"Get us moving, whether the valve's open or not. If you need to open it, find it while we're running. I won't have us sitting here as cannon fodder due to an accursed valve."

"I'll get on it, sir."

Following the stocky engineer, the colonel walked aft to the oversized electric motor. Sunken into a recess, it wielded a hidden mass that impressed him with its potential power output.

Two combat swimmers stood around the machinery, appearing unsure of their responsibilities, and the colonel attempted to reassure them. "Don't worry, gentlemen. It's an imposing machine, but you understand its basics."

One commando swimmer shrugged. "The basics, sure. If a temperature gauge gets near the red band, I make sure the cooling water valve is open all the way. But other than that, I can only yell for help. We could learn only so much without access to the real machines."

The second commando pointed to a cradled sound-powered phone. "No, you don't yell. You talk into this. Or I talk into this. Whatever it takes."

The colonel exhaled through his nostrils. "I don't care how you do it. But I trust you two are smart enough to raise the alarm before the motor would burn itself into liquid."

Beads glistening on his forehead, the stocky engineer perspired enough for two men. "None of us knows the limits of this motor. It's a custom design. So, we're making this up as we go."

"You'll understand this plant soon. But only if you get it up and running. Take me to the control station."

Waddling, the engineer turned and departed.

The colonel trailed him to the propulsion control panel where sprawling gauges and lights dizzied him. "Do you understand all of this?"

"It's all quite simple in theory. Battery bus voltage, battery discharge current, propulsion motor current, generator voltage for each MESMA plant–"

"I get it. Just get the damned ship moving."

A stubby finger depressed a green button, and pixelized images of dials indicated an electric field forming in the propulsion motor. A fleshy hand then rotated a knob, and colored needles jumped from their leftmost stops as current flowed. "Making turns for one knot."

"Faster."

"I need to watch the systems respond."

"For God's sake, this ship's a battle-tested juggernaut. Push the accursed limits."

Fat fingers advanced the knob, and a whir rose behind the colonel as dials danced, but the stocky man remained silent.

"Well?"

"Making turns for seven knots."

"How is it?"

"It's fine. The MESMA unit's bearing the load at ninety-eight percent capacity, and the battery bus voltage dipped a bit, which is normal. Propulsion temperatures are fine, but they'll rise as friction heat builds up."

"How fast are we moving?"

"Just under five knots, but we'll reach just over five."

"That's all?"

"It's due to drag when we use the rudder to compensate for single-propeller operations."

"So be it. At least we're moving. Get familiar with this plant and be ready to support faster speeds when the other MESMA systems are brought online." The colonel marched forward, and passing through a watertight door brought him into the hiss and humidity of the aftermost starboard MESMA plant.

The oxygen and hydrogen tanks fed fuel into the controlled bomb of a heat exchanger, turning water into steam that rose into a turbine to turn an electric generator. Seeing his lone MESMA system expert, the colonel leaned into his ear. "Where's your apprentice?"

The man pointed. "Over there. I sent him below to check for leaks."

A head appeared through the floor as a frogman climbed a ladder from the lower deck.

The colonel announced his edict to his two-man audience. "Keep this plant operational at all costs. Delay starting the other plants until this one proves it can bear the strain."

Perspiring, the MESMA expert yelled his response over the

steam piping's hiss. "It's holding, but barely. Don't put any more strain on it. Flow rates are at the red line for the fuels and steam."

"I need to check what's going on around us. When I know more, I'll let you bring up another plant."

The ship's impressive length became evident as the colonel hurried forward.

In the silence of the starboard hull's middle MESMA plant, he heard his heels hitting hard deck plates. Eight meters later, he entered another unused air-independent electric plant and kept marching. Then the lengthy crew accommodation compartments tested his patience while he passed the mess deck, the galley, and the sleeping bunks.

Having achieved the control room, he found his team's two undersea warfare brains. Studying the console of the ship's Subtics combat system, his submarine commander leaned over the shoulder of the sonar technician.

The duo became animated as he entered the compartment, and the commander stood, revealing a lean frame the colonel considered tall for an inhabitant of submerged confines. "Colonel?"

"What's going on?"

The submarine commander referred to his colleague, who listened to the sea. "He just heard a torpedo launch. From the *Specter*."

Fear stung the colonel's stomach as Renard's rapid response surprised him. He'd expected the submarines to make defensive moves, but not a torpedo. Not this fast.

He inhaled and reminded himself that Renard's fleet's tactics qualified the risk. "This isn't a complete surprise. The weapon should be non-lethal. They're probably noisemakers."

The lean submarine commander shrugged. "Probably. But our lives depend upon your assessment being correct."

"He won't sink this ship unless he has no other choice. It would ruin everything he's worked for."

"If you're wrong, we're dead."

"You're the expert. Is there anything to be done if I'm indeed wrong?"

The commander aimed his index finger towards an invisible distance. "The port hull's bow is a temporary fix to the damage the proper crew incurred by sacrificing the original bow to a torpedo. I suggest you let me do the same and turn the port bow towards the incoming weapon as a sacrificial limb."

"How would you turn us?"

"With the outboard motors."

"Have you found their controls yet?"

"I think so. The controls for most major systems are set up in a menu directory and are accessible from any linked console. I found the top menu for the outboards."

"Would this slow our escape?"

The commander's face darkened as he frowned. "It would halt it outright since we'd have to turn around and point at the *Specter*."

"Forget it. If the *Specter* or the *Wraith* mean to sink us, they'll sink us. We can't do combat with either of them, much less both of them."

"You want me to stay on course?"

The colonel fell into retrospective thought about his decision to forego neutralizing the submarines. When he'd considered tripling his number of commandos to silence the *Specter* and the *Wraith*, he'd given up recruiting such a large force to the clandestine mission.

Expecting to outrun the submarine crews' responses, he'd planned to escape their retaliation.

Down two men and with two unwanted submarines in pursuit, he relied upon his major advantage–his adversary's refusal to sink his flagship. "Yes. Stay on course and get us to open water."

"I need speed. We just reached five point one knots."

"I have only one MESMA system expert, and I'll get incrementally less speed from each plant I bring up. Dare I risk losing the first plant while bringing up the second?"

"You could light up a gas turbine and get more than twenty knots on just the single propeller."

"But then I wouldn't be ready to submerge. Something airborne will come for us soon, and the best defense will be submerging."

"This ship submerges rapidly as a matter of normal operations with its proper crew."

The colonel considered his words. He needed the submarine commander's loyalty as much as he needed his obedience. "Calling the prior crew the 'proper crew' implies that we're an improper crew."

"But we are improper. We're thinly staffed and illegitimate."

The colonel clenched his jaw and then answered. "True, but use a term that's less... demoralizing."

"I can call them the 'old crew'."

"That's much better. What might the old crew have done to allow rapid submergence with a gas turbine running?"

"With the expected automation of this ship, I would hope it's no more than pressing the right sequence of buttons."

"Do you know the right sequence?"

"Not yet, but I should before it becomes necessary."

The colonel recalled his lessons on submerging a vessel. "If you don't, then we'd submerge with huge air intakes open, which could lead to catastrophic flooding?"

"Yes, at least one intake, since this ship has two. But they should have automated safety shutoffs."

"If they fail?"

"Then we'd take on water and begin sinking, but this ship is large enough to give us time to fight to the surface."

"So be it. We'll take our chances. I'll tell the engine room to bring up the gas turbine. How can I communicate with them without having to make that long walk?"

"I've set up an open microphone circuit. Just yell."

The colonel raised his voice. "Engine room?"

Loudspeakers delivered the stocky engineer's response. "We're here."

"Can you bring up the gas turbine yet?"

"Yes. It's a standard General Electric LM twenty-five-hundred plus design as expected. We've been warming it up in case you needed it."

"Bring it up." Rumbling steel and howling air feeding the engine's hunger confirmed the turbine's fury, but then the sounds died. "What happened?"

The speakers issued a misplaced voice the colonel recognized as belonging to a commando. "It shut down. The geeks are trying to figure it out."

"Go to them and come back with a report."

"I will, sir."

While the colonel awaited his propulsion status, he found his mind wandering to odd concerns. He questioned what food was aboard, if he'd have clean water to drink, and whether the showers used freshwater or saltwater.

The commando's voice brought him back to pressing needs. "It was a ventilation problem. The turbine was trying to suck air from a throttled intake. It should be up soon."

"How soon is that?"

Growling steel gave the colonel is answer. "Never mind. Have them give me their best speed." As vibrations rose from the hull, ticking numbers on a prominent gauge caught his attention. He aimed his voice at the control room's occupants. "Just under twenty-four knots. Is that all?"

The commander frowned. "In this mode of propulsion, yes. One screw and one gas turbine."

"But surely we can generate more speed, even with just one gas turbine available."

"In terms of just power, I would agree. But the limiting factor is the single propeller for delivering that power to the water, and I also have to steer our rudder right five degrees to compensate for the single propeller's tendency to push us to the left. It's creating drag."

"I don't have enough experts to bring up all power sources at once. One engine room is all I get for now, and this is all the speed I have."

"Don't worry. This is fast enough to outrun the submarines, but you have a bigger problem."

The comment returned the colonel's thoughts to an important assumption he'd forgotten–the non-lethality of the incoming torpedo.

Uncertain how raw sounds fed calculations that became renderings of reality, he appreciated the simplified overhead view of the waters around the *Goliath* the Subtics system made available on screens throughout the ship.

On the screen beside his hip, a simple crosshair in the center signified his catamaran, and red icons of submarines and a torpedo represented the nearby dangers. He knew he could press buttons, tap icons, or drag a stylus to conjure answers, but he lacked time to learn the skills.

He looked to his submarine commander. "How soon until we know?"

"With our new speed, about sixty to ninety seconds. It's hard to tell when the geometry's as direct as this. We're essentially target practice for the *Specter*."

"You make it sound hopeless."

"This stands against everything to which I've dedicated my career. I know you believe the torpedo has a harmless warhead, but God help me if you overestimated Renard's love for this ship."

The colonel turned and watched the torpedo slide towards the crosshair. If his intuition of time was accurate, the answer would arrive soon. "God help us all if I'm wrong."

"You're basing your assumptions on snippets from a man's dossier."

The colonel scoffed. "I grow weary of your challenge. Either I'm right, or I'm wrong. If I'm wrong, it won't matter. And it's not snippets in a dossier. I know Renard."

The commander looked to the deck and then met his colonel's stare. "I won't speak of worst cases again, unless there's value in doing so."

"Good. So let's assume I'm right, and we'll continue as planned despite this unexpectedly rapid reaction from the submarines."

Fear consumed the commander's face. "No..."

"What's wrong?"

"I just realized how terrible this could be."

"How so?"

"Renard's arrogant enough to think he can finance and build a replacement vessel. He's arrogant enough to destroy this ship because he sees himself as bigger than its cost."

The concept generated a cloud of fear that pinched the colonel's stomach but then dissipated. "That may be true. But you're overlooking another critical–"

The icon of the torpedo disappeared, and a mini-swarm of magnetic limpets clamped themselves to the hull. The cascading and interlacing thudding echoes brought both terror and hope as the colonel recognized the attachment of benign noisemakers.

When the magnetic trackers began shrieking sonic frequencies, he sighed in relief.

The first counterstrike had arrived, and it had brought no harm. Instead, it portended an extended clash of skills and wills, as he'd predicted. With his confidence swelling, he turned to his submarine commander. "The critical point you're overlooking just revealed itself."

"I still believe he's arrogant enough to think he can lose this ship and acquire a new one."

"You're too kind in your assessment."

"Really?"

"Yes. Because he's more arrogant than that. He's arrogant enough to believe he can outwit us and take the *Goliath* back."

CHAPTER 4

Olivia McDonald leaned back in her chair, dissecting herself with her psychologist's acumen.

With relentless candor, she sliced through her outer protective layer to glimpse her pain, disappointment, and loneliness.

Rape trauma had eviscerated her innocence, leaving a broken girl. Survival demanded the aggressive protective layer she'd crafted during fifteen years at the CIA, and in a male world that provoked her reoccurring nightmares, a pillaging monster provided her best defense.

She hated the monster but understood its necessity. So, she learned to accept her self-generated inner beast, influence it, and tame it.

A decade ago, her first post-trauma assignment had targeted the fugitive Jake Slate, whom she'd ensnared with feigned love. Though she'd slipped into true love, she'd helped stop a nuclear attack through her accidental alliance with the former American naval officer, attracting strong allies within the CIA.

Success begat power and high-profile assignments, such as teaming again with Jake and his mentor, Pierre Renard, to thwart an electromagnetic pulse attack on the United States. Mastery in languages, investigations, military tactics, and psychology had allowed her continued success, and excelling in manipulation, politics, and even seduction had enabled her advancement.

Increasing power had fed a beast that grew hungrier. As she'd recognized Pierre Renard's growing need for her support, her outer animal began to sink its fangs into him.

She'd given him intelligence to capture the Malaysian submarine that had become the *Wraith*. She'd connected him with the Australian Navy, serving up Terrance Cahill as his ace to command the *Goliath*. She'd supplied him with weapons in the Falklands, subsidized his attack on Crimea, and set up regime changes in Greece and Israel for his profitable Mediterranean missions.

As Renard's fleet had grown to three ships, he'd needed more support. More intelligence. More influence on regimes. More capital. She'd supplied it all.

And now, per her reckoning, she owned him.

Where her soft skills failed within the agency, she relied upon the power of awe. Impressed allies and jealous enemies within the CIA venerated her for three coveted possessions.

Through Renard, she owned a navy. Through hunger, she owned a South American president. Through guilt, she owned a U.S. congressman.

During Renard's Falklands campaign, she'd called upon Argentina's future leader. The young politician had seen through her seductive skills but had found her growing influence attractive. His taste for power compelled him to propose, and the pending wedding promised both bride and groom synergistic clout.

She'd almost owned two presidents, but an unexpected candidate had trumped her mentor's ambitions. Gerald Rickets, a former CIA director and former Secretary of Defense, had instead retreated to a smaller political stage.

Despite graying hair and a receding hairline, Congressman Rickets kept an imposing stature.

As he entered her office, his tall, broad frame filled a conservative gray suit.

Olivia rolled to her feet and walked around her desk. She noticed her hips swinging in slinky seductive strides, and she corrected her steps to a straighter gate.

"It's not too late to visit?"

She'd waited for him past her normal dinner hour. His hand felt warm as she held it and let him kiss her cheek. "Of course not, Gerry."

"I know it's late. Forgive me for... well, for everything."

With her eyes, she absolved him yet again for placing her in peril under the knife of a human-trafficking rapist. The gesture came easily because she knew he'd always feel guilty. He'd always be under her power. "I already have."

"If you do it enough times, maybe I'll forgive myself."

She returned behind her desk and gestured for him to sit. "What's so urgent that you needed to see me in person?"

"Great news. I wanted to tell you in person. Your appointment to the next level is secured."

She'd expected it, but the validation filled her inner girl with warmth and calmed her inner beast. "That's awesome, Gerry. Thanks."

"It's going to take six months, but barring a disaster, it's yours. Then you'll be one step away from being the first female Director of the CIA, and you'll have a lot of people pulling for you."

"I know you helped, a lot more than I'm aware of."

He blushed. "Sure, I pulled a few strings for you, but that's true for anyone who climbs the ranks in a large organization. You've done the hard part by yourself."

"I've just done my job, really."

A massive ebony index finger waggled at her. "Don't feign modesty with me, young lady. You're good and you know it. Own it. A little arrogance is okay at your level. Hell, it'll be expected at the next."

"I'm not young anymore. I'm almost forty."

"Try being sixty."

"I meant I'm old enough to do what needs to be done."

His accusatory digit retreated to his lap. "Let's talk about something more positive. I heard your engagement's now official. When's the wedding?"

"Next summer."

"I'm getting an invitation, right?"

The inner girl desired his approval. The beast needed him in attendance to signal her sway. "Don't be silly. Of course, you're coming."

"Hopefully you'll have a promotion and a wedding to celebrate all in one season."

"Why not? I've worked hard to make it all happen."

"You sure have. But it's a lot to handle. Are you scared?"

"Why would I be scared? I can do any job a man can, and I can do it better. I've proven it time and time again."

"I meant about your wedding."

The inner Olivia feared the Argentine leader would leave her when he tired of her wrinkles or the graying of her auburn hair. She feared his sexual appetite, which drew him to a parade of mistresses she expected to continue during her marriage. She feared any failure in her career that would cause him to cast her aside in shame. Nothing about her nuptials seemed normal, but the promised power pulled her in. The beast gave the expected, defensive answer. "I know it's the right thing for me. That's all that matters."

Rickets' momentary downward glance revealed the sadness of his understanding. She knew he saw her as a daughter and disapproved of her marrying for gain.

"Of course, it is. I can't wait to see you in your dress."

"Celebrating my wedding and my promotion."

"Celebrating your wedding and your promotion. This is as far as I can take you, though. You're on your own after this."

"I know how to run with the big boys."

"True. I'm sure your momentum will carry you to the top."

She agreed. She had to. The beast craved it. "Can I take you to dinner to thank you for the visit?"

"Thanks, but no. I need to attend a late dinner with some members of the Armed Services Committee. Most of my work gets done after hours, unfortunately."

As she considered challenging his plans, her phone vibrated. Glancing downward, she saw an alarm notification. Though she received several per week, she sensed an urgency about this one. As her heart accelerated, the beast forced her composed exterior as she stood and escorted her mentor to the door. "I appreciate you coming here in person."

"Don't mention it. I'm always happy to see you."

After giving a requisite hug and closing the door behind him, she marched to her desk and accessed her computer.

Questioning which random world leader was doing something unexpected, what nation's military machine was grinding into gear, or what terrorist team was on the move, she found the surprise disturbing.

The *Goliath* was leaving Oman.

She clicked an icon to hail the evening's support team. A new window revealed a geeky face that seemed too young for a CIA analyst. "Good evening, Miss McDonald. You got my text?"

"Yeah. Show me the UAV footage."

A high-altitude Unmanned Aerial Vehicle's night vision image of Renard's catamaran flagship appeared. She noted the brightness from the heat of its starboard propulsion equipment and its distance from the Omani coast.

Per her last conversation with the Frenchman, his fleet was parked in Muscat for the night. "How old's this?"

"Three minutes."

She checked the computer's system time. UAV usage constraints limited her overhead snapshots of Renard's fleet to every fifteen minutes. "That's off schedule."

"I take sneak peeks for you when I can." His smirk signaled his enjoyment of the gift the beast sent him each month.

"Thanks. I'll send you an extra bottle this month."

"Can you make it a good one aged twenty-five years?"

"I will if you tell me what's going on with the submarines."

"Already done. I caught an image after I saw the *Goliath* out of place. I'm seeing heat from their engineering spaces."

Knowing Renard saved fuel costs and transportation time by carrying the submarines on his catamaran cargo ship, she hoped the *Goliath* departed with the intent to submerge and take the other two vessels onto its centerline freight bed. But she questioned why the Frenchman would leave Muscat early. She knew the replacement bow section he sought had been delayed. "Can you get me a shot of the Taiwanese ship that's carrying the *Goliath's* new bow?"

"Depends how much resolution you need."

"I just want to know where it is."

The analyst aimed his eyes off screen. "I got a free fifteen-second window coming up. I'm checking on the ship's expected location, and... I'm inserting coordinates and scheduling the shot. Done, with ten seconds to spare."

"That's why you're my go-to guy."

"Keep the whiskey coming. Okay. I see your ship, and I'm overlaying coordinates. You want them?"

"Just tell me if it's gained any time on its arrival in Karachi."

"Nope. It's fallen about another five miles behind schedule."

As she groped for a reason why the Frenchman would move his fleet ahead of schedule, her phone rang.

Pierre Renard was calling.

"I need to go." She closed her computer session and lifted her cell phone. "Pierre?"

"Yes, it's me. Pardon me for skipping pleasantries, but I must speak with you about an urgent matter."

She considered sharing her knowledge of his fleet's movement, but the beast made her withhold it as tactical edge in the conversation. "What's going on?"

The permanently poised Frenchman sounded perturbed. "I'm afraid I have dreadful news. The *Goliath* has been compromised."

The terrified inner girl quaked. Backlash scenarios of having aided and groomed a failed mercenary fleet flashed in her mind. Expulsion from the CIA, public humility, a broken engagement, and criminal investigations. Her house of cards shuddered.

She inhaled a rapid breath as the beast encircled the wounded child. Angered, the inner animal forced her focus on survival. It surprised her by cycling through options to sacrifice Renard to protect herself.

After a methodical, deep breath, she calmed herself and gave the Frenchman a chance to explain himself. "Tell me what happened and what you're doing about it."

"An unknown assault force overpowered my security team

and boarded the *Goliath*. They've taken it underway. I was able to get Jake and Dmitry to their ships to pursue with very supportive helicopter support from the Omanis."

"Shit. The Omani's know about this?"

"Unfortunately."

"Who else knows?"

"Nobody, I assure you. I considered calling Admiral Khan, but I wanted to call you before I would solicit Pakistani assistance."

Her head spun. "Wait. What assistance do you need? Put a torpedo in it and call it a day."

The Frenchman's hesitance signaled resistance. "Well… let's just say I'd rather find a less violent solution."

"Solution to what? You don't know what this is. People don't steal frontline warships for joyrides. Whatever this is, it's huge, and it's going to blow up if you don't stop it."

"You know I'm skilled at surgical sabotage. I implore you not to be hasty in calling for extreme violence."

"Sinking a problem of your own creation isn't extreme."

Irking her, he hesitated again. "I see we're of diverging opinions. I was contacting you as a courtesy, not as a request for orders."

"You know damned well you had to call me. Did you think you could lose your toy without me knowing about it?"

"It's not a toy. And no, of course not."

"Good. Then remember who you're talking to."

"And I implore you to do the same, young lady. Regardless of your opinions, the fact remains that I'm under no obligation to destroy my own property. If you won't help me, I'll deal with matters myself, including calling Admiral Khan if I must."

She knew the risk the retired Pakistani admiral posed. As the Frenchman's longtime friend, the man's loyalty would beget actions she feared.

He could influence war machines from his nation to come to Renard's aid. Such movement would trigger alerts within the American intelligence machine that pointed back to her and the mercenary fleet she claimed she controlled.

The beast considered outflanking Renard and threatening the Pakistani admiral to ignore the Frenchman, but then it realized appeasement offered a safer route. The *Goliath's* owner had proven his past adaptability to adversity, and he represented possibilities to sidestep this disaster.

But she decided he would need boundaries. "For the sake of argument, let's say I help you. What do you need from me?"

"I need your standard surveillance, centered on the *Goliath* and scanning outward one hundred and fifty nautical miles. I need to know what's happening on the *Goliath* in high-resolution in real time, and I need to know what high-value assets are within weapons range of it."

"You know I can't do that, not without identifying a mission for the *Goliath* that would warrant dedicated use."

Again, he hesitated. "I understand the rules, but I had to state my needs. Can you at least give me the scanning surveillance?"

"It would be spotty, nothing like you're used to. But I could get you something."

"That would help. However, the greatest support you could offer me is timing."

She snorted. "Shit, Pierre. Everyone wants more time."

"No. I meant a specific time, or a specific place, to bound my mission parameters. I need your help defining a terminus."

"You mean, you want me to give you a timeline where I define the final deadline?"

"Yes. You have the intelligence assets and the analytical skills. What's the ultimate endpoint of this mission the hijackers have taken against me? Who are they? Why are they doing this? I have educated guesses, but you can make quicker sense of it. I can't allow myself to chase them around the entire world forever, and I want you to serve as my voice of reason if I let emotions overrun me."

The beast wanted her to remind the Frenchman she could have the Fifth Fleet snap the *Goliath* in half before sunrise, but the inner animal also saw value in recapturing the mercenary flagship. Submergible guns with a one-hundred-and-twenty-mile reach offered unique options.

"You're right. I could help. But what confidence can you give me that this ends the right way?"

"We've attached enough limpets to the *Goliath* to track it anywhere."

"Can you keep it submerged?"

"Yes, with air support. It's the only way."

"How far are the Omani's willing to help?"

"They've promised support while I'm in the Gulf of Oman, and fortunately that covers a lot of water in all directions."

"How can you be sure they'll honor their word when weapons start flying back at them? The *Goliath* can defend itself."

His delay suggested he considered sharing a secret. "I've offered to broker and subsidize arms purchases to fill gaps in their military arsenals, and I've offered bounties for kills and major damage on the *Goliath*. I've also offered compensation for casualties for any Omani staff."

"For a man who knows subtlety, you don't hold back when you're being blunt."

"No, I don't. And let me be blunt now. I need to know your answer. Will you help me?"

The beast answered for her. "If I do, it'll be on my terms. You don't make a move or contact anyone without telling me first. If you do, I'll get the Fifth Fleet involved."

"Agreed. In fact, if I can't resolve this before the *Goliath* reaches weapons range of an American warship, I'll beg you for such intervention."

"I'll learn what I can, and I'll call you back." She hung up and invoked her computer session, bringing the geek face into view.

"What can I do for you, Miss McDonald?"

"I need to know if any American naval assets are within three hundred miles of the *Goliath*. No, wait, scratch that. Any military asset or passenger vessel within three hundred miles."

The geek frowned. "That's an unusual request."

"But we track military assets and passenger vessels all the time. It won't raise red flags, will it?"

"No, it won't. Just give me a couple of minutes."

"Okay. Call me back." She minimized the window and picked up her phone. The beast reminded her to order dinner and prepare for a long night.

It also reminded her to apply her contriving mind to a backup plan, in case the Frenchman failed, of finding a way to turn Renard's loss into her gain.

CHAPTER 5

The colonel stood atop the *Goliath*, underneath its unique domed bridge. Interlaced steel supported transparent tiles of polycarbonate windows, allowing him a hemispherical view. Discordant chirping chimed its chorus, the limpet swarm's screeches shredding his nerves. "How long will those accursed things blare?"

Beside him, the commander appeared to have accepted the annoying noise. "It could be days, I'm afraid."

"They'll drive me mad."

"You'll get used to them before we can pry them off."

"And when might that be?"

"Tomorrow after nightfall, if you still believe we must."

"You're optimistic about me staying sane that long. The noise is running through my bones."

"You could find relief in the port hull."

A sideways glance showed the silhouetted central cargo bed and then the starboard hull's twin. Farther aft, the largest cross-beam provided the solitary tunnel between the catamaran's halves. "Has anyone gone across yet?"

"The sergeant sent a commando across."

"What's he found?"

"I have no idea. He departed over fifteen minutes ago, and I haven't heard any reports since."

The colonel realized the vessel's size and shape hindered communications as his team located and adapted to the sound-powered phones. Frustrated, he focused on the benefits of his unique, captured prize. "What systems are working?"

"Most them, as best I can tell."

"Then start with what's not working."

"Weapons aren't working."

"Of course not. Those are locked out except where we can invoke manual overrides."

"Sonar is running, but only passively."

"Does this ship even have active sonar?"

"It has side-scan sonar systems, and those are locked out. More importantly, the tactical radar system is locked out, too."

"That's disappointing, but not a surprise."

"I'm sure I could energize our navigation radar, but that would give away our position more than it would benefit us."

"Keep it off."

As if spurred by the reminder of the *Goliath's* electronic blindness, the submarine commander lifted night vision binoculars to his face and scanned the circular horizon.

The colonel looked into the blackness with his naked eye. "What are we looking for?"

"Trouble."

The colonel studied the horizon and the low stars. "Okay. I'm not sure what trouble looks like."

"It must look much like the hostile aircraft you search for when you're carrying a rifle behind enemy lines."

"I'm used to looking for low-flying aircraft as black objects on the horizon, unless I have night vision, which lets me look for engine heat."

"That's what I'm doing, sort of."

"Why 'sort of'?"

"You're used to objects moving sideways across the horizon. But whoever's coming for us knows exactly where we are and will come straight for us."

"That's almost impossible to see."

"That's why I'm looking. If you want to help, you could grab night vision binoculars from the hooks at the back of bridge. They have a low-magnification search mode."

"I'll get us some help."

The colonel hovered his finger above an icon on a screen that promised to send his voice throughout the entire ship. "Have you tested this yet?"

The commander lowered his optics and glanced down. "Yes, that will work."

After lowering his finger, the colonel announced his request into an overhead microphone. "Does anyone know where the sergeant is?"

The bulldog's voice rang back. "I hear you, sir. I'm in the engine room."

"I need two more sets of eyes up here on the bridge."

"Everyone's spoken for. There's even one guy in the port hull. You're out of bodies."

"I don't need two guys watching the propulsion motor."

"I can agree to that. I'll send one man forward."

"Good enough. Take care of it."

The colonel hit a muting icon to regain his privacy. "So, I can barely see any aircraft that are coming for me. But I can't submerge without cutting my speed by more than half, which would allow the submarines to catch me."

"Right. The best estimate is that this ship can sustain twelve to thirteen knots submerged with both propellers and all MESMA plants running."

"And we can't use the Phalanx close-in weapon system."

"No. We can't use any weapons now. All weapons and offensive sensors are locked out for lack of a physical firing key that's hanging around Terrance Cahill's neck."

"Is anything working from a tactical standpoint?"

"Just the passive sections of Subtics–listening on sonar and sniffing incoming radar energy."

The colonel reflected upon the deviations from his planned hijacking. The loss of two commandos during the infiltration amounted to an annoyance, but the rapid helicopter response to place tactical teams on the submarines had unsettled him.

Compounding his concern, his sonar expert reported a new threat over the bridge's loudspeaker. "Incoming torpedo, this time from the *Wraith*."

The commander aimed his voice upward. "Very well. Do you

have a time to impact?"

"I'm not sure how this system calculates it."

"Calculate it by hand and manually update the system."

The colonel found his men's calmness about another incoming torpedo juxtaposed with the danger he sensed was coming, but he avoided panicking. "It's going to catch us, isn't it?"

"Those two big black blobs behind us on the horizon are the *Specter* and the *Wraith*. Anything they shoot will hit us, no matter what we do."

"Then why are we bothering to run from them?"

"I want to escape their torpedo range. The more time they have to ruminate over what we just did to them, the more likely they are to get angrier and shoot something with a big warhead."

With his naked eye, the colonel thought he saw an opaque orb oscillating over his opponent. "Look at the *Wraith*."

His accomplice swung the optics. "That's a helicopter."

"Damn it. A gunship?"

"No, it's just a transport vehicle. It's dropping people onto the *Wraith*."

"But does it have guns?"

"I can't tell from this distance. It might."

"Keep an eye on it." The colonel remembered the incoming weapons. "What's the chance this latest torpedo already has explosives?"

"Small. I expect it to be another limpet weapon to mark our port hull."

"That will double the amount of these maddening sirens. Can't we just submerge and disappear?"

The commander lowered his optics and glared. "With limpets on our hull?"

The colonel became a scolded child but stuffed away the shame to profit from the submarine expert's advice. "I mean if I get the MESMA plants running and go faster than the submarines. Eventually we'd be far enough away from all danger to send swimmers over the side to pry off those monstrosities.

Then we'd be submerged and undetectable."

"No. This ship can submerge, but it's a poor combat submarine. Unless we crawl at a near drift, the flow noise over this forest of metallic jagged edges will serve as a beacon to the *Specter* and the *Wraith*."

"Then I need to make a decision."

"About what?"

"Submerging now, or waiting until I can bring up all the MESMA plants and the port propulsion plant."

"Why would you submerge now? We need speed. You just said it yourself that you wanted to get far from danger."

"True, but I'm also concerned about aircraft now."

The commander scoffed. "We can always submerge under aircraft if needed."

"But how fast? One missile could ruin everything."

"The submarines have missiles and could shoot us now if they wanted to. They're not risking the damage of an anti-ship missile to their flagship."

"But what about the smaller rockets gunships carry, and what about airborne cannons?"

"That's why this ship has Stinger missiles."

"You mean, we think it has Stinger missiles."

"We'll find them. It's only a matter of time. Staying surfaced is the obvious decision."

The colonel grunted. "Then why do I have an eerie feeling that there's a combat aircraft coming for us?"

"You're paranoid. It's your job to be, I suppose."

The colonel challenged his companion's diagnosis. "It's not paranoia when it's real. There are several nations Renard can call upon to challenge us."

"What sovereign nation would attack unidentified assailants who commandeered a dangerous mercenary warship?"

"He's dining with one of them as we speak."

"Just because they're willing to fly his crews to his submarines doesn't mean they're willing to risk their lives."

"The Omanis may take our actions as a personal affront. We

stole the *Goliath* from their waters."

The commander was cynical. "I'm sure the local economy will survive."

Footsteps echoed from the stairway behind the bridge, and a commando appeared. He grabbed night vision optics, lifted them to his face, and kept his mouth shut to avoid the argument while scanning for threats.

The colonel challenged the cynicism. "I still think we should be submerged."

"But you've entrusted the naval tactics to me. We need to out-run the submarines."

"So be it. But get ready to submerge as quickly as possible."

"I found the top level of the diving procedure in the menu system, but I didn't have time to work through it."

"Meaning?"

"Meaning, you'll have to explore it yourself unless you want one of us to stop scanning our surroundings."

Fumbling through icons brought the submergence routine to the foreground. "I found the diving icon. What happens if I tap it?"

"I can only guess. Tap it and find out."

"That's cavalier for a man who wants to stay surfaced."

"I also want to understand this ship."

The colonel's fingertip's electrical capacitance invoked a deeper menu. "Nothing happened other than bringing up a new screen."

"What's on the new screen?"

"More icons. One for each gas turbine, each main air intake, each railgun, and the Phalanx point-defense system. It also looks like a status of each hatch."

"That's to prevent submerging with an open hole."

"I see. Some are highlighted with a red outline while others are outlined in green."

The commander lowered his optics and craned his neck. "My guess is that when they're all outlined in green, you can press the top icon, and the ship will submerge itself."

"What about these?"

"Those look like pumps. My guess, and it's only a guess–"

"Stop that. I know you're guessing. Let's move beyond the qualifiers for each piece of advice."

"Understood. Those look like trim and drain pumps. If you use them, you'll suck water into the ship much faster than free flooding, and we'll submerge faster."

"I like that. Should I tap them?"

"Go ahead."

The colonel's gentle finger presses turned red outlines framing pump graphics to dotted green. "I think that worked."

"My guess... assessment... is that you just shifted the pumps from off to standby."

"Call it a guess when it's a guess. Call it a certainty when it's a certainty. Just don't dwell on the uncertainty like an attorney."

"Yes. That's my guess. But it's a good guess."

"So they'll automatically start if I press the diving icon?"

A pensive look overtook the lean commander's face. "Submarines have been my life, but I don't know. Better said, I can't know. This ship is unique, and nobody but a select few understand its inner workings."

"I told you that guessing is acceptable."

"I'm tired of guessing, and your paranoia has worn me out. Let's submerge this ship now to assure ourselves we can. Then we'll surface again to run from the submarines."

"I see you're a man of action."

"Didn't you notice that from our last hunting trip? I'd rather take a mediocre shot rather than letting an opportunity pass."

"Indeed, I did notice. So be it. We're submerging. For something this complex, you'll have to do it."

The commander tapped an icon and projected his voice upward. "Engineering, bridge, make turns for nine knots."

"Bridge, engineering. Making turns for nine knots."

"Engineering, bridge, I'm going to submerge the ship as a test. Watch and study how the gas turbine shuts down, and watch how the load transfers to the MESMA plant."

The stocky engineer's voice issued from the loudspeakers. "Do you want me to shift the load to the MESMA now?"

"No, I want to see how this ship behaves under stress."

"Okay, I'll watch for it. We're ready back here."

Using the open circuit, the commander raised his voice. "For anyone who didn't hear that, we're going to submerge. Everyone watch for water flowing from places that are presently dry. If you see anything like that, shout out your location from the nearest sound-powered phone and describe what you see."

"Well said."

"I'm making another guess now."

"What's that?"

"That this ship is smart enough to stop submerging on its own instead of continuing to its crush depth while waiting for us to stop its descent. These waters are deep enough to shatter this dome."

"If something as basic as this maneuver kills us, then today is our day to die."

"I'll take that as permission to submerge."

The thin man pushed an icon, and the world changed. Gentle chimes warned of the pending dive, and pixels on screens pulsed. Then, as commands became actions, machinery moved.

A football field away, each head valve clanked shut, and the gas turbine's rumbling howl died, giving the shrieking limpets louder life. The trembling deck signaled suction from the sea through centrifugal pumps, and the colonel pointed at accumulating digits that flickered. "What are these numbers?"

"That's how many kilograms of water we're taking into our tanks through each pump."

"I find this ship increasingly impressive. I've truly taken Renard's pride from him."

The colonel noticed moonlight shimmering atop the swells crawling up the bow. Dark liquid lapped the windows and crept up the dome as the sea swallowed the *Goliath*. Opaqueness rolled over the hemisphere and the calm water's blackness blotted out the stars. The deck's slight angle leveled. "That was unnerving."

"We started this night in your commando world, and now we're in mine. But I'll admit that was creepy, looking through windows."

"This ship constantly impresses."

"And it was smart enough to level at twenty meters."

As the colonel watched the icon of the incoming torpedo, the sonar expert announced news over the loudspeaker. "The *Wraith* is submerging. It's venting its ballast tanks."

The commander aimed his voice upward. "Very well. Track it as a submerged contact, at least while you can hear it."

His enemy's choice to dive piqued the colonel's curiosity. "Why would they submerge? Who are they hiding from?"

"They may think we're trying to override the weapons lock-outs to shoot at them, but it's more likely they're submerging to begin sustained tracking of us."

"Submarines are faster underwater, right?"

"They are, but we're not since we have rakish bows designed to cut the water's surface. However, every submarine hears better underwater, and that's one reason they're going under."

"We hear better submerged, even with these damned limpets on our hull?"

"Yes, although those things compromise everything acoustically, and it's about to get worse."

On his display, the colonel watched the *Wraith's* torpedo merge with the icon of the *Goliath*. As the sonar expert announced their dispersion, magnetic drones clamped against the port hull's underbelly with echoing thuds. A new chorus wailed. "I won't make it a full day with those accursed sirens blaring. And now the port side is just as bad as the starboard."

"I think we have bigger problems." The submarine commander aimed a thin digit at a display that showed raw sounds from the sea. Two new lines appeared behind the *Goliath*, and he raised his voice towards a microphone connecting him with the sonar expert below. "Do you see those new traces?"

From the speakers, the sonar expert responded. "The first is another torpedo from the *Wraith*. The second... another torpedo from the *Specter*."

The commander wiggled a triumphant finger at the torpedoes' traces. "This is why we need to be surfaced and running. These weapons will breach our hull."

The colonel hoped his submarine commander was wrong but doubted it. "What makes you so sure?"

"There's no further value in limpets. These two will have warheads with small bomblets that attach and explode."

"Such weapons are Renard's calling card. They're supposed to minimize damage to their targets, but they could very well sink us. He wouldn't risk it."

"He's lost his patience. He fears we might get away."

"He'd risk everything out of fear?"

"These warheads are expected to have variable yields. They may have only a small number of the bomblets explode."

A commando's voice shot from the loudspeaker. "I found the Stinger missiles. A lot of them. They're forward in the port hull with a bunch of crates of spare railgun rounds."

The colonel welcomed the favorable news. "Good. Grab the launcher and as many spares as you can and get ready to head topside. I'll be surfacing the ship now."

"Understood, sir."

Concerned about seaborne weaponry, the commander retained his frown. "That's fine. But you have bigger problems than the possibility of aircraft. You have the reality of explosive warheads."

"Can we outrun them?"

"Not quite, but this ship's speed can buy us time and give us options, provided you get the second engine room online."

Facing an unquantifiable risk, the colonel sought advice. "Engineering, bridge, I need an assessment of bringing up the port hull's engine room."

After a pause, his engineer responded. "Bridge, engineering, if I head over there, I won't be able to make it back here to the starboard side if there's a problem."

"Understood. Is the starboard engine room giving you any reason to doubt it?"

"Not really. It's a solid design. The load shifted to the MESMA plant without a problem."

"How about the turbine?"

"We'll need to watch it when it comes up again. But I think I can get you propulsion on two propellers powered by one gas turbine and one MESMA plant in ten minutes. After that, we can see about bringing up the second gas turbine."

"Go to the port side and start the port engine room."

The colonel looked to the lean commander. "Now, how to reverse this submerging process?"

"I'm well ahead of you. I've already set up the icons. One more touch should surface us."

"Take us to the surface."

A tap begat a gentle incline, and digits flickered as pumps spat tons. Blackness receded down the dome, unveiling stars and the sea's shimmering surface. Swooshing air whispered as head valves opened and fed the hungry turbine.

Night vision optics rose to noses as men scanned the horizon for threats. Within seconds, the quiet commando aimed his finger off the starboard beam and shouted. "Helicopter!"

Peering with his naked eyes, the colonel saw a dark shape blocking nature's backlighting. The aircraft was low and close—close enough that he saw its twenty-millimeter guns. "Get us back under, now!"

While the commander obeyed, the helicopter angled and aimed its armaments towards the *Goliath*. Bright bursts painted the night's black canvas as bullets pelted and pushed through steel. "We can't submerge!"

Ire rose within the colonel at the rejection of his order. "What?"

"We'll flood! Those bullets are breaching the hull. They must be!"

"Damn it! Submerge this damned ship!"

Creases formed on the submarine commander's brow as

water rose up the windows. "You're sentencing men to die in the breached compartment. You could be killing us all."

"We're helpless against helicopters."

The world became silence except for cooling fans, blaring limpets, and bullets slicing water on their way to clanking against the *Goliath's* submerged stern. The sea's blackness became engulfing as the dome's light failed, and emergency diodes turned the room red. Though a hardened war veteran, the colonel found his surreal world haunting. "What happened?"

"We lost our electrical system. Speed is dropping to zero. We're drifting."

"How's the damage?"

"Incredible..."

"What?"

"This ship. The informational it gives in real time. It's amazing. There must be wetness sensors arrayed in each compartment. I can see the port engine room flooding to the second deck, and MESMA plant number five is flooded to half a meter."

"We were breached in two compartments?"

"Yes. But look." The commander's trembling finger pointed to a dynamic schematic of the trim and drain system. "The pumps are already sucking water from the internal tanks near the flooded compartments and moving water into tanks on the port side. The ship's mitigating the negative buoyancy on the starboard side, and it's creating the same negative buoyancy on the port side to avoid lateral torques."

"In layman's terms?"

"It's rebalancing the water to stabilize itself."

"Good."

"Now it's balancing water fore to aft and adjusting with the stern planes automatically to keep us level. Simply amazing."

"But we have no propulsion."

"No, we don't. The stern planes will become useless as we slow, but this ship has protected itself. Incredible."

The bulldog's voice issued from the loudspeaker. "Bridge, this is MESMA plant three."

"Go ahead, sergeant. What's your status?"

"Gunfire broke through the hull in the engine room, and water started gushing in before we could react. So we ran forward. There's five of us here, counting the two guys who were in MESMA plant five."

"Injuries?"

"None. Just shaken up."

"Can you get back into MESMA plant five?"

"Yes. The hole was smaller. Not as many bullets. You want damage control there?"

A display showing pumps keeping pace with the water level in the air-independent propulsion space's bilge encouraged the colonel. "Not now. Get everyone into MESMA plant five and use the tunnel to get to the port side. We'll bring ourselves back to life using the port propeller and the port MESMA plants."

"We're on it, sir."

As the colonel sensed himself having survived the worst of the attack, the sonar expert announced news. "Both torpedoes have shut down, the *Wraith's* and the *Specter's*."

His face ashen, the commander appeared as shaken as the colonel felt. "They had wire control and issued shutdown commands."

"Why?"

"Because I was right. They were going to damage us with bomblets. But after the helicopter attack, there's no need. We're compromised and slowed, and they know it."

The colonel grunted. "Then they didn't mean to sink us."

"No. They could have done so a dozen times already, but here we are."

"They may be counting on capitalizing on our mistakes, such as forgetting that a transport helicopter can carry machine guns and move with enough speed to surprise us."

"Capitalizing on our mistakes could sink us. There's only so much damage to us they can risk."

The colonel scoffed. "Not in Pierre Renard's mind. He believes he can recapture his ship, and as long as he thinks so, we hold the advantage."

CHAPTER 6

Terrance Cahill stood behind the *Specter's* commanding officer, wanting to replace him as the video feed's conversation put the *Goliath* in jeopardy.

Thankful for the linguistic gesture of inclusion, Cahill participated in the meeting of the commanders over the data link in English. He thought Volkov's translator spoke French, but he preferred to leave that theory untested.

He cringed hearing his colleague's warmongering tone, as Jake sounded irate. "Okay, Pierre. I shut down my slow-kill weapon, and so has Dmitry. But I did it under protest, and I don't like it."

In contrast to the American, Cahill's French boss appeared calm. "What's not to like? You and Dmitry have tagged the *Goliath* with enough limpets to track it across the globe, and the helicopter flooded its starboard engine room."

"But those thieves still have an operational ship. They'll have the port side up before we know it, and God knows what's next on their agenda."

"You'd risk sinking our flagship?"

"No. If they're smart enough to steal the *Goliath*, they're smart enough to surface it if I put a few small holes in it. Let me cripple it."

The comment irritated the Australian commander, and he interrupted the conversation. "It doesn't have the reserve buoyancy of a standard submarine. Have you ever heard me brag about the size of its main ballast tanks?"

Jake's ire rose higher. "No. What's your point?"

"It doesn't have any main ballast tanks! How do you expect it to get to the surface if you riddle it with holes?"

The American shot an annoyed glance over his shoulder.

"Your trim and drain pumps are enough to turn that thing into a cork."

"Me pumps–their pumps–'that thing's' pumps... are running on an undersized battery system. They'll die out with the MESMA systems down."

"But they can blow the drain tanks with high-pressure air."

"If they know how. And the ship's only designed for a hundred meters. There's not nearly as much stored high-pressure air in the air banks as you're used to."

"You're downplaying its abilities."

Unable to restrain himself, Cahill raised his voice. "The hell I am! Get it through your bloody head that it needs its power plants to survive. Flooding multiple compartments would sink it with a band of clueless frogmen mongrels tripping over themselves trying to do damage control."

The Frenchman's assurance lowered Cahill's blood pressure. "Gentlemen, please calm yourselves. I've already resolved this debate by ordering our weapons tight. We'll think through possibilities together as opposed to rushing through reactions. We can afford this luxury since we've turned time to our advantage."

Jake remained hostile. "How? Last I checked, Dmitry and I can sustain twelve knots best transit speeds, and the *Goliath* can hold twenty-four with a gas turbine and one propeller."

"I've negotiated air coverage. With our security system lockouts, the *Goliath* presents no threat to aircraft and will be forced under."

"Who are you negotiating with? You don't even know where it's going."

The Frenchman became snappish, signaling an informational boundary. "I can get air coverage as needed. Leave it at that."

The American dragged a stylus across an electronic chart of the Gulf of Oman. "We're two hundred miles from the Strait of Hormuz. Even if you can keep the hijackers submerged, that's roughly twenty hours until the Fifth Fleet is bound to hear them."

"We don't know if they're going that way."

"They're heading that way now, and they won't turn unless it's west to shoot over land and hit Dubai. Maybe they want to hit the Burj Khalifa. They'll be in range in less than ten hours."

"I'm working a plan that will preclude this."

Again, Cahill interrupted his colleagues' exchange. "And they'd need weeks with supercomputers to break through the weapons' safeguards." He then felt like an idiot guilty of wishful thinking as his words replayed silently through his head.

After a slight hesitation to process Cahill's oversimplification, the Frenchman clarified. "For automated firing, I agree. But manual firing of the cannons and setting of the rounds' coordinates can be achieved easily enough."

"Yeah. That was stupid of me. At least I think we just concluded that the railguns are the reason they stole me ship."

"Indeed. And they'll be going after stationary objects since they have no way to guide the rounds into moving targets."

The American remained agitated. "No way that we know of. Who's to say they haven't figured out how to program their own guidance information into the rounds? They could be ripping into spare rounds now and reverse engineering the guidance encryption."

"Possibly. But it's all speculation. I urge you all to stay calm."

Cahill shared a thought his team had left unspoken. "We need to know who did this."

The comment backfired with the American. "No, we don't. We need to hit them with little bomblets from the weapon I personally conceived to deal with a situation just like this, make the little bomblets go boom, and force them to surface. Then let a helicopter put an end to this so we can go finish desert."

Cahill stepped back to distance himself from Jake. The rift forming between himself and the American concerned him. "You designed the slow-kill weapon to let crews abandon sinking submarines, not to spare me ship."

"But I can dial down the weapon to a one-third the yield.

What the hell, Terry? You know this. Why are we even arguing?"

"Even if they could manage the damage control, what if they scuttle the ship in your happy scenario, genius?"

"They're not suicidal."

"How do you know? And if not, they can still scuttle it and swim away from it as easily as they swam to it. You can't assume anything about these mongrels."

Cahill welcomed his boss rescuing him from the impasse with Jake. "Enough, gentlemen! Focus on your duties. The second helicopter has dropped its last crewman to your deck."

The new crewmen came through the forward hatch and then shut it. At the ship's control station, the silver-haired Henri faced the newcomers, queried them, and looked to his commanding officer. "Jake, the ship is rigged for dive."

"Good. Now I can dive us below those railguns. Henri, submerge the ship."

Cahill watched the subtle interplay between Jake and Henri. The quick glances, gestures, and body language communication they shared became a graceful dance of effective informality.

In a blink, the French mechanic aimed the *Specter* below the waves. A slight dip brought the submarine below its radio mast's highest reach, and Renard's face froze before the screen darkened. Then the mechanic nudged the ship's mass upward, and the conversation recommenced.

To Cahill's relief, Renard restarted the discussion in his favor. "Terry has a good point."

The American remained doubtful. "Which point?"

"We need to know who did this. We can better react if we know our adversary and what he's doing."

"I know who did this. The bad guys. What the hell does it matter?"

"Don't be so hasty, Jake. Statecraft is a complex art. I could receive a ransom call any minute, for example."

"And that would be a good thing?"

"It would present options that remain available only while our adversaries believe they control our flagship."

The American appeared uncomfortable as he adjusted his seated posture. "You think they're just thieves? Like a Somali pirates all-star team?"

"I'm saying there are multiple possibilities. We have hours to react–not minutes. So keep your wits about you while we have a time to think."

Cahill's mind was a beehive of thoughts. "I've been thinking about how to get it back. I have several ideas."

Jake's tone was more accusatory than questioning. "Anything foolproof?"

"Nothing we do is foolproof."

"Our torpedoes are foolproof."

Unsure how to deal with the American's stubbornness, Cahill welcomed the Frenchman's rescuing. "Enough, Jake. I implore you to redirect that energy towards devising a tactic to disable the *Goliath*."

The American aimed a frown at the monitor. "I've already been racking my brain on that, and the only answer is a slow-kill."

"We must analyze other options. I urge you all to keep your hopes up. We have the skills and resources, and I'm sure we'll have a plan soon."

"What plan? We all know this is going to end with a slow-kill weapon. Period."

Cahill saw his French boss' rare anger as he barked words in French. The American snapped a response in the same language, and then Renard spat a final volley. Jake looked away, weighed his words, and reverted to English. "It won't happen again."

"Let's move on, then, shall we?"

The American sounded calmer during a shift into a productive dialogue with Renard. "We need some rules of engagement."

"Right. Let's set trailing parameters. Despite your limpets, I want you to stay close to minimize torpedo run times if, God forbid, you do need to shoot."

"Let's go for broke. Two miles."

"Aggressive, but appropriate."

"We'll need depth separation between me and Dmitry."

"Right. I want you shallow so I can have easier access to Terry. Jake, take eighty meters and above. Dmitry, take below one hundred meters. We'll arrange two-dimensional separation if Dmitry needs to snorkel."

On a quiet screen, the Russian commander scrunched his face while listening to his companion's translation. Cahill hoped his colleague would voice an idea to regain the transport vessel, but Volkov remained silent as the American responded. "What about tripwires?"

Cahill sought a meaning for the slang. "What's a tripwire? That sounds like American jargon."

"A parameter that gets crossed which requires action."

"So, you're looking for reasons to shoot me ship?"

"Yeah. Like if its cannons start shooting at an American aircraft carrier, I'm sending a heavyweight up its tailpipe."

The gravity of the possibility silenced the conversation. Cahill reflected on the heightened American naval activity around the Arabian Peninsula, including the home base of the Fifth Fleet, three hundred miles away in Bahrain.

His heart sank as he grasped the risk his former ship posed to innocent people. If his colleagues failed to stop it, they might face a situation in which decency forced its sinking.

Cahill accepted time as a constraint. "That's about a day away from the *Goliath*."

With the new opening, the American's defiant tone resurfaced. "You got a plan to get it back in a day? Or how about before it gets within range of Dubai? Or Bandar Abas? Or whatever the hell it's going to attack?"

"You know bloody well there's no plan yet."

His respect growing for his boss' conversational skills, Cahill appreciated Renard's quick redirection. "Then we'd better start making one."

"Is that Sheila at the CIA willing to give you friendly combatant ship locations? I mean, without telling anyone about our predicament?"

The Frenchman's face assumed a shade the Australian found odd. It seemed plasticized, even for the seasoned negotiator. For a moment, Cahill suspected his boss spoke with a half-truth. "Miss McDonald has been on my mind since this disaster struck. Soliciting her is dangerous, based upon the concern you expressed. She may use news of our predicament against us."

"Meaning she might order me ship sunk as a safety precaution?"

A Marlboro's butt turned amber as the Frenchman inhaled. Squinting, he exhaled while framing his response. "She has the power to destroy the *Goliath*."

Seated under Cahill's chin, the American stirred. Having once been Olivia McDonald's professional target, and then her heart's target, Jake had an old connection with the fleet's CIA link. "She's not the Director of the CIA yet, is she?"

Renard confirmed that the power within the CIA of the American's pursuer-turned-lover-turned-ally remained limited. "No. She's still too young, and she'll always be too female. She can overcome one of those obstacles, but not both. She's still one promotion, or more accurately, one presidential appointment away, from being next in line."

"You're sure she could have Terry's ship sunk, but would she betray us like that?"

"She may see no other option. Consider her position. Knowledge of our predicament makes her responsible to prevent the *Goliath* from reaching strike range of any NATO asset, much less an American ship."

Cahill wanted to ask if his boss had shared their difficulty with his CIA contact, but he read a subtle clue in the Frenchman's face warning against it. "So we may get no help from American intelligence?"

"Let's not rely upon it. In fact, I can't promise any help beyond that of the Omanis."

Images of his new love flickered in Cahill's mind. "What about Ariella? She can gather intelligence for us."

"I hesitate to place such a burden on your new lady friend. She was a stranger to you only a month ago."

"You don't trust her."

"I can't afford the luxury."

Unsure if infatuation or true love clouded his judgment, Cahill checked his hopes of seeking support from his Israeli girlfriend. "Then what do we do, mate?"

"Perhaps you and I should begin brainstorming options while Jake and Dmitry take their trailing positions."

Taking the hint, the Australian excused himself and walked away. He headed aft and felt the cramping confines of a normal-sized submarine. The crew's mess seemed small, and he realized how accustomed he'd become to his huge ship.

He stepped into the tight space and saw a moving body. "Excuse me."

"Yes?"

The man's thick French accent and hesitance caught Cahill off guard. The Australian then realized that aboard the *Specter* he was a misplaced reminder of the fleet's victimhood. "I'm Terry Cahill, commanding officer of the *Goliath*."

"Of course. I'm Jean-Paul. What just happened is terrible. But don't worry. Jake is the best. He'll get it back for you."

"I'm sure."

"Can I get you something to eat or drink?"

"No, thanks. I was hoping you could help me get a tablet or a laptop with a communications link."

"Sure. You can use mine. I'll set you up at the dinner table. There's a LAN connection there."

Minutes later, Renard offered the Australian qualified privacy. "Jake and Dmitry can see my face, but they can't hear me since I've muted their audio."

"You're mastering your fleet admiral's technology."

"It's an art."

"Where are you?"

"I've turned my hotel room into tonight's command center. I'm using my phone's hotspot as our communications channel. I'll wager that it's the most secure device in the Arabian Peninsula."

"It might just be."

"Unless the others can read lips, we have our privacy."

He tested his boss. "I appreciate you ordering Jake and Dmitry to shut down the slow-kills."

"Since we're alone, I'll share with you that the decision was a difficult one."

"But the right one."

"For now. Jake's correct, though. This will end with a slow-kill if we can't create a better option."

"There's got to be a way. You and Jake invented an entire industry based upon stealing or disabling submarines."

"This is no mere submarine. It's my flagship, and I want it back as much as you do, perhaps even more."

"Sorry, I forget it's your ship. I keep calling it mine."

"That's acceptable. Though I own it, you command it. I applaud your pride in ownership."

Cahill embraced the sentiment. "Well, then. I want me damned ship back."

"Understood. Shall we compare notes?"

"I haven't really sorted through my ideas yet."

"Stream of consciousness is fine."

The Australian recalled his first foray with the Frenchman's fleet. They'd stolen a Malaysian submarine by landing divers on its snorkel mast and injecting the ship with poison. "What if we did what we did when we took the *Wraith*?"

"Possibly. But I don't know how long it would take to get canisters of poison ready or if there's any predictability on the *Goliath* using its air intakes."

"I know. There's enough MESMA fuel for it to run hundreds of miles submerged, unfortunately."

"That's a good idea, though. We need to come at this with several ideas in parallel."

Cahill prioritized his backlog of ideas and revealed the next one on his list. "We could alter a slow-kill to deploy only one or two bomblets."

"That might work, but it's tedious. Imagine if we were to place one hole in the control room. Then one in the crew's mess. Then one in a MESMA plant. And so on and so forth until we'd sink it by a death of a thousand cuts."

"I see. If we never hit the port engine room, those mongrels may keep pressing their luck and running."

"I lament that the Lynx helicopter couldn't finish the job, but the hijackers submerged too quickly."

"I'm sure it took several hits for twenty-millimeter rounds to make a sizeable hole in me ship."

The Frenchman frowned and looked to his arm. "I must take this call. Excuse me."

As his boss stepped away, Cahill pondered the identity of the culprits. He reckoned the *Wraith's* original Malaysian owners might be settling a score–with interest–by grabbing the more expensive combat cargo ship.

After joining the Frenchman's fleet and taking command of the *Goliath*, he'd helped rescue a South Korean submarine from its northern adversaries. He questioned if the North Koreans sought vengeance through the theft.

Next, he'd challenged the conquerors of Crimea by vandalizing its connecting infrastructure, and he wondered if the hijacking represented Russian revenge.

Then, his attack on Greece had created a NATO enemy with a reason to seek the *Goliath*.

Finally, Cahill's interference in an Israeli civil war had left a failing prime minister who'd enjoy a public relations coup by stealing the ship that had ruined him.

The Australian then recalled what he knew of his boss' history prior to his employment. The Chinese, Pakistanis, Syrians, Iranians, and Argentines could claim scores worth settling. Then his mind flitted over a mental map of random nations and rogue actors that could benefit from the *Goliath's* stealth, speed, and firepower.

He accepted that the hijacker could be anyone as the Frenchman's face returned on the screen. "I wish I had better news. I need you to keep a secret."

"Of course."

Cahill's boss leaned forward and lowered his voice. "I mean from our team, especially Jake."

"From Jake? What's wrong?"

"His state of mind is too bellicose. I shouldn't be surprised, since he's wrestled with a deep anger since his childhood, and it still underpins his personality."

"Okay, mate. I'll keep the secret."

"I stretched the truth earlier when I implied I was hesitant to call Miss McDonald. In fact, I called her immediately when I had the chance, and I shared everything."

"That was risky."

"And she just called me back. She's threatened to share our predicament with the Fifth Fleet."

"Bloody hell. Is she trying to kill us?"

The Frenchman shook his head. "I released her from any confidentiality."

"Dear God. Why?"

"Because, if I'm honest with myself, I'd rather destroy the *Goliath* than let it become an instrument of wanton destruction in hostile hands. If we fall short of stopping it, I want the Americans to sink it before it could damage their assets."

Cahill considered the *Goliath* part of his identity. He credited it with attracting his lover, the Israeli intelligence officer who'd become enamored with his deeds before meeting him. He equated losing his command to losing his manhood. "Well, shit. What's that mean for us?"

"I know her well, and most of the implications were expressed in the words she didn't say."

"Okay, what didn't tell you?"

"She understands the concept of a choke point, and I expect she'll formally inform the Fifth Fleet before the *Goliath* reaches the Strait of Hormuz. Nothing gets through the strait unheard by the U.S. Navy, and it's a proper point for them to engage. It would be irresponsible to let the *Goliath* pass into the Persian

Gulf."

Cahill's mental map placed the American naval base more than one hundred miles outside his ship's railgun range from the Strait of Hormuz. "That's harshly conservative. But I understand."

"Even if she's not planning to draw the line, I will. I'm declaring the line of longitude running through Bandar Abbas as our terminus for having assets from the Fifth Fleet sink it."

Cahill trusted his boss' judgment, but he wondered if informing his CIA link had caused more harm than good. "I don't mean to be rude, but did she bother to help us?"

"She'll give us some surveillance, and she was able to accelerate a transiting American destroyer out of harm's way ahead of the *Goliath*. She also convinced the American fleet's admiral to divert an Indian frigate from entering our flagship's weapons range."

"She did that without raising suspicions?"

The Frenchman waved his fingers. "She has tricks to request modest course changes. She can claim knowledge of Chinese spy satellite coverage, for example."

"Okay, then. I'm glad you made the call."

"But the Bandar Abbas limit remains."

"A line is drawn, then."

"Indeed. I suggest we outline our reaction plan immediately. The clock works against us."

CHAPTER 7

The colonel scolded his submarine commander. "I shouldn't have let you talk me into remaining surfaced."

"We were going to take damage either way. It would have been worse with the bomblet torpedoes."

"You may be right, but let's not argue the past. I shouldn't have brought it up."

"I'd rather have you vent your frustrations than see them overwhelm you at the wrong moment."

"Good point. Are you ready?"

"Go ahead."

He grabbed a latch and opened the door to the damaged MESMA plant. The wailing grew louder, and he realized he'd adapted to ignoring the limpets' whining.

After stepping into the compartment, the colonel closed the door behind the commander and faced the spray. A handful of high holes spat liquid onto the propulsion plant's piping. Thin sheets cascaded down the heat exchanger, rolled over pumps and panels, and formed a placid pool in the bilge. "How bad is this?"

"With shoring, we could slow the influx and run the plant. But it should remain our last priority."

"We may need every knot we can get."

The commander shrugged. "Maybe, but we can bring this plant online last."

"Shouldn't we do something about this now?"

"Maybe. Hold on."

Raising his arm as a shield against droplets, the commander stepped into the salty rain and then disappeared behind the electric generator. Following bursts of metallic banging, he appeared with a waterproofed bag over his shoulder.

After a return trot through the rain, the commander dropped the sack to the deck. He unfurled it, opening an array of twine, mallets, rubber matting, cutting tools, and wooden blocks. Kneeling, he grabbed conical wedges and a rubber hammer and then stood. "You're strong. I'll get on your shoulders."

"How'd you know where to find all this?"

"It seemed like a proper place for a damage control locker."

"I'm wiser than I thought for having recruited you."

The commander scoffed. "Don't flatter either of us. Not while we're fighting for our lives."

The colonel nodded at his companion's hands. "That's all we need?"

"I'll plug some holes, and that should be enough for the pumps to get ahead of it."

"So be it." The colonel turned and squatted, and his companion felt like a feather mounting his back. He stepped into the droplets and steadied himself against the twisting torque of his partner's hammering. As wooden plugs filled holes, the spraying pattern widened but the steadier streams disappeared.

The commander yelled from the colonel's shoulders. "Okay! That's good!"

"That's it? It sounds worse than before."

"It's like a garden hose when you block it with your thumb. It looks more violent, but the flow is less."

Escaping the seawater shower, the colonel lowered his haunches to lighten his load, and then he reached for an elevated door. He turned athwartships towards the tunnel that connected the halves of his stolen bounty. Reaching through the circular doorway, he hoisted his torso into the cramped space and began crawling.

The commander's voice rang with a tinny tone in the tunnel. "I'll stay on this side, then?"

"Get back to the control room and keep us going as fast as our propulsion limits allow. I'll return when I can." At first, crawling through the confines bothered the colonel. Difficult to clean, the intra-hull tunnel smelled stale, and the atmosphere seemed weighty. But as he approached the midpoint between the hulls, distance muffled the grating chirp of the magnetic parasites.

At the deepest point in the tunnel, he considered the crawl-space that confined him an elongated coffin filled with damp, thick air that tasted dusty.

Bowing his head to avoid the air-intake cross-connect, he watched his symmetric shadows stretch under the thin grating that served as a floor. His regulated breathing echoed off the bilge, where condensation reflected light from the twin rows of LED bulbs that ran beside the crossing air duct.

He hastened his movement as he squirmed by hydraulic lines that fed an oversized block of metal. He craned his neck and watched steel arms move outward through grease-coated holes into an invisible nook that shaped the hydrodynamic rear of the ship and housed the rocker that swung the stern planes.

Scrunching his shoulders, he slipped past the planes' controller and forced himself onward to a door that gave way to the heat and hissing of the port hull's MESMA plant six.

As his head emerged into humidity, he twisted and grabbed a bar. He pulled his shoulders through the portal and then reached for a higher bar. With his waist freed, he walked his heels out and pushed his buttocks free. He drove his haunches backwards, making space for his legs and feet to back into the compartment and transfer his weight to rungs mounted below the door.

He stood and gathered his bearings.

Within the ethanol-liquid-oxygen propulsion MESMA plant, the hiss of steam rang, and soothing heat wafted over him, but a new grouping of limpets howled.

"Accursed sirens."

He found the sixth air-independent propulsion plant humming but void of occupants, and he marched to MESMA plant four. As he stepped into the space, he saw three men stepping out its far, forward door. Making eye contact with the last, his bulldog, he gestured to him and met him in the room's center.

"Is this plant bearing load?"

"Yes, sir. We just got it up and running and coordinated a speed increase with the control room."

"What's our new speed?"

"We're making turns for nine knots on MESMA plants four and six, but we're moving at six point three knots using just the port engine room's propeller."

"Understood. I assume you sent the men to get working on MESMA two now?"

"Of course."

"They can do it without you, right?"

"Sure. They have a handle on it now."

"Good. Show me the Stinger missiles."

The sergeant marched ahead and ducked through a frame into the port hull's forward propulsion plant. Trailing him, the colonel stepped through the dogged-open door and saw men obeying the instructions of the MESMA expert in bringing up the equipment.

After giving quick congratulations about succeeding with the power generation, he ushered the bulldog into the next compartment. There, he found an open space that paralleled the starboard side's galley and mess. The quiet compartment had dining tables, housed spare parts, and served as the recreational space for the *Goliath's* proper crew.

Hundreds of spare railgun rounds covered the free spaces between pieces of exercise equipment. Some crates formed short walls around a treadmill, and others concealed the lower half of a Bowflex machine.

Disordered from the weapons' methodical inventorying arrangement, a lone, opened rectangular crate stood out and caught the colonel's attention. "I suppose that's a Stinger?"

"It is, sir. We were getting it ready when we were attacked."

"Yes. I learned quickly that a flooding problem can make one's day stressful. How many Stingers did you find?"

"Twenty-four missiles and two launchers. I don't think we'll run out."

"No, we won't. Stage four missiles by the hatch and have all the soldiers know where they are."

"Of course, sir."

"And make sure there's always a soldier in MESMA two who can grab a Stinger and head topside every time we surface."

"Every time. I see."

The colonel calculated the numbers underlying his survival. "If we stay submerged, the submarines will keep pace with us, and that's unacceptable. I never planned for them to react so quickly, and I blame myself for underestimating Renard. I won't do it again."

"Our guys are warriors. If you give me thirty seconds of warning each time you surface, I'll have two guys get a Stinger up there and ready to launch within ten seconds of you saying 'go'."

"Do I really have to say 'go'?"

"Something like that. How else would they know it's safe to open the hatch?"

"Right. I'll say something more obvious."

"How about 'Stingers topside'?"

"That's fine. Stingers topside."

The colonel weighed a risky move. "Get a team ready now."

"For training, or for real?"

"For real."

"Then I'll send myself up with a Stinger."

"I can't afford to lose you."

"You sound like you know there's a helicopter above us."

"There is. Even with these accursed limpet parasites, our sonar operator can hear it. It's following us off our port beam, like it's waiting to shoot our port engine room."

"Then let me go up."

Needing to play God, the colonel did. "You're not our best Stinger operator."

"I've trained on it."

"Everyone's trained on it. I want the best man to go up and send the message that needs to be sent."

Fighting what seemed a battle between bravado, self-respect, and utilitarianism, the bulldog offered a cold stare. "It should be me, sir."

"You know the man I want. Get him."

The sergeant marched away, and the colonel pulled a sound-powered phone from its cradle. "Control room, MESMA two. Come in."

The commander's voice reverberated from its reflection off equipment in the control center en route to an overhead microphone. "This is the control room. Go ahead MESMA two."

"I'm stationing a man below the port hatch with a Stinger missile. I'll want you to surface to allow him to take down the helicopter. Once that's done, I'll want you to shift propulsion to the port gas turbine."

"If your man fails?"

"Then you submerge immediately. You'll have to be on the bridge to watch this in real time."

"Actually, I don't. I found access to the camera system with lights that illuminate our hull underwater. Remember that this ship was built for loading and unloading cargo submarines underwater."

"Would that also allow you to watch the helicopter?"

"Yes, there are cameras mounted atop the weapons bays."

Sighing through his nostrils, the colonel wanted to accuse the officer of cowardice for avoiding the exposed bridge. But he conceded the man's safer tactics were sound. "Agreed, then. If you see him fail, submerge immediately."

"When should I surface?"

"I'll tell you. Contact the engine room first and make sure they're ready to use the gas turbine."

The bulldog reentered the compartment with a young soldier behind him. Wearing a mask of bravado, the youngster projected a commando's air of invincibility. "I hear you need some ass kicking."

"You heard correctly. You know what you're up against?"

"A Westland Super Lynx, Mark One-Twenty. Omani Air Force. Two twenty-millimeter cannons. It's capable of carrying eight anti-tank missiles, but it's a coin toss if it's got the launchers attached on such short notice."

"Impressive. You know what you're facing. But do you know why the men shooting at you will do so with resolve?"

The warrior shrugged. "Because we insulted their nation by stealing this ship from their capital city?"

"That's part of it. But would you like to know the real reason these men will stare down your Stinger missile and shoot back with true aim to kill you?"

After swallowing, the youngster mustered a courageous tone. "Yes, sir. I would."

"I've studied Pierre Renard's history. I know him, and I know his tactics. He's offered each man in that helicopter crew one hundred thousand Euro for each man on this ship that they kill."

"You can't be serious."

"Can't I? Based upon his history, he's already paying out a quarter million Euro to each member of the last helicopter's crew for taking away our starboard engine room."

The warrior's voice weakened. "A quarter million each? How can you be so sure of the amount?"

"He's consistent. He's methodical. He repeats what's worked in the past. And the worst of it is, he has a deep sense of guilt, and he compensates for it by giving a full one million Euro to each widow he creates. That does a lot for a man's courage."

After absorbing the danger, the young man furrowed his brow while steeling his nerves. "Then let me make some rich widows."

"I commend your fighting spirit."

The sergeant stepped forward and continued towards the weapons stores. "I'll rerun the diagnostics on these and have them ready."

The colonel raised his palm. "You'll 'rerun' them, will you? Would you rerun them if it were you going up?"

The bulldog lowered his gaze.

"Then bring both launchers over here."

With the young commando's aid, the bulldog carried two

loaded Stinger systems under the hatch.

The colonel clarified the tactics. "You'll go up the ladder, open the hatch, and climb until your shoulders are high enough to hold the launcher. Then we'll lift it to you, and you'll do your duty. If you need a second shot, drop the first launcher and we'll hand you the other. Don't worry about us getting out of the way."

With the youngster standing below the exit, the colonel lifted the phone receiver to his cheek. "Control room, MESMA two, come in."

The submarine commander's voice issued from the speaker. "This is the control room. Go ahead MESMA two."

"Are you ready to surface and shift propulsion to the port gas turbine?"

"I'm ready. I'm watching the hatch on video, too, and I'll be looking for the helicopter with our rear cameras."

"Let me know immediately over the loudspeaker when we're surfaced so I can send up the missile launcher."

"I will announce it immediately."

"Very well. Surface the ship."

Seconds passed like days until the announcement rang from the speakers, and then time accelerated into a compressed crunch.

In a blur, the young warrior pushed open the hatch, and a circle of starlit darkness appeared. The commando's silhouette engulfed a third of the twinkling, and the colonel grasped the weapon and heaved it up. Metal pelted metal in a brief staccato chirping, and then rocket exhaust burned the blackness.

The youngster's limp frame fell, and the colonel caught him while his bulldog darted up the ladder, dragged down the missile launcher, and then sealed the hole.

The sergeant grabbed the phone and screamed to the control room to submerge.

Silence.

Then the commander's urgent order rang from the loudspeakers. "Medic, lay to MESMA plant two. Medic, lay to MESMA plant two."

With a history of coolness under pressure, the sergeant remained calm. "We were already submerging before I called the control room. I'll grant that our submarine commander was paying attention and was quick to act."

The colonel feared he'd lost a man. "What happened?"

"He couldn't get off a good shot. The bastards were ready for him and shot fast, and they had flares to draw away the missile."

"Damn." The colonel looked into the terrified eyes of the bleeding warrior, who faced death.

Kneeling, the bulldog compressed the entry wound above the man's left lung and urged the colonel to press the wound he feared gave entry into the right lung.

"Am I going to die?"

The sergeant was convincing. "No, lad. We've got the best medic in the world. He's on his way."

As death teased the youth, the colonel wondered if he could create a better outcome by sending multiple men topside together to overwhelm the countermeasures and assure that one missile found its mark.

CHAPTER 8

Jake glanced at the system time on a Subtics monitor and mentally calculated twenty-eight hours separating the *Goliath* from its destruction by the U.S. Navy's intervention. "Henri, set up a tracker to give us distance and time until the *Goliath* reaches the tripwire. Have it update every thirty seconds based upon the *Goliath's* position and speed."

The Frenchman stood from his station and turned to the central plotting table. Within a minute, a new window tracked the submersible ship's speed, its distance from fifty-six and a quarter degrees east longitude, and the time remaining until the *Goliath* reached the U.S Navy's declared demarcation of death.

With two hundred miles to travel and the three port MESMA plants providing a speed of seven point two knots on the port propeller, the system showed twenty-seven hours and forty minutes.

"Good enough, Jake?"

"Yeah. We're in trouble if the Omani flight crews lose their nerve. I'd be heading home now if I were them."

"I think not. Imagine if you loved helicopters as much as you loved submarines. With your confidence, you might fight for the sake of the challenge."

Jake considered helicopters his natural enemy but agreed. "Yeah, maybe. For self-respect."

"Or purpose. I assume you agree there are purposes worth dying for."

Jake appreciated Henri's timely philosophical witticisms, which distracted him from his stressors. But this comment made him question if the *Goliath's* theft marked the beginning of the end.

He teased himself that it might be a divine sign for him to abandon violence and seek peaceful ways to carry his share of humanity's burden. But beyond his lead role in Renard's fleet, he foresaw nothing, and past prayers had left a future outside the realm of mercenary combat murky.

Barring supernatural guidance to the contrary, Jake was in his proper realm, regardless if caught by surprise and reacting to an ambush. But his mood remained somber, like the crew around him, with their flagship's uncertain future.

He stepped down from the conning platform, joined the French mechanic by the plot, and murmured a retort. "I don't think anyone out here's trying to get killed. That's a bit dramatic, don't you think?"

"Dramatic perhaps, but consuming the thoughts of the men in battle."

"I have no idea what an Omani airman might be thinking."

"Officially, per the state religion, they all should believe in an afterlife."

"Officially, per my beliefs, so do I. I believe that the consciousness can survive death, but I'm not planning on dying early just to find out. And neither are they."

His distraction apparently exhausted, the Frenchman looked to his panel. "Pierre will make this work."

"I'm sure he's paying them well."

"Pierre can tell when people are receptive to monetary motivation. I expect he's issued bounties and other rewards."

"Well, shit. This has grown into a full-blown mission, and the Omanis are getting our paychecks."

"Perhaps we should go on strike."

Jake liked the joke but could muster only a snort. "Thanks for trying to cheer me up. But I was bitching for the sake of bitching."

"Understood. I was attempting levity as much for my own sake as yours. I don't imagine we'll feel anything but twisted until we recapture the *Goliath*."

"Was I out of line when I tried to get Pierre to let me finish this with a slow-kill?"

"No, not given the tension we're under. You needed to speak your mind. But I can't say that I agreed with your intentions."

"Well, what the hell do you think we should do?"

"I've been considering a few possibilities."

"But you've got nothing better than a slow-kill?"

"I don't yet unfortunately, but I agree with Pierre and Terry that we need to use the time we have to pursue safer options."

Jake remembered stealing an American submarine and the leeway from his pursuers which had allowed his narrow escape. "I suppose I'm the only guy who thinks this gets worse before it gets better."

Hearing movement behind him, he turned to see his Australian colleague. "You may not be the only one. But you're the only guy with the guts to say it."

"Thanks, I guess. Was that a compliment?"

"Sort of. A bit of mending of figurative fences, but I may just be preparing you for bad news. Pierre's got new orders, and you may not like them."

"Try me."

The Australian explained them, and he was right.

Jake disliked them. "I don't suppose this is up for debate?"

"No, mate. Pierre likes it, and I wouldn't muck around. Save any more of your hard challenges for orders you really hate."

Thirty minutes later, Jake leaned over the central plotting table watching data from the *Specter's* hydrophones draw lines to the *Goliath*. "Have you ever seen anything like this?"

The Australian stood beside him. "This close and this accurate? Never."

His submarine aside the *Goliath*, Jake counted dozens of sonic lines shooting from the chirping limpets to his hull. The separation between the ships measured less than the *Specter's* length from its bow to the last hydrophone of its toward sonar array.

On the *Goliath's* far side, the *Wraith* held a symmetrical position to that of the *Specter*. "It doesn't get any tighter."

"No kidding, mate."

Jake looked at the toad-shaped head of his sonar expert. "Antoine, are you sure about the depth?"

"With those limpets being so close, yes. The depression angle on sonar puts the *Goliath* at twenty meters."

"That's right where you'd expect me ship to be per the automated diving routine."

"Are the starboard MESMA plants still down?"

Remy's toad-head swiveled. "Yes. It's still running on only three. Speed is holding at seven point two knots. But I hear sounds of them starting MESMA plant number one."

"They'll only go faster if we don't stop them. What the hell's holding up Pierre's air cavalry?" Jake's noticed the deck's rocking in the shallows and the gentle rumbling of the diesel engines while he charged his battery.

Over the loudspeakers, the Frenchman responded. "This is delicate flying. But the first two helicopters will be in position within three minutes. They have your periscope and Dmitry's on infrared."

"All they have to do is fly down the middle."

"I see that you've never flown a helicopter."

"I did once during summer training at the academy. It was like riding an angry bull."

"Then you have respect for the effort."

"I do, but good pilots can handle it. I'm just concerned what will happen if they don't release the nets fast enough."

"A valid concern. Which is why the nets aren't bolted to the aircraft. They'll be spooled out manually."

Jake envisioned airmen unrolling nets yard-by-yard from lockers aboard hovering helicopters and dropping them into the sea. He'd heard horror stories of submarines snagging rigging and dragging fishing ships underwater. An uncareful aircrew would turn their Lynx into the *Goliath's* sea anchor. "I imagine it could work."

"It will. Our fish is large and predictable, and the location is precisely between you and Dmitry."

"I don't suppose you'll tell me where you found the nets on short notice."

"The gillnets I'm using are common commodities in Muscat's fishing fleet. I specified the longest nets the helicopters could carry, and the rest was accomplished by a sense of duty on the part of the Omani team."

Jake silently appended the Frenchman's thought to include the thorough financial award structure he knew he'd created for every task. He respected his boss for his career of recruiting traitors and outcasts into people he could motivate. "Two hundred meters should be good enough."

"The *Goliath* by design is limited to one hundred meters of depth. You're tracking it at twenty. We have more than enough netting to succeed."

"Good job getting them out here so fast. We'll have to wait to see if this works."

"You sound dubious. Work the plan, and trust the results."

Glancing at the incoming sonar data and then at his control room team, Jake convinced himself the *Goliath* maintained its course and speed. Ignoring his concern about colliding with his quarry, he indulged in spectatorship by opening a window on the plotting table to the periscope's view.

Through a night vision filter, he watched the lead of two helicopters hovering two miles away. Cooler than the humid air, a thin rectangular form fell from the closer Lynx.

Renard confirmed what Jake saw. "The first helicopter is deploying its first net."

"Yeah, I see it. How many nets do they have?"

"Two each. That's all they could fit."

"Four nets should be enough to make a difference."

"So far, so good, they report. I'm having the second helicopter deploy its first net now."

While the aircraft fished for the *Goliath*, Jake watched them unfurl their snares with glacial lethargy. "How long's this going to take?"

"A good five minutes. It's a gravity feed limited by a hand-cranked spool."

The screen below the American's nose showed the *Goliath* reaching the snares in ten minutes. Facing uneventful moments, Jake freed his mind and aimed it beyond the rogue flagship. "Antoine, how easy will it be to hear the nets hitting the *Goliath*?"

Remy shrugged. "Not too hard. Even with the limpets, the rubbing and scraping will be loud."

"Put one of the other guys on it, and start searching for threats around us."

The toad head rotated towards Jake. "What sort of threat? I need to optimize my search."

"Keep it local. Submarines from Iran, Pakistan, India."

"That's it? Just three large fleets with submarines built by at least five countries?"

"Now that you mention it, throw in Malaysia. They're pissed at us for a good reason."

The sonar expert frowned and faced his monitor. "I'll just listen for fifty-hertz electric plants."

"That's too broad. You'll hear surfaced contacts."

"I can sort them out."

"I know you can, but it will take time and distract you."

"You have a better idea?"

Jake pulled an ancient tactic from the submarine archive. "Use active."

The toad-head rotated back towards Jake. "How active? Secure chirps?"

"No. Go all out, full power."

"Seriously?"

Making use of free expert advice, Jake stole a glance at Cahill, who nodded his concurrence and boosted the confidence in his decision. "Yeah. We're close enough to the *Goliath* that it won't matter that we're announcing ourselves. Anyone out there will think our sonar bursts are coming from the *Goliath*."

Remy needed extra convincing. "But the *Goliath* doesn't have an active sonar. At least not a tactical search system."

"Anyone who knows that is working with the hijackers and

won't shoot us for fear of hitting them." Jake raised his voice and continued. "Do you have any heartburn with this, Pierre?"

"It's unconventional, but I agree. Something could be out there waiting in ambush, and this is the only way to counter such a threat. But I'll have Dmitry keep his active sonar secure, since only one of you needs to do this."

"Thank you, Pierre."

"All out active it is." Remy tapped icons, and moments later, powerful tones boomed outside the hull.

Jake discerned the clockwise march of sheets of sound moving from left to right as the *Specter* pounded the gulf in a methodical sweep in hopes of uprooting hidden dangers. "Shit, that was loud."

"Bloody loud."

Silent seconds passed as the sonar guru studied the echoes. "Nothing. I see only the *Goliath*, which is blocking the *Wraith's* return. It's blocking a large sector, actually."

Jake found the sonic pounding less intrusive during the second active search sequence. "I'm sure we'll get used to this."

"Part of me hopes not, mate. It's not right to run with our active sonar blaring."

"This whole day's about things not being right. We need to make them right. Somehow."

"You still want to end this fast, don't you?"

"Yeah, I do."

"I'd agree with you, except for one thing."

"What's that?"

"Once you blow holes in me ship, you can't un-blow them. We need to try the other options first."

"No need to argue. The boss is on your side, and I know when to shut up and follow orders."

"But you looked spewing mad, mate."

Jake assessed his anger and sensed some truth in the Australian's observation. "I thought I was hiding it."

"Not really. You're pretty transparent."

After the *Specter's* third active sweep seemed to slide into a tolerable background cadence, Jake welcomed the distraction of a young sonar technician. "I hear the first net hitting the *Goliath*."

Jake aimed his voice towards the youngster. "What do you hear, specifically?"

"Metallic banging. It sounds like there are weights spread all across the net."

"Good. That makes sense."

"The second net has caught now."

The night vision scene from the periscope showed the lead Lynx dipping towards the water, compelling Jake to raise his voice towards the overhead microphone. "What's going on, Pierre?"

"The helicopters are flying forward now to assure that the nets become draped over the *Goliath's* cargo bed."

"They're cutting it close to the wave tops."

"Don't worry. Military pilots enjoy testing their skills, and as you noted, good pilots can handle it."

Jake watched the first aircraft drop a pulsating light atop a buoy that marked the end of its net. The helicopter shot upward, freed from its load. A minute later, the second Lynx sprang skyward and joined the first in repositioning itself ahead of the *Goliath*. "So that's it?"

The Australian submarine commander aimed his voice upward. "That's it for the first run only. Right, Pierre?"

"That's correct."

Jake grunted. "Doesn't sound like either net is doing us the favor of catching the *Goliath's* propeller."

Cahill shrugged. "That would have taken some luck."

"I could've told you this isn't our lucky day."

"Then we'll win with skill. Look, speed has dropped."

Jake saw lines between the limpets and the *Specter's* hydrophones showing the *Goliath* lagging the submarine. "Seven knots. Already an hour of helicopters flying around just for two tenths of a knot of drag."

"Let's see what the next pass brings. They'll dump the lockers overboard with the nets to act as sea anchors."

As the aircraft lowered their second nets, Jake noticed the *Goliath* complied by maintaining its course. He questioned why the hijackers feared turning away, but he realized the time invested in steering clear of the helicopters would create worse delays than the unwanted drag–at least in the short term.

His reasoning convinced him the assailants sought a nearby target, a goal close enough to taste. The conclusion abraded his thinning patience.

Anxiety became tapping fingers, inviting a glare from his Australian colleague. "Are you always like this? You're behaving like a wuss."

Behind Jake's shoulder, the mechanic failed to bite back a guffaw. The American turned and offered his French retort. "Shut up, whore."

"Sorry, Jake. It's just that he's right."

"That's enough, you bastard asshole." Jake switched to English for Cahill's sake. "You might have a good point, my friend from Down Under. So good, in fact, that I'm going to excuse myself and let you serve as my command duty officer, to include weapons launch authority."

"I was just trying to cheer you up, mate. It's just a joke."

"There's something I need to do in the torpedo room. Now's as good a time as any to hand the ship over to you. That is, if our fleet admiral will allow it."

Over the loudspeaker, the French boss sounded skeptical. "It depends where you're going with this."

"I'm going to break into a slow-kill warhead myself and see if I can modify it to yield a single bomblet."

"At least see what the second set of nets does to me ship."

"No, let him go, Terry. He's creating another option. I won't have any more helicopters for several hours due to readying assets at this time of night. I was lucky the Omanis could pull three crews together on short notice. I'm afraid we're at a limit."

"One on station with guns to keep me ship under, two running back and forth for more fuel and more nets."

"Right. And barring the luck of a net entangling the propeller, each net would have a diminishing effect. I'm inclined to discontinue this fishing expedition and dedicate the helicopters to a reliable rotation of gunships over the *Goliath*."

Jake glanced at the periscope optics before stepping away. "Looks like the second nets are catching."

A young sonar operator cried out. "They're harder to hear the second time with all the noise from the first nets, but I can hear them now."

"You're sure you don't want to stick around and watch me ship get slowed even more?"

"No, thanks. I've got work to do."

"All by yourself?"

Jake looked to his silver-haired mechanic but knew Henri's ship control skills were vital in supporting Cahill this close to their submerged prey. His thoughts gravitated to his crew's other technical genius. He lifted a sound-powered phone to his cheek, flipped its address to the engine room, and whipped the dial.

LaFontaine answered. "Engine room."

"Claude. You're just the guy I'm looking for. Meet me in the torpedo room and plan on spending a few hours with me."

"May I ask what this is about?"

"Care to guess?"

"It can mean only one thing."

"You like the idea enough to try it with me?"

Jake waited while the Frenchman gathered himself. "I'll bring my tools and a pack of cigarettes."

CHAPTER 9

Olivia scrutinized the message behind the Frenchman's comments. His tone, his pace, the chinks in his emotional mask… they informed her faster than his words.

He'd been afraid, but now he held hope. "Four nets are applied, and I slowed the *Goliath* to seven knots."

"My latest update has it moving at eight point seven."

"Yes, that's true. After my team laid the nets, the hijackers brought up the remaining MESMA plants."

The monster threw a jab. "Your claim of seven knots was misleading."

"No, it was true at the time, for reference. But with all six plants running, the *Goliath* should be making over nine knots. So now that it's making only eight point seven knots, the nets are performing well at the higher speed."

Acknowledging the Frenchman's confidence, the monster receded, but Olivia questioned if the outcome justified the effort. "It still sounds like tin cans tied behind a car of newlyweds."

"It's a powerful ship and hard to slow, even with just the one propeller. But the time invested in the fishing operation has paid for itself in the added delay between the *Goliath* and the tripwire."

"The netting may help, but it sounds like a stalemate in a game we need to win."

"A stalemate or perhaps better, depending when we recapture the *Goliath*."

"Let's cut to it, then. What's your plan to recapture it?"

The Frenchman's hesitance suggested uncertainty. "I have several options I intend to exercise in sequence until one works, or in parallel wherever possible."

"I'm listening."

"My security team's developing a plan to attach swimmers and force the surfacing, and Jake's modifying a slow-kill weapon to yield a single bomblet, with the same desired outcome. There are other options, but these two are the most viable."

She tested his confidence. "Those ideas are your most viable? Why not just send in Dmitry's dolphins?"

"They'd attack windows and only damage the dome. They're useless in slowing the *Goliath*, unfortunately."

The Frenchman's serious response negated the jab of her sarcastic dolphin comment. She admired his subtle shrewdness and shifted her tactics. "Okay, Pierre. I'll trust your planning since you've got a perfect track record. I've got updates for you on the positions of naval assets, and–"

"One moment, please."

His tone tightened her chest, and she strained to speak. "What's wrong?"

"Jake and Dmitry both report the *Goliath* turning."

"Which way?"

"To the starboard, steadied already on course zero-zero-six."

Having spent weeks aboard a submarine with Renard a decade earlier, she remembered the patience required in resolving a submerged target's change in direction. The Frenchman's rapid response surprised her.

Then she remembered an obscure benefit of the limpets chirping at a constant sonic frequency. Antoine Remy needed only seconds to identify the Doppler shift of the limpets and tell which way the *Goliath* turned.

She recognized a discrepancy. "That's the wrong way. That's away from Hormuz."

"And it's towards the Iranian coast."

"Do your guys have a new direction, uh, what do you call it? Heading? A new heading for the *Goliath*?"

"Possibly. Allow me to enquire."

"Go ahead."

After taking several deep breaths to calm herself, she heard the Frenchman's response. "Due north."

She compared the stolen ship's new direction against her memory of the Gulf of Oman chart. "That's the shortest route to Iranian waters."

"So it is."

"You can't follow the *Goliath* into Iranian waters, and you can't ask the Omanis to fly into Iranian air space. Your deadline just got tightened."

His hesitance catalyzed her hypersensitivity to his mood, and she noticed a slight tone of defiance in his voice. "Agreed. The *Goliath* is ninety-six miles from Iranian waters. That gives me an earlier tripwire at eleven hours."

She considered challenging his compliance. Although he voiced his recognition of the new time constraint, she detected his dismissal of it. But she kept her sensation secret.

The chilling concept of the Iranians crushing her world froze the inner girl, but the monster stayed cool. It made her withhold her challenge of Renard's intentions–to judge him innocent until future evidence would implicate him threatening to cross the Iranian nautical boundary. Instead of attacking the Frenchman with a premature accusation, her beast made her use the new clue. "This means something. I'm going to take a harder look at possible Iranian involvement."

"I wouldn't rush to a conclusion. It's possible I simply scared the thieves into running towards a border they believe their pursuers won't cross. I've made them desperate."

The *Goliath's* turn towards the Persians tickled her mind, and she considered a connection. "This is the first clue pointing to any nation, and if the Iranians are involved, I need to know."

"I've always trusted your instincts. I'll defer to you."

"Yeah... this is what I do best." Her head drifted towards the human psyche and its governing motivations. Then she morphed her mind into the perspective of a Persian man, rooted in the religion of submission, possibly wronged by Renard, and equipped to enact vengeance.

Her thoughts tumbled and ricocheted through myriad mazes,

seeking possibilities but leaving her lost.

An Iranian faction seeking an electromagnetic pulse attack against the United States had suffered nine years ago from Renard's intervention, but the hypothetical chain of vengeance from that source seemed vapid.

She recalled recent hostilities Renard had inflicted on the Iranian submarine fleet, but Volkov's dolphin attack against a *Kilo*-class vessel amounted to an insult she doubted would compel Persian vengeance.

Later, she'd give it deeper thought, but for now, she had nothing.

"Olivia?"

"What? Sorry. I need to probe for suspicious activities that don't get automatically flagged."

"Yes, of course. But before that, please remember to send me the tactical update."

"I'll have someone send you the data of nearby naval assets, but the summary is that you're clear."

"You mean I'm clear on what's known—surface combatants."

"If I help with friendly submarines, I'll draw attention by asking the question, and I can't help you with non-friendly submarines at all."

He paused, seeming to collect his thoughts. "Non-friendly around here means Iran. And given their massive numbers, they're a problem. I need whatever information you can give me on the Persian fleet."

"I can find out which submarines are in port and when the rest deployed. I'll make sure you get that information ASAP."

"I appreciate it. I'm speeding into the jaws of the world's fifth largest submarine fleet, and it's a competent one."

She tapped her memory banks of the Frenchman's victims. "The *Kilo* submarine Dmitry damaged almost five months ago is repaired and deployed again. That's one angry commanding officer with one angry crew."

"I doubt the minimal damage I inflicted on just one submarine would put me on a nation's most wanted list."

"It's hard to say. Wounded pride can motivate men, but I agree that Iran barely breaks the top ten list of people who want to disembowel you."

"Well, I never killed any of them."

"They may still be trying to even the score."

"Regardless, I assume you wish to become knee-deep in dossiers, and I need to return to tactical matters."

"Yes, you do. Don't screw me, Pierre. Don't screw this up."

He scoffed. "Have I ever?"

"Argentina. Crimea. And probably a few other times you covered up before I found out."

"And I covered up–adapted my plans, rather–in those situations because I excel at turning chaos into control. And I will return the *Goliath* into my possession in one functional piece."

"I can't afford to share your confidence. Not when you've been caught off guard like this."

"Young lady, my own interests aside, I'd win this ship back to protect you as a gesture of our friendship, which I hold dear despite your view of me as a manipulator."

The monster insulated the inner girl from feelings. "I also can't afford to trust a friendship."

"It's unfortunate, but I understand why you cannot."

"But I can trust your interests. While they're aligned with mine, we're more powerful together than apart."

"It's a synergy, if you'll excuse the cliché."

"Get the *Goliath* back. I'll be watching."

She hung up and slid her phone into her pants pocket.

Looking away to clear her mind, she saw December's early darkness blotting her office windows, and she recognized the challenge of supporting the Frenchman after hours. Any assistance she might seek beyond normal intelligence traffic risked being construed as suspicious within the CIA's self-policing machine.

Curious in the Iran possibility, she needed private help–a favor that might require a gift in return.

She remembered her Iran expert, Matt Williams, who had

helped her six years ago. Back then, he'd given her overt advice, and she'd limited her gratitude to polite greetings when they're paths crossed and to positive comments about his abilities when the topic arose with CIA colleagues.

Her informal approval had earned the junior analyst immediate advancement and had given him momentum for his next promotion.

She suspected he retained his gratitude for her backing of his success, but she acknowledged the fickleness of memory and the inaccuracies in the accounting of intangible favors. If he considered himself free of her debt, she'd need to offer him something.

Scanning her mental inventory of influence, she remembered a drunken flirtation at a holiday party two years ago with his boss. The sloppy kissing amounted to nothing beyond ammunition to blackmail her victim, but the threat of one phone call to a jealous wife gave Olivia leverage.

Her inner child recoiled while the beast tallied the count. A threat to his boss would beget a gift to Matt Williams–if he had the audacity and courage to demand something in return for the favor she prepared to request.

She found his number, dialed it, and put her phone to her ear.

His voice was strong and confident, like a man who'd grown accustomed to being revered in his position. By casting a shred of her luminance upon him years ago, she'd made him. "This is Matt."

"Hi, Matt. Olivia McDonald. Is now a good time to talk?"

His tone remained strong but carried the expected reverence. "Olivia McDonald? Of course. How can I help?"

"I'm running a special operation tonight. I can't explain it on an unsecured line, but you'll like it. The only thing is, I need you in my office ASAP."

He feigned the requisite hesitance, but she heard the enthusiastic edge she'd remembered from years ago and hoped he'd accept as his compensation the unspoken promise of a reward to be defined later at her leisure. "Well, it's date night with my wife."

"I'd be happy to treat you and your wife to an extra special makeup date night, if that would be okay."

"Can I call her and get back to you?"

"Of course." After she hung up, she glanced at a screen showing the latest infrared UAV image over the *Goliath*. With the stolen ship submerged, the pair of pursuing periscopes marked its position. The fifteen-minute lapse between the *Wraith* and *Specter's* past two locations gave Olivia her estimate of the *Goliath's* speed at eight point seven knots.

A timer in the window's corner reached zero, and a new image rolled down her screen. Under a distant force's influence, a mouse cursor jumped to the fuzzy hues of the periscopes and stopped. The time and distance between consecutive UAV snapshots generated a new speed for the *Goliath*.

Eight point four knots.

A geeky support analyst's face in another corner window looked at her, and its mouth moved. "I just marked a change in speed, Miss McDonald."

She unmuted her microphone and responded. "I noticed."

"That's an average, of course. In reality, it's got to be moving slower than eight point four knots. The UAV was in use. So, I couldn't sneak a peek for you. If you'd authorize it, I could–"

"No."

"Um, okay."

Her inner girl felt shame for snapping, but the beast reminded her of her status. Then the monster reconsidered and commanded her to display gentleness. "I mean, it's not possible."

"You mind if I ask what's going on with these ships?"

She lied. "It's a training exercise. At least that's what they're telling me. I want you to help me watch them and make sure."

"Got you covered, ma'am."

A form in the finalized night vision image caught her eye. "What's that new lighter patch?"

"I just saw it. I'm not sure yet, but whatever it is, it's partially submerged."

"You don't know what it is?"

"Sorry, ma'am. I'm best with urban areas."

"Did you capture a visual spectrum photograph?"

"Yeah, but I didn't look at it yet. Hold on."

As the dark sea replaced the night vision hues, her eye adapted to the overhead view of moonlit nature, and she shifted her mind to resolving the maritime riddle. "It's got a feather, like the periscopes, only it's softer."

"A feather? You mean those small wakes?"

"Right."

"Okay, ma'am. I'll have to trust you on that. You know a lot about submarines."

Noting the new feather's motion in the same direction as the submarines, she realized it was either part of the *Goliath* or attached to it. She then deduced the new wake's source. Renard had ordered buoys attached to the nets, but the transport vessel had dragged them under until it slowed. Now one of them was breaching the surface. "I know more about submarines than I wanted to know. It's amazing what you learn by spending weeks on one."

"Your secret knowledge is safe with me."

"Much appreciated."

"Who'd believe a chronic whiskey abuser anyway?"

Her cell phone's vibration signaled Renard's hailing.

"I'm putting you on mute. See if you can get me an image during a free UAV window."

"Will do, ma'am."

She answered her ringing phone. "Calling to gloat prematurely?"

Renard sounded positive. "How I do enjoy your subtle jousting."

"We're racing a clock. What's on your mind?"

"I thought by your greeting you already knew."

"You called to tell me you slowed the *Goliath*. I'm dying to hear you brag about it."

"And then negate it as a premature celebration."

"Depending on your tone."

"My tone is rational."

She agreed. "Okay. I didn't mean to be a bitch. It's just that…"

"I understand. We're all reeling from this, but we'll succeed if we endure together."

"Go ahead. I noticed you slowed the *Goliath*."

"Well, no. Temperamental MESMA plants slowed the *Goliath*. Two of them tripped offline. The new speed is seven point six knots. That now leaves us twelve hours to Iranian waters."

"That's still the blink of an eye in submarine time, and they'll get a plant or two back up soon enough."

"They may, but I trust they'll struggle to hold eight knots from here."

As she dissected his mood, she sensed a dichotomy. A strong optimism masked a weakened but lingering fear. "At least the nets and your finicky power plants are giving us breathing room. You got anything else?"

"No, young lady. That's all the good news I can muster in one telephone call."

"Get at least one of your plans in motion, Pierre."

"Already in progress. I shall update you soon."

She hung up and reclined in her chair to rest her mind. Closing her eyes, she sensed her anxiety draining her energy, and she questioned how long she could endure the risk of the *Goliath's* escape.

Her phone vibrated, and when she looked at it, she noticed she'd missed a call from CIA agent Matthew Williams, who was calling her again.

This time, she answered. "Hello, Matthew."

"My wife's okay with me working tonight. I'm on my way."

"Good. Text me what you want for dinner, and I'll have it delivered with some good coffee. It's going to be an all-nighter."

CHAPTER 10

Terry Cahill sensed a dark force pervading the *Specter,* and he feared confronting it.

But he had to face it.

With the *Goliath* tracking north, he kept the *Specter* a mile abaft the transport ship's starboard quarter. The mirror image *Wraith* trailed the stolen vessel on its port side, deeper than Cahill.

He sought a private conversation with Henri and joined the Frenchman at his ship's control station. "How are you doing, mate?"

"As well as can be expected."

"Not our best day, is it?"

"It's taking an effort to maintain my composure."

The Australian challenged the dark force. "We're all still in shock. I think Jake's taking it the worst."

The Frenchman's assertiveness surprised him. "Are you challenging his frame of mind?"

"I wouldn't call it a challenge. Nor would I necessarily call it his frame of mind."

"Perhaps you can clarify your meaning."

Cahill considered tempering his response, but he opted for candor. "Right, then. I'm challenging his frame of mind."

"Watch yourself."

"I don't mean to start a power struggle, but it's a valid concern."

"That depends on what your concern really is. He's obviously emotional, but what do you hope to achieve by confronting him?"

"Nothing viscous, mate. I just want to make peace."

"I wasn't aware there was a war."

"Maybe it's all in me head. But to be sure, I should have a candid discussion to make sure we share the same goal."

"If you want to approach him, I suggest you let me help you."

The Frenchman's stare was strong, and Cahill took the hint to retreat. "Of course. I appreciate the offer. Since Jake's busy at the moment, we can do this at a more appropriate time."

He returned to the captain's foldout chair and sat. The tactical display showed the *Specter* holding a steady location relative to the unwavering *Goliath*, and Cahill realized he could leave the ship in junior hands.

After letting several minutes pass to allay the Frenchman's suspicions, he stood and called out. "Henri?"

"Yes, sir."

"I could use a short break."

The Frenchman gave a blank stare.

"You know what I mean, right, mate?"

"No, I'm sorry. I don't."

"To use the head."

"Ah, yes, of course. Jake normally uses the facilities and trusts me to handle the control room while he's gone. But in this case, I'm concerned about our proximity to the *Goliath*."

"You have no one who can conn this ship competently in Jake's absence?"

"Well, there is Julien." Henri tilted his head toward the young French sailor seated beside Remy's squat body.

"Does 'Julien' speak English?"

Julien answered for himself. "Yes, of course, I do. Jake lets me drive the ship quite often during our quiet hours."

"Would you know what to do if the *Goliath* turned towards us?"

The youngster looked upward in thought. "I'd turn left and keep turning until it was on the edge of our baffles. We're too close together to risk any fancier responses."

"Excellent. You can handle the basics for ten minutes. Do you have a man who can relieve you at your sonar station?"

"Noah can handle it."

Cahill looked to Remy for confirmation. As the toad-head nodded and then returned to its own distant world, the Australian commander accepted the gesture as a vote of confidence. "I believe that's a plan. Henri, please call Noah up here to fill in for Julien."

Two minutes later, the young Frenchmen exchanged roles at the sonar console, and Julien stepped up to the conning platform. "I'm ready to relieve you, Terry."

"I won't be gone long. I'll be back well before you'd need to snorkel."

"I can manage."

The Australian raised his voice. "Attention in the control room. I'm taking a short break. Julien has the conn and the deck."

Walking towards the *Specter's* bow, Cahill left the control room's humming air-conditioned consoles behind him and continued his walk forward.

When he arrived at the torpedo room's doorframe, he heard two men speaking in French. The words streamed over his ears as gibberish, but the speakers' tones revealed their meaning.

Jake and his engineering ace were arguing.

Risking a quick view, Cahill held his breath, stole a glance of the torpedo room, and then stepped back. As he processed the image of two frustrated men hunched over an opened warhead with an oscilloscope and test probes, he grasped the problem.

Jake's effort to reduce the explosive yield on a slow-kill weapon was stalled.

He opted to avoid the *Specter's* frustrated commander and to seek a different route to find an ally in recapturing the *Goliath*. He headed aft, searching for unusual company.

As he stepped into the mess deck, he found his targets—the francophone security team.

Wearing dark T-shirts and bluish camouflage pants, the six men huddled around a dinner table. Becoming the room's seventh inhabitant, Cahill silenced the French conversation.

The eldest warrior, a former legionnaire who revealed graying whiskers in his beard stubble, turned his nose towards the Australian and greeted him in a thick accent. "Are you lost?"

The man's tone and hardened edge intimidated Cahill, but he kept his composure. "No, mate. I'm right where I need to be. Do you blokes mind if I join you for a minute?"

"Nobody speaks English but me."

"Then can I have a minute with you?"

The elder legionnaire issued an order in French, and his team dispersed. "I sent them on a break. What's your question?"

Unsure how to articulate his concern, Cahill groped for words. "I... well."

"Yes?"

"Whatever your team's planning with the *Goliath*, I want to be a part of it." The blank stare made Cahill question the legionnaire's English and compelled him to clarify. "I mean I want to participate. I want to join you."

"You want to swim with us?"

"Yes."

"I don't think so."

"But I really want to."

"It's a very bad idea."

"Why?"

"We're going to land on a ship moving at almost nine knots that is twenty meters underwater. A mistake is deadly."

"But it's me ship, and I want to get it back."

The legionnaire leaned over a sheet of plotting paper his team had spread across the table. Crude sketches of the stolen catamaran appeared in varied perspectives. He tapped his finger against a penciled rendition of the *Goliath's* port stern. "My men are trained well, but I am concerned for them. Loss of our grips could have someone to fall into the propeller. I do not know you or your training."

"I'm in decent enough condition."

"Maybe, but you train for life inside a submarine, not outside. This is not for you. You can only get in the way."

Unsure if the elder legionnaire voiced a valid hazard, Cahill questioned his heroic intent. Wondering if he'd overextended himself in asking to join the swim team, he shifted his tactics. "Well, perhaps I can help with your planning. Nobody knows the ship better than me."

"Maybe after we finish you can review."

As the security team trickled back into the mess area, Cahill deemed his welcome expired and retreated. He headed forward and stopped to relieve himself in the restroom's urinal.

He then found his way through the small but unfamiliar ship to the rear entrance to the control room.

The quiet space showed no signs of change since he'd left it, and he relegated the young Julien back to his sonar technician role.

Cahill retook his captain's chair, glanced at the *Goliath's* incoming sound data, and appreciated his quarry's unchanging and predictable path.

After settling into the routine of monitoring the absconding transport ship, he felt doubts creeping into his mind.

He questioned if efforts to recapture his ship were delusional delays to Jake's inevitable intention to use torpedoes. A thickening sadness enshrouded his spirits, and he slumped into his chair, letting the sea's swells rock him.

As he sulked, he heard his boss clear his throat over the loudspeaker. Cahill peered at his display and mustered the energy to lean into his console. "Pierre?"

"The mood seems rather subdued on the *Specter*."

"Are you saying it's a party on the *Wraith*?"

"Of course not. But Dmitry seems to be enjoying the chase."

"I don't know how he can enjoy this."

"He loves his work. He doesn't care about who's paying the bills or the politics or the embarrassment of having been victims of a hijacking. He's in his element, and that's all that matters to him."

"Yeah, mate. But I thought I had that going on in me head, too. But this is the worst I've felt commanding a submarine since…

well, since forever."

"I'm sure you feel victimized."

"But I'm the only one who's showing it. Jake should feel victimized, but he's just pissed off. You should feel victimized, but you've found your damage control groove without a hitch. Dmitry's blocked out everything and enjoying this like just another normal mission. Why am I taking it so hard?"

"I own it, but for all intents and purposes, it's your ship. That's why it's hitting you the hardest."

"It can't be that simple, can it?"

His hotel room's lights casting shadows over his face, the Frenchman fell silent to focus his thoughts. Cahill allowed the delay in hopes of enlightenment, and then Renard sounded pensive. "I believe you've revealed something important."

"Go on, mate."

"Each of you–Jake, Dmitry, and you–all came to me after losing commands. Jake was younger and had never been an official commanding officer, but his career had been taken from him, and he commanded the submarine he stole for me. So the loss of a submarine's a commonality you all share."

"I know that. We've joked about it before."

"But it's no laughing matter. For all of you, the ships you command represent redemption."

The words lifted to the surface a realization that had been lurking within Cahill's subconscious mind. "Yeah, you have a point."

"You were relieved of your prior command, though wrongly per my estimation, leaving you broken at the time."

"Every man who's relieved of command is broken. It was a brutal feeling I'd like to forget."

"The *Goliath* was your solace, and its loss is a redoubling of your pain. What Jake and Dmitry don't yet feel is that its loss will destroy this fleet and take their ships of redemption away from them, too. You, however, are feeling the loss in real time."

During an uncomfortable lull in the conversation, Cahill let the realization settle.

He welcomed Remy's interruption. "Water hammer, MESMA plant four. They're bringing it back online."

"Water hammer? Is that what you call it when steam tosses condensed water droplets against the piping?"

"Yes."

"How can you hear that on the *Goliath*? That steam system is encapsulated behind... I mean it's sound-mounted within..."

The toad-head turned, looked at Cahill, and offered a knowing grin.

Henri shook his head. "Don't argue, Terry. Jake's tried to call his bluff many times, to his shame."

"I'm sure, mate."

"Now I hear steam ring."

"I won't argue. I believe you, Antoine. That will take the *Goliath* back to five MESMA plants online."

The silver-haired mechanic lifted a makeshift placard covered with grease pencil markings and read its notes. "With the single screw and drag friction of the nets, that correlates to eight point two knots."

"Understood, mate. Eight point two knots."

The Frenchman lowered his placard and ran his finger over a faceplate mounted at his station. "If we increase speed to eight point two knots to keep pace, our new time to snorkel to avoid going below thirty percent battery is now forty-one minutes away."

"Very well. We're now forty-one minutes away from snorkeling." Expecting a slight change to the transport ship's speed, Cahill looked to a tactical display and noticed lines of acoustic direction from the shrieking limpets sliding off track.

Before the Australian could voice his observation, the toad-head turned. "And now, the *Goliath* is accelerating."

"Got it. The *Goliath* is accelerating. Let's keep pace. Henri, have the engine room make turns for eight point two knots."

As the mechanic acknowledged, two men scurried through the room's front door. "What's up, mate?"

Jake seemed giddy. "We figured it out. Well, Claude did,

mostly, but we got it."

"You mean you figured out how to reduce the slow-kill's yield?"

"Damn straight."

LaFontaine's wiry frame appeared too thin to support his weight. "It will take time to implement, but we've removed one bomblet from the detonation sequence."

"How much time will the whole thing take?"

LaFontaine looked to the American. "Well, it took us almost, what... two hours for the first bomblet?"

Jake tilted his head and shrugged. "Yeah, but most of that time was figuring it out. If I had to guess, the actual time to make a bomblet inert is only about fifteen to twenty minutes."

Cahill recalled his knowledge of the customized Black Shark torpedo. "The Subtics system allows you to make two thirds of the bomblets inert automatically before launch, right?"

Jake spoke with a pride of ownership in his design. "Yeah, sure. They come in three rings of eight bomblets each. We've got a routine in Subtics that lets us turn off one or two of the rings as we like."

"So, to reduce the yield to just one, you need to manually detach seven on the same ring. That leaves six, which is conservatively an hour and a half of work."

The wiry engineer stepped forward. "Not exactly. I can get two teams working on different bomblets at the same time. They can reach without interfering with each other. But they'll need to stop halfway through their work and have our torpedo technicians lift and roll the weapon. The bottom three bomblets are inaccessible as the torpedo is resting."

Cahill had lost track of the math. "So, what's it all add up to?"

The engineer crossed his arms, looked upward, and calculated. "You were right, after all. It's an hour and a half of work."

Before Cahill could voice his newfound enthusiasm, he heard footsteps passing through the room's aft door.

The elder legionnaire stopped below him next to the elevated conning platform and posed a question in French.

Jake corrected him. "In English. If you need to say some of it in French, we'll translate it."

"I have a plan. My team can plant explosives on the *Goliath* and force it to stop."

Redemption. Hope. Possibilities. Cahill sensed the claws of depression receding. He also saw a break in the dark clouds covering Jake, and he dared to trust in the return of his teammate. "Well then. We have ourselves some progress. Let's get started on the warhead modifications and review our new opportunities."

CHAPTER 11

The colonel stood under the domed bridge, doubting his bulldog. "Is the team preparing to mutiny?"

"That's not what I said, sir. I said they're disgruntled."

As the bulldog offered an unreadable grin, the wailing limpets grated the colonel's nerves. He blocked out their incessant whining and commanded himself calm. "I heard you, but a disgruntled crew doesn't concern me. What are you getting at? Are they afraid?"

"You can't blame the geeks for being afraid. They're not used to the stresses of combat."

Realizing his fervor for revenge had blinded him, the colonel accepted a problem.

He'd expected frayed nerves from his technicians, but he'd banked upon the resolve of his steeled commandos to generate steadfastness. By turning them into deckhands on a crippled submarine, he'd sapped their control of their fates. Men accustomed to driving their destinies were helpless passengers.

He'd marginalized their courage.

The only opportunity for his commandos to fight back had left his best Stinger missile man clinging to life.

But he needed his warriors to remain warriors. "I understand the technicians aren't accustomed to the stresses of combat. I don't care about that. What I care about is you keeping our men in line and them keeping the technicians in line."

"Of course, sir." His demeanor negating his words, the bulldog remained a stone edifice.

"I've known you too long to expect blind obedience. What's bothering you?"

"I'm only the messenger, but I need to share what I've heard.

It's not pretty."

"Out with it."

"The team isn't just afraid. They're afraid the mission is lost. The doubt is building the more they talk."

"Doubt is normal. I'm concerned only if it's excessive fear."

The bulldog stepped forward and lowered his voice. "It is fear, sir. And futility. It's the combination."

The colonel's ire rose. "The warriors I recruited are not cowards."

"A man can be brave and afraid, sir. A coward shirks from duty while a warrior fights on. The problem is, your bravest men can do nothing to improve their lots, while the geeks who keep the ship running are the most likely to crack."

Exhaling through his nostrils, the colonel sought serenity. "Are you still strong?"

"Of course, sir. You needn't ask."

"But I did ask because you raised the concern, which means you believe there's a measure of truth to it."

"It doesn't mean I'm afraid or frustrated."

"But are you?"

Bright lighting highlighted the cracks and scars on the bulldog's worn face as he weighed his response. "Of course. I'd be a fool to claim otherwise. This is dangerous work, and I'm dependent on strangers to succeed."

"Strangers? You've known everyone for at least a year. You've known our fighting men much longer. We've taken bullets for each other."

"I meant the Iranians."

Another realization billowed into the colonel's lucid mind. Everything had hinged on escaping before the submarines had scrambled to trail him. He'd expected to fend off any helicopters with Stinger missiles, manual use of railguns, or hiding below the surface.

But Renard's rapid response had rallied the submarines and had forced him to flee surfaced, exposing him to the helicopter attack. Flooding damage and dragging nets had slowed his underwater speed below that which his submerged hunters could sustain, and a steady cycle of armed helicopters hovered above him.

Though he possessed his prize, everything beyond the act of taking it had gone wrong.

Respecting the adage that no plan survives contact with the enemy, he'd prepared contingency plans with his Iranian clients, who awaited far to the north.

But after Renard's inspired retaliation, he considered his contingency plans to be his best option to escape–and he remembered that his allies thought he was somewhere else. "You may be right. We may need to rely upon the Iranians. But they didn't expect us to turn north so soon to hasten our arrival to their waters. We need to tell them where we are."

"You could patch your phone into the Subtics system and reach your contact through one of the radio masts."

"If a helicopter doesn't pelt us with bullets while trying it."

"Ask the expert, sir."

The colonel stepped to a console, tapped a screen, and aimed his voice upward. "Control room, this is the bridge. Over."

The commander's voice filled the dome. "Bridge, this is the control room. Over."

"Can you use the radio mast to inform the Iranians of our location, course, and speed without giving the helicopters a clean shot at us?"

"It should work, sir. A radio mast presents a small target for bullets."

"Is the Farsi translator with you?"

"Both translators are with me. As long as we're raising a mast, I'll listen for whatever unencrypted communications I can sniff and translate. Merchant vessels may be saying something that's useful."

"Good idea, but minimize your exposure of the antenna."

The pause suggested he'd ordered the obvious to an expert, like reminding a surgeon to scrub in before an operation, but the commander kept his response's tone respectful. "Of course.

I'll lower the mast once the Iranians confirm they have all they need."

"Also, is there anything of tactical value about the *Specter* and the *Wraith* you can send them?"

"I've got notes written down, but it's limited to what can be said during a phone call. We can't send a data link from Subtics without a password."

"Send them what you can."

"We'll mention the primary frequencies we hear, but they're just standard *Scorpène*-class tones. The most useful data is their constant use of active sonar. That's something the Iranians can exploit, as long as the *Specter* and *Wraith* keep using it."

"Let's hope they do. They'll be vulnerable, I assume?"

"They will be. Any submarine that blares its active sonar is vulnerable. In fact, if they keep it up..."

The colonel coaxed the idea he sensed forming in his submarine commander's mind. "You've got an idea. Perhaps something we or the Iranians can exploit while the *Specter* and the *Wraith* keep their active sonar systems energized?"

"It's dangerous for the Iranians, but I'd like to give them the opportunity to test their mettle."

In a flash, the colonel understood, and he simultaneously derided himself for failing to conceive the idea and praised himself for recruiting a submarine commander who did. "You want them to be the aggressors. Instead of waiting for the *Specter* and the *Wraith* to enter their waters, you want them to move forward, use their active sonar against them, and surprise them in international waters."

"Yes, I do. But only a couple of submarines, because that's all it should take. And it should work."

"Very well. Make that recommendation in your update. Take control of the ship, take us shallow, and call our Iranian contact."

"I'll see to it."

For quiet minutes, the deck rolled harder under the waves while the depth gauge revealed the *Goliath's* shallowness. Expecting the staccato chirp of helicopter rounds at his exposed mast, the colonel realized in the silence that the wise aircrew above him conserved its ammunition for choicer targets.

As he made a mental note to be liberal with future radio communications if needed, the commander announced success. "We've got confirmation from the Iranians. They'll adjust their plans for our new course and speed, and they'll consider the aggression opportunity beyond their waters we suggested."

"Very well. Take us back down." The deck's rocking weakened. "That's good news, but then again, we're not completely incapable of fighting back ourselves."

The sergeant looked to him. "You don't mean to challenge the helicopters again?"

"Per our sonar expert, there's only one harassing us now."

"Okay, then. Do you mean to challenge the one helicopter?"

"Perhaps I do."

"Given the last result, you'll need to come at it with more than a single Stinger launcher."

Shooting down an aircraft would be a bonus, but the colonel believed he needed only to break the Omani airmen's courage to stop their harassment. "Then I need to know when the railgun will be ready. I'd like to test the Omanis' resolution against hypersonic metal."

"My last update is ten minutes old, but the technicians were still wiring their way around the capacitor charging circuit."

"Was there a timing estimate?"

"They said two to three hours."

"That's too long. Get them on the phone."

At the console, the bulldog tapped an icon selecting the populated weapons bay and aimed his voice upward. "Port railgun, this is the bridge. Over."

A technician's voice filled the dome. "We're here at the port railgun."

Disliking the tone of anxiety that validated the bulldog's report of fear and frustration, the colonel interjected his concerns. "What's taking so long?"

"We're installing our homegrown step-up circuit to convert the main battery's two hundred and seventy volts of direct current to one thousand volts. If we go any faster, we'll blow up our equipment, or worse."

"But there must be a faster way than taking three hours."

"Not unless you want an undercharged capacitor."

"What's so bad about that?"

The pause suggested he'd asked either a foolish question or a great one. After a moment, the technician answered. "If you run the firing capacitors off the battery, you'd get much less power from the gun."

"Can it fire with less power?"

"I'm sure it can."

"How much less power are we talking about?"

Again, a pause while the technician calculated. "The energy in a capacitor is proportional to the voltage squared. We're guessing these capacitors run on one thousand volts. So, charging directly off the battery gives roughly one fourth the voltage, or one sixteenth the energy."

"What's that mean in terms of muzzle velocity and range?"

Another pause and a background conversation while two technicians verified the answer. "The energy of the bullet is also proportional to the muzzle velocity squared. So, one fourth."

"One forth the muzzle speed?"

"Yes, sir."

"That still gives us almost Mach two?"

"Right, sir. Mach one point seven five, based upon our assumption of a nominal Mach seven."

"That's good enough to take down a helicopter at short range. How fast can you modify the railgun to run straight off the battery?"

"Faster, for certain. I'm not sure, but it might even be a standard backup operating mode to charge the capacitor banks off the battery. We'll figure it out."

"Is everything else ready to fire the weapon?"

"Probably, but we won't know until we run a live test."

"How much do you know, and what's still unknown?"

The technician paused again before sharing his thoughts. "Hydraulics work. We lifted the gun about half a meter and lowered it again. Manual loading is tested–of course, we can't load automatically with the Subtics system lockout. We can run cooling pumps, both fast and slow speed. We can also aim the gun vertically and in azimuth with manual control of the steering motors, but that's a lot of slow hand cranking."

A second voice the colonel recognized as belonging to his gas turbine expert interrupted the conversation. With the ship submerged, the turbine technician had become useful applying his knowledge to diverse engineering problems.

When the side chatter ended, the first technician, the team's *Scorpène* engine room expert, reported. "He reminded me we can also set each round to break into smaller pieces prior to impact. It appears that Subtics normally does this for rounds in the muzzle queue, but we found switches on each round we can twist with a screwdriver."

The colonel appreciated the workaround that suggested his men were finding ways to dictate their own fate. "Excellent. My intelligence suggested that Renard's fleet uses this mode against surface targets. I'm certain they use this mode against aircraft, too. That's what we'll do."

In the loudspeaker's background noise, the colonel heard the two technicians breaking into an argument about waterproofed cables, followed by indistinct talk. Then the engine room expert returned to the main conversation. "He also thinks we can bring up the starboard gun, but I'm not in complete agreement."

"How? The starboard engine room's isolated from the rest of the ship's electrical grid. There's no way to get power to the starboard railgun."

"In theory he's right that we can route waterproofed power cables to the gun, but I'm not sure I trust the ship's cabling."

"Why not?"

"Because I haven't tested it, and the electrical grounds failed when the starboard engine room flooded. That doesn't give me confidence in the insulation."

"Forget the starboard gun for now. I only need one gun against the helicopter. Get the port railgun ready to fire, and get me an update in thirty minutes." The colonel waved his hand.

Obeying his leader's gesture, the bulldog terminated the communication connection. "I didn't want to challenge you with the men listening, but you do understand that attacking the helicopter can create more problems than it solves."

"I disagree. Explain yourself."

"If you remove the helicopters, you'll force the submarines to get nasty."

"I would agree except for one vital fact. Renard is far too arrogant to admit defeat until it hits him in his smug French face."

"You're the boss. I've trusted you this far."

"This is a just mission, and justice must be rendered."

"We all agree with that. None of us is here for the money alone. We want to right the wrongs that were done."

The colonel wondered if he'd pushed too far. He questioned if he'd been arrogant thinking he could inflict retribution upon the guilty Frenchman. Then he realized that moving forward required stifling all doubts, beginning with his. He stuffed every impulse causing him to hesitate behind iron doors and turned himself into an engine of action. "But fear and futility are challenging that desire."

"Yes, sir. Couldn't you hear it in their voices, even over the loudspeaker?"

"Of course, I did. But did you notice how they focused when I asked them pointed questions? If I can keep each man concentrated on his duties, thinking ahead, we can overcome this."

"Fair enough, sir."

"That's where I need you."

"I'm your man. What's your plan?"

The colonel reflected. "I'm going to recover our morale by creating the option to fight. We're going to get the men ready to take down the helicopter."

"The option, but not the commitment?"

"Right."

"I see where you're going, sir. Nobody has to know if you really intend to take on a helicopter again, but the purpose and possibility of controlling our fates will help matters."

"You're wise and insightful, for an old dog."

"You've got this old dog motivated again. You should let me get to my job of rallying the troops."

"Not alone. I'm coming with you. This walk through the ship will require both of us."

"Lead on, sir."

Upon the colonel and sergeant's arrival in the control room, the submarine commander stood, revealing his lean frame. "Good morning."

"Huh. You're right. It's already after three o'clock, isn't it?"

"Three hours to sunrise, colonel."

"Does daylight work for me or against me if I surface and send Stinger teams topside against a helicopter?"

"In a normal situation, I'd say against. But this isn't normal, now is it? The helicopter knows exactly where we are. So, I'll say that daylight works in your favor."

The colonel looked to his silent bulldog, who nodded his concurrence. "Agreed. If I order the attack, it will be after sunrise. But let's keep this a secret within this room."

The sergeant leaned into him. "To keep the sense of urgency on getting the railgun ready?"

Looking at each man in the room, the colonel made eye contact with the translators first. The academics, one fluent in English and French, the other in Farsi and Arabic, nodded emphatic agreement. As he continued scanning faces, his warfare experts offered rote gestures of approval. "Yes. To keep the urgency on the railgun."

The commander raised an eyebrow. "You're readying the railgun? It's a noteworthy tactic, but I wouldn't take a single railgun against a helicopter at this range. Our shots are too infrequent, and the target can reposition too quickly. And the aircrew can walk in their rapid-fire rounds to our railgun. We'd be too susceptible."

To keep the conversation about actionable results, the colonel countered. "Susceptible, but capable of fighting."

The commander sounded cynical. "Perhaps if we ever have the luxury of shooting at something that's not right on top of us."

"That will be our status as soon as we reach our Iranian supporters."

The submarine commander walked to the central plotting table, leaned his long torso over it, and pressed his weight into his palms. "If you can keep the five MESMA plants up–"

Instilling confidence, the colonel clarified his trust in his technical team. "I'll give you the five."

"With the five MESMA plants up, we'll hold eight point two knots. That puts us nine hours from Iranian waters."

Garbled watery tones clicked through the overhead speakers and reminded the colonel of extraterrestrial aliens. "What was that?"

The solitary sonar technician turned from his seat. "That's the *Specter* talking to the *Wraith*, sir."

A similar sound filled the room.

"And that was the *Wraith* answering the *Specter*. I've heard it a couple of times an hour ever since the *Wraith* went deep. It's an encrypted audio signal."

The colonel moved to the submarine commander at the table. "They can talk in real time and in code?"

"Yes."

"Can that code be broken?"

"Any code can be broken. It's a matter of time and resources. We happen to lack the resources."

"I can't argue that."

"As a submarine sailor, I'm bothered knowing that two superior undersea hunting vessels hold me at such a disadvantage. I still believe in your cause, but I must be candid. If our Iranian support fails us, there's no undersea combat tactic I can dream of that would rid us of this twin *Wraith-Specter* menace."

"Don't worry. I still have several options to overcome Renard. You know most of them, but not all. Have faith."

Unwilling to wait for a possible retort, the colonel ushered his bulldog towards the stern. In MESMA plant five, he followed the sergeant through the hatch into the tunnel connecting the catamarans.

After a claustrophobic crawl, he contorted himself into the aftermost port-side plant, MESMA six. Finding the humming compartment void of life, he led the bulldog forward.

In MESMA plant four, he found his air-independent-propulsion expert glaring at a heat exchanger. "How's the plant holding up?"

"Not bad, sir. Not good, either, really. This one needs constant watching and adjusting."

"Is it any worse than plant one?"

"No. They have about the same temperament."

"You speak as if they're alive."

The technician cocked his head and shrugged. "Well, aren't they?"

"You have a point. They're keeping us alive."

"Yeah, but for how much longer?"

The colonel seized the opening. "Until you're wealthy beyond your wildest dreams. We're going to rally and fend off the airborne threat."

"But it was horrible last time. They fought back, and they dodged our missile."

"They won't again. When we defeat them, it will be with two Stinger launchers and one railgun. We will overpower them."

The technician glanced at a dancing display and grunted. He then darted to a throttling valve and dialed down the cooling water's flow. When he returned to his leader, he accelerated his cathartic outpouring of doubt. "But even so, the submarines. The limpets. They're a constant reminder that we're a wounded fox within snapping distance of the hounds."

Needing to instill confidence, the colonel pushed his position. "You're aware that I've created a contingency plan for our Iranian clients to assist us?"

"I know of a plan. Everyone does. But none of us understand it. You've never explained the details."

"That's because I didn't want to focus on it. There was no need to confuse our first steps by focusing on the downstream events. Now that it's coming closer, I'll share more as the time approaches. But trust me, it's going to be our deliverance."

The man seemed to grope through final objections. "But if not, sir. Then what?"

"Then remember, always remember, I have something in my possession of immeasurable value to Renard. I can always use that to my advantage."

"How can you be so sure?"

"Let me remind you of our ultimate safety net. If it comes down to it, I'll call him directly and arrange to give his ship back to him in exchange for our freedom. I'd beach this thing, leave it for him, and walk you home before I'd let you perish."

"Even with how badly you've wanted this?"

"I would give it up to save our lives. I'm no monster."

The technician's shoulders lowered as his stress receded. "Well, I can keep five plants running for you. Four of them are behaving, and I'll keep on top of this one."

"Good enough. Keep it up."

Retreating to MESMA plant six with the sergeant, the colonel stopped and addressed his bulldog. "I may need to hold a few more conversations like that."

"Maybe, sir. But I wouldn't be surprised if he's calling the others now and sharing his newfound hopes. Your confidence will spread. You did great. That's why you're the boss."

"And you're my right arm."

"You say it, and I make it happen."

"Get them ready to fight with the port railgun and two Stinger teams, one from each hull. Within two and a half hours, I want them ready to bring down the helicopter."

CHAPTER 12

Olivia McDonald examined the man in his mid-thirties seated across her desk. He seemed unsure of his purpose but excited to serve the CIA's most powerful woman. "Thanks for coming in."

"My pleasure, ma'am."

"Call me 'Olivia'."

"Thank you, Olivia. What can I do for you?"

She recognized his improved confidence since she'd last needed him years earlier. "You've probably heard rumors about my involvement with the new mercenary navy that's been handling unique missions."

His eyes lit up. "Yeah. Of course. The one that's been handling surgical strikes against some of our allies. Russia, Greece, and Israel?"

"That's the one."

"So, it's true. You do have your own navy."

"Don't rush to conclusions."

"Sorry, ma'am, Olivia. It's just… the rumors are practically legendary."

"And exaggerated. If you believe half of them, you'd think I was Poseidon's daughter."

He nodded and crossed his ankle over his leg. "Okay. There's always exaggerations in rumors. The human imagination fills in the gaps. But there's also usually some element of truth behind most rumors."

"Let's just say I have an interest in that fleet. I watch it."

"And I'm here because it's tangling with the Iranian navy, or it's getting ready to do so?"

"They're heading towards Iranian waters."

"I'm no naval expert. Are you looking for an assessment of Iran's motivation for state-driven action against your... excuse me, the mercenary fleet?"

"That's right."

"Is there any evidence you've seen suggesting hostile action, other than your fleet's movement?"

She offered her half-lie, a type of misleading and conditional half-truth her monster created to manipulate people while easing the inner girl's guilt. Though powerbrokers abused such linguistic sins on instinct, Olivia despised the practice, and she despised herself for succumbing to it. "Of course, if I had anything useful I could share with you, I would. But you're going to have to speculate for now."

"That's a lot to speculate about."

"Maybe I can narrow it down for you. Do you remember five months ago, an Iranian *Kilo* submarine took damage and headed to the repair yards?"

"Yeah. They were tight-lipped about it. Collision damage was the official story, but we've got photos showing something much cleaner. It looked like explosives planted by divers."

"For the sake of argument, let's say the mercenary fleet was responsible. What the hell? Let's say it's hypothetically my fleet to keep it simple."

He looked away in thought and then responded. "Okay. If your fleet did that, then that could lead to a retaliation. But it's hard to say without more data."

"My fleet has no other bad blood with the Iranians."

"You're sure? They haven't messed with any Iranian allies or sympathizers?"

"That's an awfully small population."

"But non-trivial. You have the usual suspects, Syria, Lebanon, Palestine, Venezuela, and Russia. After the fall of Saddam, you have Iraq, too."

"I don't see much chance of a connection there."

"But your fleet attacked Russia recently, right? The Iranians could be doing secret puppet revenge work for the Russians."

In the Black Sea conflict, she'd helped bail Renard out of a stalemate, paying the Russians double the amount of damage the Frenchman had inflicted. "They did attack Russia, but they paid off anyone who'd still be pissed off. Plus, they staff one of their submarines with veterans from the Russian Navy. The Russians wouldn't be too quick to kill their own sons."

"That's got a hint of ancient Rome to it. Conquer and recruit. Not bad for a bunch of mercenaries. But what about their Israeli work? Could they have upset local Iranian allies?"

"Quite the opposite. They spent their own money to break a blockade and feed the Gaza Strip, and then they stopped a tank battalion from rolling into the Golan Heights. If anything, the Iranians should be thanking them."

"Huh. And no interactions with the other allies?"

She shook her head. "Not that I know of." The monster added requisite flair. "And I'd know about it."

"The last time I helped you, you captured an Iranian woman who was seducing an American destroyer captain. If your fleet was connected back then, maybe there's some motivation there."

She respected his thorough questioning, but it wearied her. "Even if my fleet had participated, the Iranians from that operation died or fell from power."

"Then you're saying it comes down to that... let's call it an incident, where your hypothetical fleet hypothetically placed explosives on an Iranian *Kilo*."

"I think so."

"This fleet? It's got what? A couple of submarines and that half-destroyer, half-submarine catamaran that can carry them?"

"Two top-of-the-line *Scorpène*-class submarines commanded by the two brightest commanders on the planet. And that catamaran makes thirty-four knots surfaced, thirteen submerged, and it has twin railguns with a range of one hundred and twenty miles, guided rounds, mind you."

He wiggled and switched the crossing of his legs. "You know

so much about it, I think it is your fleet."

"I know my subject."

"Well, like I said, I'm no naval expert, but I know a lot of Iran's money's been going into its navy over the last decade."

As part of her real-time homework during the evening's crisis, she'd verified the count. "They've got two dozen submarines and half a dozen frigates. But most of the submarines are small coastal subs."

"Coastal... That sounds innocuous, but I'm sure that's the point. A deceptively small vessel with full-size weapons?"

"Exactly."

"And their sheer numbers could be a problem for your fleet in Iranian waters?"

The question overstepped the bounds of her undersea warfare knowledge. "Yeah. Let's assume so."

"It's hard to assess Iran's motivation. Everyone likes to think of them as madmen, but I see them as selectively fanatical. When it comes to making people believe they're committed to a cause, you'll see fanaticism. When it comes to using their resources, they're rational actors."

"You don't see revenge as a motivation for them going after my fleet?"

Thinking, he looked away before answering. "They'd probably be willing to risk a couple of midget submarines, maybe as part of a reactionary plan of opportunity. For example, if your fleet happened to take the Strait of Hormuz... you said your fleet's heading towards Iran."

The monster forced a half-truth as a query. "They are, but I'm questioning if it's a preemptive strike. Is it possible my fleet's aware of and trying to stop a premeditated Iranian attack against them?"

He shook his head. "I doubt it. The Iranians wouldn't go after your fleet just for that insult on the *Kilo*. Even if they were upset, there's no upside. Your fleet officially belongs to nobody. So, there's no public image value in attacking them. It doesn't align with their normal routine."

"What about a show of strength? They could claim success where Russia, Greece, and Israel failed in getting revenge."

"To which audience? Again, I'm no naval expert, but isn't it really hard to prove who sunk whom with submarines?"

She leaned back in her chair and pondered. "Yeah. You're right."

"Are you sure your fleet isn't attacking Iran as part of their own agenda? By definition, they're mercenaries. Have you considered the long list of actors who'd pay for that?"

"If they were attacking Iran, I'd know about it."

"Fair enough. So, what's left to consider?"

Her psychological razor cut through the thoughts of caricatures of Iranian political and military leaders, but she couldn't link their mindsets to the attack on the *Goliath*. If anything, an Iranian attack would've sunk all three of Renard's ships and claimed a quick and decisive victory. The hijacking was something more complex. If the Iranians were involved, they weren't alone. "Spend a few hours looking through financial transactions, arrests, and border stoppings in the last three months, and see if anything pops up for someone sympathetic to Iran who has any links to naval activity.

"I can do that. I'll need to do some digging at my desk."

"Dinner's on my secretary's desk. Enjoy, and call me ASAP if you find anything."

After he passed through her office door, she turned her attention to her computer screens and unmuted her speakers. In a corner window, her supporting technician looked frustrated. "Where've you been, ma'am?"

"I had the sound turned off during a meeting."

"I've been trying to get your attention. The commander of the U.S. Fifth Fleet wants to talk to you."

She'd wanted more time before confronting the vice admiral who ruled the seas surrounding the *Goliath*. As the inner girl wished away the pending challenge, her geek's supervisor appeared in the window.

As a mid-ranking watch captain, he had respectable authority within the CIA, but he had fewer stripes than her. Everyone but a handful of old men had fewer stripes than her.

But the supervisor made no apparent effort to hide his discomfort. "Miss McDonald, the executive assistant for the commander of the U.S. Fifth Fleet has been trying to get your attention for ten minutes. You weren't answering your phone or computer."

She pulled her phone from her pocket and glanced at it. Realizing she'd let her battery run empty, she wondered how many other mistakes were escaping her attention tonight. As she plugged her phone into a charger, her inner girl wanted to run home and hide, but the monster redoubled her strength against all challengers.

In a corner window of a screen, she checked the image her laptop captured of her. Despite her buried fear, she appeared strong and presentable. "Fine. Tell the executive assistant I'm ready for a video conference."

"It's not a conference. The commander will be calling you on your secure cell phone. We'll handle the encryption and route him from here."

She fiddled with her phone until it turned on. "Give me a minute for it to boot up."

The supervisor left the camera's view and then returned. "Confirmed."

After muting her speakers, she waited until her phone rang, and then she answered. "Olivia McDonald."

Though she knew the vice admiral by reputation as a thoughtful man, he sounded irritated. "Good evening, Miss McDonald. This is Vice Admiral Schmidt. How are you ma'am?"

"I'm fine, sir. How are you this morning? It's three o'clock in the morning for you, right?"

"It's two o'clock."

She realized the one-hour time difference between Bahrain and Oman. "My mistake. Two o'clock."

"I've had better mornings, and I understand you're to blame for my rude awakening."

Years of conditioning had braced her to absorb the verbal jab without volunteering knowledge. "That depends on why you were awoken."

"I'm being cordial with you, Miss McDonald. I expect that should earn me your candor. You should know I rank among the senior staff who know about your personal naval task force. Can we skip the political gaming talk?"

The triple hit of him highlighting her political wiggle words, his knowledge of her connection to the *Goliath*, and him reducing her fleet to a task force weakened her. Her tough outer monster recoiled to a defensive posture. "Of course. I apologize. It's a habit."

"Your task force was supposed to be parked in Oman all night and then head to Pakistan for repairs. But I was just informed that all three of your ships are sixty-five miles away from Iranian waters and driving straight north. That requires an explanation."

She suspected he had access to satellite feeds, to spying aircraft, or to a nuclear submarine in his fleet that spied on Renard's machines. As she inhaled deeply, her cold monster calculated half-truths and arranged her sequence of words. "It's true that I watch the task force and that I have influence over it, but I don't have direct control. Sometimes, the ships' owner heads out on independent operations without telling me, and he updates me after the fact."

"The owner. You mean Pierre Renard?"

The ease with which the vice admiral used a name hidden for decades behind espionage and aliases saddened Olivia. Though she used Renard, she admitted she considered him a friend and considered his growing exposure dangerous. "Yes. Pierre Renard."

"Are you saying you have no idea what he's doing?"

"No, that's not quite right. You rightfully demanded candor from me. Pierre called me tonight. He won't share everything that's going on, but he assures me there's no need for alarm."

"That sounds like political gaming talk."

The monster reminded her that candor required truth but omitted volunteering information. Nobody but Renard knew she knew of the hijacking, and the beast protected that secret. "I'm sorry, but Pierre holds all the cards, so to speak. I normally trust him for weeks of independent operations without telling me what he's doing, but I understand your concern given his proximity to Iran."

"I trust you'll put these games to bed and get clarity by the time I call you again."

"Yes, sir. Of course."

His voice became grim. "And let me be clear. Whether you can clarify his intent or not, I need to draw a line. You know that. This shouldn't be a surprise."

"No, it's not. I appreciate you mentioning it. Can you tell me where that line is, so to speak, so I can convey the proper sense of urgency to Pierre?"

"I know what his ships can do. I don't care if they harass the Iranian navy. That's between them and Iran, and my fleet is smart enough to stay out of the way. But if your ships try to pass through Hormuz, I'll enforce my authority in the strait. I can't afford to let them pass into the Persian Gulf."

She knew better than to ask what he meant by enforcing his authority. At best, it meant ordering Renard's ships to turn around and then escalating if they disobeyed. At worst, it meant sinking them without warning. She knew the vice admiral had such power. "I appreciate your honesty, sir."

"That little task force of yours is useful. They don't follow the rules of engagement I hold sacred, but I understand how they might serve our national interests. But don't think for a second that I won't do my duty. I need to protect my fleet and the allied nations in the region."

"I'll take the appropriate action with proper urgency, sir."

"I trust that you will. Have a good and hopefully productive evening, Miss McDonald."

Holding her silent phone, she felt her inner girl starting to cry, but the monster clamped down and reminded her to celebrate.

The commander of the U.S. Fifth Fleet had declared an irrelevant boundary, given that the *Goliath's* fate would be sealed long before Hormuz.

Renard would have it back in his hands before it reached Iranian waters.

If not, she'd use the young agent, Matt Williams, to slip the *Goliath's* information to the Iranian navy, and let the Persians purge the waters of her problem.

CHAPTER 13

Terry Cahill paced the control room. "How long does it take to plan a bloody swimming party?"

He started to appreciate the soothing influence of the silver-haired French mechanic, Henri. "Give them time. Let them get it right."

"We know exactly where me ship is. Just grab hold of it and leave a few explosives. It's not that complex."

"Trust the experts."

The Australian ceased pacing beside the Frenchman. "What do you know about them? I know next to nothing."

"You mean the security force?"

"Yeah."

"The network Pierre befriended as a student at *l'École Navale* is strong. He's close to a former marine who connected him to top veterans of the marines, army, and foreign legion. Our security team is excellent."

"I don't mean to be rude, but if they're so good, why are six of them dead and me ship in some mongrel's hands?"

The mechanic's face tightened. "I've been asking myself that question."

"It's a toughie, isn't it?"

"No security scheme is perfect, and I believe it's a matter of gamesmanship. Pierre estimated the amount of effort a belligerent force would bring against his fleet, and he staffed his security team appropriately. But someone studied our defenses and was willing to invest the resources to overcome them."

"Someone wanted the *Goliath* badly."

"Badly enough to risk their lives."

As he considered calling Julien to relieve him and free him to join the swim team's planning session, the Australian remembered the session was happening in French. He'd be alienated, and he had to trust Jake to provide a submarine expert's insight into the *Goliath's* peculiar pitfalls.

But Cahill noted Jake didn't command the *Goliath*. He did. And though the American could recite specifications of the combat transport ship like a walking technical manual, he lacked real-world knowledge of the stolen prize.

And despite a burst of enthusiasm in reducing the yield of a slow-kill torpedo, Jake showed a continued coarseness towards the transport ship. Per Cahill's perspective, the American viewed the *Goliath* as an investment to be forfeited before its hijacking crossed a threshold of risk–a hidden threshold defined in Jake's head.

As he observed the team on the *Specter*, he realized how each man adapted to Jake. The commanding officer's rash gestures, quick words, and minor tantrums seemed engrained in the ship's communication protocols and even in the staff's DNA. Cahill wondered if the crew needed the ongoing experience of an animated Jake to function and feel alive.

What he grasped with certainty, though, was their obedience. Other than the rare challenges afforded to Henri, Jake's orders were final. If the American ordered a weapon launched at the *Goliath*, his crew would attack with ruthless efficiency.

Worse, Cahill knew his boss kept a similar threshold's parameters locked within his mind, as did the CIA queen who ruled Renard's life at inopportune moments.

Multiple secret clocks counted down the *Goliath's* doom, and the first to reach zero would leave him with no ship, no fleet, and no future.

He felt helpless, and desperation forced him to act despite his rational judgment. "I am going with them."

Henri raised his eyebrows. "What?"

"With the swimmers. I don't care what their plans are. I'm going to help them get the *Goliath* back."

"You don't need to convince me. I have no say in it. But if you can get Jake to agree, I'm sure Pierre would follow."

"Well, mate. You offered to be a conduit to Jake."

The mechanic gave a sheepish green. "I guess I did."

"Can you get him for me?"

"Give me a few minutes." The Frenchman lifted a sound-powered phone, flipped its calling destination, and whipped the dialer. He spoke in French, paused as his conversation appeared to shift from one speaker to the next, and then he continued. "Jake says they're finishing now. He'll be up here in fifteen minutes."

Twenty minutes later, Cahill huddled around the central plotting table with Jake, Henri, and the elder legionnaire. Though his boss remained quiet, he knew Renard was listening.

The penciled sketches the Australian had seen earlier in the crew's mess area had become more complex with timing, tick marks, and hand-written notes.

Thankful for a briefing in English, he listened to the American's explanation. "The first order of business is using a second helicopter. We'll use one helicopter to lower the swimmers, and we'll keep one ready as always to punch holes in the *Goliath* if it surfaces."

Cahill disliked the American's word choice. "You mean punching holes in the port engine room, specifically? Those are the standing orders to the aircrews, I hope. If you meant random holes, that's something entirely different."

The American flicked his fingers backwards. "Yeah, yeah. Of course. I'm just focused on the swimming mission here."

"Right, mate. I didn't mean to interrupt."

"We're using two pairs of two swimmers. The first pair will be lowered to a depth of fifty meters, straight in front of the *Goliath's* track. The submarines will be marking that track with their periscopes like we did when they laid the nets. So, we know we can get the swimmers where they need to be." Jake tapped a mechanical pencil in front of the bow of a free-handed profile of the transport ship. "The line holding the first team will be attached to the second team. It's only one hundred meters long, which is perfect."

Cahill had inferred from side conversations that Jake had held private talks with Renard about the swimming plan. It had been set in motion before anyone had uttered a word about it in English, the language he appreciated Jake using as he continued explaining it.

"The *Goliath* will drive into the line. Once that tension hits the line, then the second pair of swimmers jumps."

In four dimensions, Cahill envisioned his transport vessel marching through time into a cable holding two dive teams together.

The second pair of assailants would arrive above the cargo bed with the *Goliath* pulling them askew of its centerline as it angled itself to adjust for single-propeller locomotion. The team would land tethered near the starboard stern, facing eight knots of artificial current to reach their goal. But they'd have gravity helping their effort of swimming and pulling themselves forward, unlike the first team that would fight upward.

Opting to leave the herculean tasks to the trained commandos, Cahill decided which team to join.

Both teams would tangle with four fishing nets, but he trusted himself to find a way to overcome those obstacles. He swallowed back the fear of wedging his ankle in the netting with the *Goliath's* water flow pinning him down to drown.

He needed to touch his ship, and he let the American continue. "The line between the teams will catch on the *Goliath's* front crossbeam. The top guys will swim to the starboard hull. They'll get there and then use the closest crossbeam to crawl to the port side. They'll probably get to the engine room first."

The Australian nodded and noticed the three other men watching him for concurrence. "Sounds good, mate. Keep going."

"The bottom guys will have a tougher time. They'll be climbing and swimming uphill. Since communications will be sketchy, both teams will run parallel missions to lay their explosives. To avoid fratricide, the top team will place charges on the aft half of the compartment, the top team on the front half. Still with me?"

"Yeah, mate. We're good."

"The charges are small enough that they shouldn't hurt any diver who's nearby. They're from our spares we keep for our dolphin friends when they're our guests. But I'm not taking chances on getting ourselves hurt when they go off."

Cahill saw a possible flaw. "Why not lay the charges below the compartment?"

Pushing his torso from the table, Jake straightened his back. "I don't think anyone brought it up. At least nobody suggested it. It's extra effort and risky work to get down there."

"But you see why I asked?"

Jake cocked his head and looked at a sketch with an intensity suggesting he ran a mental physics simulation of the port engine room flooding from its underside. "I do, actually. If we attack from above, the *Goliath* could drive to the surface and save the engine room. But if we attack from below, they'll flood at least to the waterline. That will take out the propulsion equipment."

"But now that I've brought up the idea, I can't think how you'd get the divers down there."

"The guys can tie up to the *Goliath*. You've got a harness track running over the engine room, don't you?"

Cahill tapped his finger on a penciled circle representing a rear view of the transport vessel. "Yeah, of course. The track goes all the way back to the weapons bay. But I'm thinking it'll be tough for the guys to get to the ship's underbelly. The cylindrical shape doesn't give them any leverage outside the widest part."

"It might be good enough to place the charges anywhere on the bottom half of the hull. Even at the widest section, which is accessible."

"Right. Got it. Any penetration that's below the waterline when surfaced will do the trick."

Jake checked with the two Frenchman and then stated his decision. "They'll lay the charges as far down the hull as they can get. Terry, can you help an estimate of freeboard for the *Goliath* so that we know how far down the side is good enough?"

"I'll do you one better, mate. I'll show you."

"Great. Let's draw it up."

"No, I mean I'll show the men meself. On the *Goliath*." Cahill hoped Jake would agree for the self-serving reason of ridding himself of the extra commanding officer aboard the *Specter*.

"You think you can handle it?"

"Yeah. I'll get it done. Nobody wants me ship back more than I do."

The elder legionnaire protested. "I want it back. We lost six of our men. I must bring these…"

He looked at Jake and queried him in French. The American plugged the gap in the man's English. "Assholes."

"These assholes to justice. They killed my friends."

"Right, mate. We all want it back."

"I'm okay with you going, Terry. Nobody knows the ship like you, and your presence could come in handy. But I don't know enough about frogman ops to give an intelligent opinion."

The legionnaire frowned. "You don't know enough about what frogs?"

"Frogmen. That's what Americans call experts in combat swimming operations."

"No, you don't know about frogmen. But I do, and I don't like it."

"Bringing Terry's a compromise. You'd give up a man's swimming expertise in exchange for knowledge of the target."

"Maybe." The legionnaire walked around the table and studied the Australian's physique. Cahill felt naked.

Then the commando hoisted his buttocks onto the table, arched his back, and reached for Jake. "Hold me."

Though surprised, Jake obliged. Then he broke into a smile as he realized the commando was setting up a physical demonstration and test. As the American provided leverage, the French fighter extended his legs. "Push my legs down with just your arms."

Cahill pressed his palms into the elevated thighs, which felt like laser-cut steel. When his shoulders and triceps proved powerless, he gave up. "I can't budge them."

"Make it easier. Now push my feet."

Cahill tried with better leverage, and again he yielded. "I can't."

The legionnaire slid off the table and to his feet. "Now you and your legs."

Jake sounded giddy. "I hope that bare hairy ass of yours is strong."

The Australian wiggled his buttocks onto the table and then leaned back into the American. As he extended his legs, they became lead weights, and his stomach began to tremble.

His routine of jogging and light resistance training three times a week gave him a respectable build, but it failed to optimize him for swimming.

The legionnaire's tone was condescending. "You no swimmer. I could blow on your legs and make them fall."

Defeated, Cahill started to relax and quit.

"No! Not a swimmer, but don't quit. You hold strong for one minute, I let you swim. You have no training, but show me toughness."

"Give him credit for ten seconds already?"

"Okay, Jake. He goes for fifty more seconds."

The world turned red, and sounds became distant, but Cahill's burning, trembling muscles held.

Jake's encouragement gave him strength. "Thirty seconds. Come on, Terry."

A yelp of wincing pain escaped the Australian's throat, but he kept his resolve.

"Twenty seconds to go, man. Are his feet still high enough?"

"Barely. I grade very nicely since he tries very hard."

Just when Cahill thought everyone supported him, Henri poked fun. "But what if he dies? I think you're giving him an aneurism."

But the mechanic's chiding gave the Australian commander

the needed spark. "Henri?"

"You can still talk? I'm impressed."

"Kiss... me..."

Jake started the countdown. "Ten seconds!"

"Bare... hairy..."

"Five, four, three, two, one!"

"Arse!" Cahill rolled sideways and lowered his feet to the deck. He pressed his torso into the chart and let it bear his weight. Blood coursed through his sore abdomen, and he feared his first steps. So, he delayed them and became a statue against the table. "I'm going swimming, then?"

The legionnaire nodded. "I must teach you much in a short time. But you can come. Meet in crews dining area in five minutes."

Jake's support sounded sincere. "Good job, Terry. That was impressive. Let's get everyone geared up. Swimmers topside in twenty minutes, boarding the helo in thirty."

Jake and the legionnaire departed while Henri cocked his head and stared at Cahill. "It seems impossible as I say it, but that might be more painful than it appears."

"I didn't peg you as the sadistic type, mate."

"Nor did I picture you as the masochist."

"Good, then. Off you go. Back to your station."

"Of course, of course. But first, how about a small wager?"

"What the bloody hell's wrong with you? Did you pull the wings off flies as a child? Did you slap kittens for fun?"

"It's completely harmless, and you can only win."

"Just get it over with."

The Frenchman extended his palm. "If you can stand straight, face me, and kick my hand, I'll give you one hundred Euro."

Cahill scoffed and stood. Then fire consumed his belly, and after he realized he'd be lucky to place one foot in front of the other, he leaned back into the table. "Go to hell, you mongrel."

A wide smile cut across the Frenchman's face. "You've been a wonderful sport."

"Thanks, I think."

Twenty minutes later, Cahill stood behind the *Specter's* surfaced conning tower. His wetsuit pinched him in private places, and the diving equipment strained his steps. As the deck rolled, the smoldering flames of his tired abdomen burned, and he wondered if his muscles retained any usefulness.

Standing in a vertical wall of rotor wind, he awaited queueing from the elder legionnaire, who watched a fellow commando rise in a harness towards the hovering helicopter.

While waiting, the Australian's adrenaline flow slowed, and a mix of soreness and fatigue crept over him. Realizing he'd skipped a night of sleep, he considered himself unready for his pending challenge.

Judging himself a dunce for having forced his way onto the dive team, he wanted to quit and turn back.

The dangling harness returned to the legionnaire's reach, and the commando held it while yelling over the whipped air. "You go now, Terry."

With his pride, the *Goliath*, and the fleet's future at stake, he choked back his doubts.

He waddled forward in his swim fins, wiggled into the constricting web of belts, and then gave the legionnaire a thumbs-up.

The *Specter* became an oblong abyss of blackness below, and groping gloves pulled him into the aircraft's cabin. Red lighting bathed the helicopter's interior.

When the legionnaire reached the door, he wiggled from his harness and joined an Omani crew chief in snapping and checking cables between the winch and the men.

The deck angled, and the aircraft climbed.

Cahill's nerves tingled as he slipped his face into his mask and tested his air.

Appearing like an alien astronaut, the legionnaire stood before him and studied him through his face shield. A transducer over the commando's mouth spat forth electrified words. "You look good, Terry."

Cahill's amplified voice sounded foreign as he responded through his transducer. "It doesn't feel good."

"You're not used to it. You are fine in the water."

"Okay, mate."

"You know not to speak unless emergency? Too loud. Alerts the people on *Goliath*."

"Right. Keep it quiet."

"How is your breathing?"

The air from Cahill's rebreather tasted like metal and chemicals. "Good."

"You have plenty of air. Not a problem. Get ready. Stand here." The legionnaire pointed to the deck behind the first pair of jumpers.

Cahill turned and stood, bumping the buttocks of the second man. Through the open door's frame, he saw blackness, and the *Specter* escaped his gaze.

He realized the submarine had submerged to periscope depth, marking one point of a line between itself and the *Wraith*. Invisible to his eyes, he trusted the exposed optics to guide the helicopter to a drop point in front of the *Goliath*.

Before he could question the logistics, the first team leapt out the door. Coiled cable unfurled behind them, and the legionnaire ushered Cahill to the aircraft's edge. "Wait, Terry."

When the first team splashed, the cable's unspooling slowed. As the coil unraveled, the Australian's eyes followed its trailing end to the belt of the legionnaire, and then to his own body.

"Now get ready."

The Australian waddled to the door, and the moonlit shimmering waves seemed close enough to touch.

The legionnaire slapped him on the back. "Go!"

Cahill gasped for breath, closed his eyes, and jumped.

CHAPTER 14

Unsure where to swim, Cahill floated until he saw the light from the commando's facemask.

He reached towards the luminous beam, cupped his hand, and pulled water down his body. As he kicked his fins, his abdomen, groin, and inner thighs ached, and he welcomed the helping force of the line joining him to his partner.

Though shrieking limpets blanketed his target, the audio beacons spanned many degrees surrounding him. Their random chirping calls were like mythical Sirens luring him to danger.

Disoriented, he relaxed as his course became obvious and his effort easy when his lifeline to his commando yanked him. It dragged him behind the frogman's fins, giving him a relieving sense of direction.

Loose cable bends appeared beside him as he swam behind his buddy, who kicked and clawed his way up the line. After several strenuous minutes, his breathing became labored. Though aching, the Australian continued swimming to minimize the strain on his partner and to keep the self-respect of making the effort.

The flowing water was an undersea river, and as it shifted over Cahill's frame, the milky glow of the *Goliath's* dome became a diffused beacon marking a fake undersea horizon. Then, in front of the backlit elder legionnaire, dark lines became visible.

Seeing the commando clamp himself against a retracted hydraulic arm, Cahill kicked the final exhilarating strides to reach his ship. Beside the former legionnaire, he grabbed the arm's rubber pad and rested.

The legionnaire pulled coils of the cable, pinched a length between his thigh and the hydraulic arm, and reached for the knife sheathed at his chest. When he had three meters of slack, he gestured for the Australian to hold an end.

Confusing Cahill, the commando started severing and fraying the interlaced metal fibers that had guided him to the *Goliath's* back. Unable to voice a protest, he frowned and watched his partner with cautious optimism. After creating two frayed ends, the legionnaire detached the useless cut cable from his belt and wrapped the remaining length around the hydraulic arm.

Cahill understood his buddy's intent as he interlaced the coils and pulled the last wrapping tight. He'd anchored the cable for the other pair of divers who swam in the invisible depths.

As Cahill wondered how he'd reach the ship's port side, the commando turned his head and pointed his light into the abyss behind and below them. His eyes adjusted to the slight contrast between black metal and the water's void, and he saw the *Goliath's* aftermost crossbeam.

The inter-hull tunnel's outer shell seemed low and difficult to achieve with a rapid downward swim, but Cahill judged the commando capable. Communicating presented a challenge, but the legionnaire mimed enough gestures for the Australian to understand his desire to be followed.

Cahill trailed the commando down the hydraulic arm to its attachment to the starboard hull. Grabbing it with both gloves, he extended his body in line with the fluid flow, aiming his flippers toward the targeted tunnel. The other swimmer then released himself and drifted into the void.

Alone, the Australian heard his labored breathing, and then a loud chirp pierced his skull. Though most limpets clamped to invisible perches hidden against the *Goliath's* underbellies, one had landed halfway up the starboard hull's side.

Aiming his light at the sonic demon, he lamented its location. Two meters away, with its top visible above the cylindrical ship's curvature, it mocked him with its proximity. Like a smoke alarm with a dying battery, it taunted him with its maddening tones.

The taut cable at his belt distracted him from the annoying

noise, and he redoubled his grip. Concerned he'd tethered his partner short of the tunnel, he considered dropping and drifting to the next hydraulic arm, but the angle from that anchorage to the crossbeam would be too steep.

Unsure how to assess his partner's safe arrival, he felt harsh yanks and assumed his buddy fought for their next perch. Fearing futility, he was relieved to feel rhythmic rapid but gentle tugs. Risking a single-hand hold to afford himself a view, he contorted his torso and aimed his forehead-mounted light under his arm.

Looking back at him with his artificial beam illuminating flowing particles of plankton and algae, the commando propped his fins' edges against the tunnel's smooth front. When Cahill made eye contact, his buddy gestured for him to follow.

Releasing his grip, Cahill pushed himself downward. Doubting he could reach the tunnel, he prayed the commando had envisioned a workable plan.

He had.

A strong force at his waist pulled Cahill down, and he groped for the nothingness. Then the line stopped him, and he grabbed it. Pulling himself forward against the current, he reached the back of the tunnel.

His body pinched to the tunnel's front, the commando greeted him with a nod and then scrambled atop the crossbeam. Wincing with the pain of exertion, the Australian climbed the rounded steel to crawl behind his partner.

The slippery surface alarmed Cahill, but it provided adequate friction against the water. He noticed his partner's skewed movement to adjust for the artificial current, but then a fishing net slowed their progress.

The first of the expected four, the net intersected the beam and extended into the darkness in both directions. Taking hold of its fibers, the commando crawled while panning his light back and forth for hooks and other sharp traps.

Discovering a hook, the elder legionnaire aimed his light at it and held it there until Cahill nodded his awareness of the dangers.

When Cahill's turn atop the net arrived, he moved with caution, but the fibers provided a welcomed stability. As the fibers gave way to smooth steel, he looked up and saw his partner laboring over another net's width.

A glance to his left showed the second net overlaying the stern planes, which glided in static silence while the huge ship maintained a shallow depth.

After passing over three more nets, Cahill saw the crossbeam's far end where the tunnel entered MESMA plant six. From there, he could pin himself in front of the cross beam and tether his partner's drift to the engine room. Finally, the victory seemed certain, and the nightmare's end within reach.

Then, an undersea sun rose.

Blinding lights from multiple angles illuminated the *Goliath's* cargo bed. Like an escaping prisoner in a guard tower spotlight, Cahill was exposed, stunned, and vulnerable.

Marking from memory the locations of the transport vessel's lights and cameras, he knew he was visible. He wanted to enable his voice transducer and warn his partner, but wise words of advice eluded him.

Would he compel his buddy to crawl faster? Could he tell him to hide? No, there was no option but to hope the prying eyes within the *Goliath* missed him.

They didn't.

Sensing a shift in the flowing water, Cahill looked over his shoulder and saw the stern planes rolling to their full dive position. "Shit." With his transducer off, his voice went nowhere. Then he probed his mask for a switch, toggled it, and called out in an amplified voice. "They see us!"

The legionnaire's amplified response reverberated off the port hull. "Yes. Keep moving."

With the nearby attentive ears aboard the *Specter* and the *Wraith*, Cahill expected his sonar technician comrades to overhear the desperate conversation.

Gravity thwarted his balanced crawl as the crossbeam angled

down. His ears began to hurt as the depth and pressure increased.

Then the Australian's world moved forward, and he slid backwards. He and the legionnaire pressed their chests to the crossbeam to stabilize themselves.

Cahill grasped the problem. "They're using the rudder. They're taking us deep and trying to shake us loose."

Fearing the pressures awaiting him at the *Goliath's* one-hundred-meter limit, he welcomed the ship's leveling less than halfway down. Wondering why the hijackers spared him the deepest depths, he recalled they lacked a definitive knowledge of the ship's formal limit.

They couldn't know the dome's pressure tolerance, and an ignorant but wise hijacker needed to stop short of its capabilities. The beam tilted from right to left as the huge ship began ascending again, and then the crossbeam reversed direction with a rudder shift, knocking Cahill's voice transducer against steel.

He started sliding off the tunnel's back, and he kicked his flailing fins to push himself forward. But his chest slipped down the sheen steel, and he forced his forearms into the metal, seeking decelerating friction.

As he looked to his companion, he noticed the commando lacked the leverage to hold them both to the ship. Fearing he'd slip away and become a chopped sacrifice to the *Goliath's* propeller, he cried out. "I'm slipping!"

With impressive agility, the commando rolled to his side and pressed his fins into the crossbeam. Their connecting line slid over the smooth metal but tightened, giving the Australian the stability he needed to brake with his waist dangling in the abyss.

Scrambling for a toehold yielded nothing, and Cahill stopped struggling. As he tried to catch his breath, he heard screams echoing from the blackness.

Failing to understand the French words, he recognized the scared shouts coming from the bottom pair of divers. Their voices started ahead of Cahill, fell silent, and then rose again underneath him as their white conical beams cut swaths below the ship.

As the lights turned away, the Australian heard a final exchange between his dislodged teammates and the elder legionnaire. Then the white orbs of the swimmers receded into the darkness.

Doubting his decision to swim, Cahill hoped his companion knew what events were unfolding. "What happened?"

"They slipped off. They dived under the propeller."

"So now what?"

"The helicopter gets them."

"What about us?"

"We finish the mission."

The crossbeam leveled as the *Goliath* ceased ascending and began another descent. Despite a rapid rudder turn jerking the tunnel, Cahill flipped a fin over the edge and pulled himself up.

But as the transport vessel dipped downward again, the commando fell over the crossbeam's forward edge, and his weight tugged the Australian's gut. Fearing he'd topple over the same edge, Cahill whipped his legs back below the crossbeam's trailing side.

The connecting line cut a forty-five-degree angle over the tunnel, one man's fall precluded by the other's torso against the beam, and the Australian struggled to move. "I'm pinned down."

"Can you move to me?"

Cahill groped and kicked, but he closed the distance to the commando by only inches. Lacking leverage to slide the line, he exerted himself, and when his stomach ached, he rested. "I can get there, but it will take time."

"We have until our air runs out."

"You said we had plenty of air."

"That was before we are caught."

"How long?"

"I can't see. Maybe fifteen minutes."

With the *Goliath's* resistance slowing Cahill's progress, its engine room seemed inaccessible. He kicked and strained again, but he made less ground. "This is taking too long."

"You have maybe ten minutes working that hard."

As the crossbeam angled up again during the next ascent, it started shimmying back and forth. Cahill recognized the constant cycling of the ship's rudders exacerbating his situation. He became a dangling limpet again as gravity and water flow pushed him back. Seeking hope in his partner's new position, he noticed his companion pinned to the crossbeam's forward edge. "Can you move?"

"No. But you can. Let go and swim back."

"What?"

"Let go and swim back close to engine room."

After envisioning the physics, Cahill risked it. He quit kicking and lifted his forearms, freeing himself. The line rose from the metal and aligned with the fluid flow, leaving him two meters behind the beam. He kicked and pulled forward, reaching the tunnel's back edge. With his companion facing him from the other side of the crossbeam, the Australian spoke despite his labored breathing. "I can hold here."

"You're stuck. We're stuck."

"There must be a way."

"No. We give up."

"Wait."

"What?"

Cahill expressed his idea to mitigate the failed sabotage attempt. "Flood the tunnel."

"You sure?"

"Yes. It won't cripple the ship, but it divides and conquers the crew."

"Okay." The commando groped behind his back and then pulled a small charge upward. He extended his arm and slapped the explosive down against the metal. The dolphin-mountable device's magnetic field held it on the crossbeam while the commando tapped its manual trigger and then wiggled away from the explosive. "Get ready."

"For what?"

"To swim up."

A pop stunned Cahill as a black hole replaced the bomblet. Then the commando pushed himself up and over the cross-beam, freeing the diving pair into the water above the *Goliath*.

"Up! Up!"

Cahill kicked and pulled, but the commando outpaced him, tightening their connecting line. Assisted upward, he continued striving for the surface.

Then his buddy's light met his face, and Cahill slowed.

The legionnaire issued an order. "Stop!"

"Why?"

"The bends. Must wait."

Cahill was frustrated with his swimming endeavor and wanted to breathe fresh air. "How long?"

The commando swam to him and examined his dial. "You have maybe six minutes left. We use it all. I lend you mine if needed. We need a minute here. Then nine meters higher. Then another minute."

"Not sure I'm going to like this."

"Don't need to like. Need to live. Get back to submarines and work on next plan."

CHAPTER 15

The colonel stood behind the lean submarine commander. "How bad is it?"

"Unnoticeable. Our men managed to close the doors on both ends. The tunnel's our only centerline compartment, and it's also our smallest. So the ship adjusted easily and automatically."

"But we've lost our passageway between the hulls. From now on, our port crew is the port crew, and we're the starboard crew."

"That may not matter. Did you get a headcount?"

"He's handling it." The colonel pointed at his bulldog.

The sergeant scribbled notes into a pad while pinching a phone receiver between his ear and shoulder. "I'm done. The only damage is to the tunnel. Our men are evenly split, seven starboard and seven port, counting our casualty."

"How is our injured teammate?"

"Still stable, but the medic says he'll need surgery within twenty-four hours."

"He'll get it, if we can keep working as a team."

Including the sonar operator and a translator who tried to glean secret insights from the *Goliath's* English-language technical manuals, the colonel counted five men in the control room.

The sixth and seventh starboard occupants were a commando and a translator who patrolled the MESMA plants in search of new leaks, noises, and blunt signs of obvious problems.

The colonel's technical experts had migrated to the *Goliath's* inaccessible port side. Instantly, they seemed distant, his team severed and his ship compromised.

And after the near miss with the divers, he felt vulnerable.

His new perspective provoked a decision to share with his submarine commander. "Helicopters have denied us the surface long enough. Let's bring them down."

"There's only one over us now. The farther we are from Oman, the longer they have to travel, and the more taxing their fuel management."

"Removing one from the rotation may clear us of this problem until we reach our Iranian support."

"It might."

"I want two Stinger teams topside, fore and aft on the port hull, and I want riflemen topside as well. Most importantly, I want to test the railgun against them. Can you optimize the ship's maneuvering for such an attack?"

The commander scoffed. "I've been considering this. If you want to use every weapon you have, the best way is the simplest way–straight up with a level deck."

"Very well. I'll brief the team. Let's get it done."

Twenty minutes later, the deck rocked under the surface swells. Trusting his submarine commander, the colonel let him drive the ship from the relative safety of the control room while he, in contrast, volunteered a showing of courage. He stood with his bulldog under the dome as a tactical distraction, daring the helicopters to shoot him.

With his teams staged and the circuit open throughout the ship, the colonel aimed his voice to the microphone. "We've faced a great deal of adversity since we first stormed this ship. I must credit our adversaries for the speed of their response. It made an otherwise flawless plan challenging."

He looked at his bulldog for immediate feedback. The sergeant's expression indicated approval, and the colonel continued. "You've all been with me for two years, some of you longer. You know why our cause is just. This mercenary fleet was born in a cauldron of greed and arrogance, and its founders have caused undo suffering to our countrymen and to hundreds, even thousands, of families around the world. Now, we'll cast away the airborne menace and retake our right to flee on the water's surface."

Again, he looked to the bulldog, and this time, the sergeant whispered. "Keep going. What's the reward for success?"

The colonel continued to his crew. "After we succeed in this anti-air defense, we'll quickly reach the submarine support we need to turn back the *Specter* and the *Wraith*. We've coordinated with our Iranian contacts, and all is ready. We hear the helicopter off the port quarter. Get ready to shoot straight, overwhelm it, and fulfill the greatest mission of your lives."

The bulldog nodded his final approval.

"That's all. Stand by."

"Well done, sir."

"This is going to happen quickly. You should get downstairs before it starts."

"I'm on my way, sir." The bulldog headed towards the stairs.

"Aren't you going to argue? I know I ordered you the lead the group if I fall, but it's not like you to leave me standing alone in danger without a protest."

The sergeant stopped. "Sir, I..."

"Don't bother explaining. I saw the rifle staged under the forward hatch. I know you're heading topside."

"I meant no offense by disobeying you, but you know I can't avoid a good fight."

"Shoot straight, and come back in one piece."

"I will, sir." The sergeant left the bridge.

The colonel waited thirty seconds for him to grab his weapon, and then he queried his crew. "All stations report in order, starting aft at the railgun and moving forward, starting port then to starboard."

The loudspeaker issued a sequence of voices.

"Railgun ready."

"Aft Stinger team and rifle ready."

"Forward Stinger team and rifle ready."

"Aft starboard rifle ready."

The sergeant's voice carried the final report. "Forward starboard rifle ready."

The colonel gave his multifaceted order to his submarine commander and his shooters. "Surface the ship. Shoot all weapons."

The black hemisphere around him receded, and as opaque sheets pooled over the dome, he pressed night optics to his face.

Scanning the low sky behind the *Goliath*, he saw the hovering helicopter.

Then he heard the port railgun's crack and celebrated aloud. "Excellent! It works!" Though poised to strike the exposed port engine room, the helicopter swerved. "It must be a hit."

A technician from the weapons bay confirmed his leader's hopes. "It's a hit! At least we think it is. There's no smoke or visible signs of damage."

"You're too close to miss. Keep firing."

Before the railgun spat its errant second round, the helicopter veered behind the *Goliath*. With its rapid cut across the water, the aircraft challenged the riflemen to adapt. Then a strong wave pitched the ship, delaying the Stingers.

When the missiles flew, they both followed flairs into the void behind the helicopter and splashed.

Scanning the port hull, the colonel saw his forward Stinger soldier on his stomach, half in the ship and half out, reaching for his dropped launcher. The fully exposed rifleman who stood beside him helped grab the missile.

His aft missile man faced a similar challenge recovering from his shifting perch on the ladder leading to his hatch.

When the Stingers and railgun recommenced their attacks, the seas shook the ship again, and their target was a shrinking spec in a dark sky.

The colonel looked to his display and tapped an icon sending his voice to external loudspeakers. "Excellent job, men! The helicopter's still flying, but it's going in the right direction. All riflemen head below. Stinger teams remain on your ladders with your missiles ready."

A technician spoke over the loudspeaker. "Ready to start the port gas turbine, sir."

"Start the port gas turbine." The colonel heard the accelerating and loud whine reach the bridge.

"The port gas turbine is ready, sir."

"Make flank speed on the port propeller."

As the dome heaved, the colonel looked aft to verify his men had returned inside the starboard hull, but his bulldog appeared far away, bent over the flooded engine room. "I believe I ordered everyone back inside."

The bulldog straightened his back, turned around, and extended his arms for balance while walking. Then he disappeared into the open hatch and closed it behind him. Moments later, the sergeant's voice crackled through the dome's speakers. "Bridge, this is MESMA plant five. Over."

"MESMA plant five, bridge. Go ahead. Over."

"We can weld a patch over the damage above the engine room. Nothing pretty, mind you, but it's mostly a big clean hole. Except for some scattered rounds, it's a tight grouping."

"We can't recover the engine room. Not with salt water damage throughout it."

"I know, sir. But we can recover the starboard gun at the very least. And who knows, maybe we can recover the starboard propeller. These motors look watertight to me."

"What about manpower and equipment?"

"I can do it with one man helping, and there's a welding kit in the engine room. You'll have to pump the engine room dry for me to get to it, though."

Envisioning the danger, the colonel hesitated to let his bulldog enter a deathtrap. "If I do that, you'll be vulnerable to God knows how many electric shorts."

"I'll lay rubber mats and wear rubber boots and gloves."

"I'm getting a second opinion." The colonel brought the submarine commander into the conversation. "Control room, bridge. Over."

"Bridge, control room. Over."

"Is it possible to enable safe entry into the starboard engine room if I pump it dry?"

"I don't like it. Even with the space isolated from the ship's main battery, it's dangerous. There's enough stored energy in the backup batteries to kill several men."

"That's not what I asked."

"I wouldn't call it safe, but a man can survive with proper precautions and deliberate movement."

The colonel looked to a new screen and worked through menus to the drain system. He opened a suction line to the engine room's bilge and energized a centrifugal pump towards the sea. "I'm draining the engine room."

The commander argued. "I'll advise you on the safety precautions, but you have to consider the need to submerge again. There's nothing I can do to assure the safety of men in a space that would be flooded upon diving."

"Of course not. But now we can shoot back at whatever might attempt to drive us under."

"Except the submarines, which we can no longer hear while we're at twenty-four knots."

"You could hear a torpedo coming, though, could you not?"

"Not until active homing, which is too late."

"Too late for what? We're already running at maximum speed."

"I would like options to maneuver, but I admit there aren't many. Handling this hybrid destroyer-submarine still seems bizarre."

"Bizarre, but turning back towards our favor." Before allowing a silent celebration, the colonel examined the rules of engagement from his adversary's perspective.

Renard would still expect to regain his property, but his oozing arrogance would erode as the *Goliath* approached Iranian waters, fifty miles away, and his tolerance for risking attacks on the ship would grow.

The colonel wondered if the Frenchman would chance an Exocet anti-ship missile from the *Specter* or the *Wraith* if he outran the reach of the submarines' less-than-lethal torpedoes.

Doing quick math, he calculated that he'd force Renard into that decision within an hour.

The commander's voice returned his focus to shorter-term thoughts. "May I share our update with the Iranians?"

"Of course. Tell them everything." Through night vision, the colonel watched the radio mast rise from the starboard stern.

"The translator's talking now. May I also raise our navigation radar? It's not locked out since it's not tied to any weapon system."

"What can it do for us?"

"It will tell us where nearby surface vessels are located."

"I know that. I mean, what's the value in that?"

"It gives us knowledge that creates options."

The colonel grew weary of the generalities. "What options? Out with it."

"If it comes to it, we may need to try to use a merchant vessel as a sacrificial anode for a hostile torpedo."

"I see."

"Or possibly we could temporarily hide among a group of ships. I won't know all the possibilities until I examine the data."

"Very well, use the radar." Through the optics, he watched another pole rise from the *Goliath's* starboard stern. At its top, a thin horizontal plate began rotating.

"The translator's finished with the Iranians. They're ready for us at any speed as long we hold our course."

"Very well. What about radar?"

"I'm gathering data now."

A tingle crept up the colonel's spine as the silence endured. "What do you see?"

"Damn. Two combatants are chasing us."

"How do you know?"

"They're making thirty-eight knots and coming right for us."

"How far away?"

"Ten and half miles. You might be able to see them on the horizon, but they'll be small."

From his low height, the colonel sought the intruder at his short horizon, but his eyes and mind struggled with the distance. "I can't see them. Maybe. I'm not sure. Just tell me what this means to us tactically."

"Given the speed, I'm assuming they're Omani *Province*-class patrol boats. They hold a fourteen-knot speed advantage over us and will catch us in forty-five minutes."

"Damn Renard and his abuse of wealth. How much did he promise to whom to rally these boats?"

"We've shot at Omani helicopters. We're giving the Omanis enough intrinsic motivation against us."

"But those patrol boats were sent after us hours ago. Can we shoot them with the railgun?"

"Unguided rounds with fractional muzzle velocity? Against ships that small and nimble? I doubt we'll hit, but we might slow them by forcing them to dodge rounds."

The railgun operator interjected. "I can see them, sir. I'm higher up than you. I may need a few shots to walk my rounds in, but I can aim at them."

For their meddling, the colonel wanted to send away the Omanis. "Go ahead. Take your shots at the patrol craft. Fire the railgun at will."

A plasma fireball lit the sky, and then another erupted ten seconds later. Lacking its locked-out charging circuit, the railgun worked at half speed.

Thinking himself immune to a counterstrike, the colonel cringed when the sea exploded one hundred meters in front of the dome. At the limit of their cannon's range, the Omanis were showing confidence in their marksmanship. He moved to the forward consoles and yelled. "They're shooting back!"

The commander sounded tense. "I know. It's just a warning shot."

"Are you willing to bet your life on that?"

"You said Renard doesn't want to sink us."

"This isn't Renard. It's the Omanis. Get us under!"

Assuming the Omanis were willing to send a crippling seventy-six-millimeter cannon round into his ship, the colonel sought submerged safety. With a quick tap of an icon and the barking of a command, he sent his commands inside and outside the hulls to bring the Stinger teams inside and close the hatches.

As opacity crept up the windows, he lamented his short-lived burst of surfaced speed, the new thirty-eight knot threats, and the abandoned hope of salvaging the second railgun.

CHAPTER 16

Jake looked over the *Specter's* control room and singled out his sonar ace. "What's the range now?"

"Four and a half miles."

Jake did a mental calculation but wanted a second check. "Terry, if I make twenty knots for half an hour, how far ahead of the *Goliath* would I be?"

The Australian, his toweled hair damp from a shower, worked a stylus over the central table. "About a mile and a quarter. You can get a full mile ahead by making twenty knots for twenty-eight minutes."

"Very well. I'm going deep and sprinting at twenty knots for twenty-eight minutes. Once I'm ahead, I'll deploy a drone and drift behind the *Goliath*. You good with that, Pierre?"

His boss' voice crackled from overhead speakers. "Yes. The patrol vessels will keep the *Goliath* submerged. Now's the time to catch up again, but do it one at a time so you and Dmitry can cover each other."

"Got it. I'll go first, and I'll deploy a drone straight ahead at first but then steer it right after Dmitry catches me. I suggest that Dmitry deploys a drone to the left when he catches up so that we can broaden our coverage."

Renard sounded approving. "You would then use the drones instead of your bow sonars for active searches?"

"Sort of. We can use secure active from the bow sonars. Between that and the drones, we'll have good active search coverage without giving away free information on our locations."

"I agree. Dmitry will need to direct traffic while you sprint. I want the patrol craft to keep station next to the *Goliath*, assuming it may surface at any moment."

Jake looked to the screen with the Russian commander and his translator, who rattled off their boss' concerns. "You got that covered, Dmitry?"

After the translator interpreted Jake's question, Volkov answered for himself. "*Da.* Yes."

"Also, can we use your dolphins? We'll be moving slow enough, and now's a good time."

"Yes. Dolphins. No problem."

On the screen, Renard nodded. "I agree again. Now's the time to use the dolphins, given your proximity to Iranian waters."

"Shit. We are getting close to Iran, aren't we?" Jake looked to the chart but feared the answer. With the Persian tripwire approaching, he sensed the inevitability of the violence he'd advocated but secretly was unsure he desired.

The slow and melancholy movement of the Australian suggested the *Goliath's* commander drew the same conclusion.

"Terry?"

"Yeah?"

"How close will we be to Iranian waters?"

"When we get ahead of the *Goliath*, we'll be thirty miles away. When Dmitry catches up, we'll be only twenty miles away."

"That's cutting it close."

"We'll still have time to send in divers again. We can do it this time." The *Goliath's* commander oozed a contagious courage.

But Jake remained the voice of reason. "How? You almost died last time."

"We won't cut the long cable. We'll use the bottom team as an anchor, and the top team will make it to the engine room."

"Against more than eight knots of current?"

"Sure. Why not?"

"Because of physics. Leverage. A hundred-meter-long cable keeps you anchored, alright. It keeps you anchored dead center in the current. You can't make any lateral movement, and the best you'd do is get wrapped around the tunnel again."

"Come on, mate. I can do this."

A confirming voice of reason issued from Renard, trumping

Cahill's hopes. "It's too dangerous. Regain your positions relative to the *Goliath*, and assure your safety with the active sonar and the dolphins. I'll determine our next attack from there."

Jake wanted to call out the next attack as the finale, but he trusted his boss to realize it, and he wanted to avoid a French tirade. He turned to the screens to face Renard and Volkov. "Okay. I'm going deep and fast. You know how to contact me if you need me." After ordering the *Specter* to begin its dive to three hundred meters, he watched the world tilt downward, and the screens went dark and silent. "Henri, make turns for twenty knots."

The Frenchman conveyed the order to the engine room, and the ship shuddered.

As gravity hastened the submarine's acceleration, a cold fear gripped Jake, and he needed to share it. "Terry."

The Australian walked to Jake. "Yeah."

He wanted to blame Cahill for the vulnerability of sprinting into danger, but in ignorance of a defined enemy, the accusation would be vapid. Instead of bitching, he sought a sanity check. "We're sprinting blind, you know."

"Yeah. I know."

"Am I forgetting anything?"

"No, mate. It's a bad position, but it's only as bad as whatever's out there waiting for us."

"And we're still far enough from Iranian waters."

"Far enough? Sure. I guess. We have no idea if the Iranians even know or care about what's happening, but we're going to resolve this in international waters, one way or the other."

"I can't wait to hear how Pierre thinks we're going to end this."

"That's why he's the big boss."

Jake wanted to continue bridging the divide between himself and the Australian, but he decided the *Goliath's* commander could benefit from unperturbed silence, and he let him go. "Thanks, Terry."

"No problem." Cahill returned to the chart.

Jake aimed his voice at his sonar ace. "Can you still hear the limpets?"

"Of course. It's the only thing I can hear at this speed, but they're still loud."

"Very well." As the *Specter* settled into its rhythmic run, Jake sank into his foldout chair and waited for his French mechanic to make eye contact. When he did, he waved to him.

Henri slid behind the Australian and found his way to Jake. Stooping, he spoke softly in his native tongue. "What can I do for you?"

Jake responded in the same language. "Why are you asking in French?"

"I sensed you wanted privacy."

"Yes, I do, but speaking French gives us privacy from only Terry. Don't you think he'd pick up on that?"

"Yes, but isn't he the one you're most concerned about?"

"Okay, fine. I can't hide anything from you. The point I wanted to make was, no matter what Pierre says, I'm not letting the *Goliath* reach Iranian waters."

The Frenchman nodded. "I understand your position."

"But do you respect it?"

"Respect it? Yes. Agree? Thankfully, that's not a decision I need to make. But I will give you this. Whether it's right or wrong, it's a logical position."

"Thanks, my friend. That's all I wanted to know."

"Shall I load a drone now, while we're making noise?"

"Yeah. Of course. Use tube five. Flood it and open the outer door. I'm going to launch it as soon as we're shallow."

For the next fifteen minutes of presenting an easy target to any nearby adversary, Jake silently prayed the *Goliath's* hijackers were working alone. He exhaled in relief when he passed under the transport ship and left it in his baffles. "Henri, it's time to let the *Goliath* catch up to us again. Slow us to three knots and take us to periscope depth."

Friction and gravity slowed the ascending submarine. The sprinting vibrations gave way to a smooth and rapid rise, which then became a leveled but rocking deck.

"Antoine, begin an automatically repeated secure active search, minimum duration bursts, twenty-degree increments, full sweep."

The guru tapped icons and turned quiet hydrophones into transmitters. "I've commenced the automatically repeated secure active search, minimum duration bursts, twenty-degree increments, full sweep."

"Give me the status of the drone in tube five."

"The drone is connected to and powered by its wire. Ready for launch."

"Launch tube five."

The toad-head twisted as Remy reported. "Drone one is swimming out of tube five. Drone one is clear of our hull and deployed. I have wire connectivity and confirmation of propulsion."

"Set the drone's speed to ten knots, straight ahead of our track, depth one hundred meters."

The toad-head looked downward as fingers danced over a capacitive touchscreen. "The drone is at maximum speed, straight ahead of our track, depth one hundred meters."

"Set drone one to a full-power active search."

Again, the sonar ace tapped his display. "Drone one has begun a full-power active search."

With his acoustic position optimized, Jake had his radio mast raised, and he reconnected with Volkov and his boss, who greeted him. "You made it."

"Yeah. I've got the drone deployed on an active search, and I've got the bow system on secure active. I haven't seen any returns yet, thankfully, and the sonar guys aren't hearing anything."

"Sometimes it's good to be alone."

"Let's hope it lasts. Now it's Dmitry's turn."

"Agreed. Go ahead and sprint, Dmitry."

The Russian commander acknowledged the Frenchman's order, and then his screen went blank, leaving only Renard's face on the connection. "Send me a data link so I can share it with the Omani patrol boats."

Jake looked to his mechanic, who nodded and offered his raised thumb.

"Henri said he's already linked with you, Pierre."

"Sorry, Jake. It must've been a delay. I see it now."

Paying attention to the background noise behind the Frenchman's voice, Jake glared at his boss' image on a display. Red lights and shadows replaced his plush hotel room. "Where are you?"

"Aboard the Omani patrol craft, *Dhofar*, one nautical mile behind you. More accurately, one nautical mile behind where Dmitry will be. We're holding to the port side of the *Goliath*, to strike its engine room, should it surface."

"How'd you manage that?"

"Helicopters have been flying nonstop through the night. I took a ride and requested a detour to the *Dhofar* when the patrol boats approached the *Goliath*."

"I have to admit, that's a nice personal touch."

"I wanted to be near the action."

A heavy swell lifted and then lowered the submarine, freezing the Frenchman's face while the mast submerged. Jake grabbed a polished railing to balance himself.

The deck steadied, and the Frenchman's face reappeared.

"Can you hear me, Pierre?"

"Yes. Go ahead."

"Have you made a decision yet?"

"About stopping the *Goliath*?"

"Yeah."

"I've made a decision, but I'll share it when Dmitry's available. I'll tell you all at the same time."

Jake doubted his boss had reached his verdict, but he trusted Renard enough to believe he was finalizing a solution. "Okay. I can wait another twenty-five minutes."

As the *Wraith* sprinted behind the *Goliath*, Jake had his *Specter* scouring the seas ahead of him for threats, discovering nothing.

But his sonar ace heard his twin submarine racing forward. "I hear the *Wraith* behind the *Goliath* now."

"Antoine, let one of the junior guys keep tabs on the *Wraith*. I want you listening out there for surprises."

"Okay, Jake. I will. You've drifted far enough behind the *Goliath*, haven't you? Time to speed up?"

Jake looked at the central chart, where Cahill nodded, and he agreed with his sonar ace. "Henri, make turns for eight point two knots." As minutes passed, time tested his patience, but he trusted in his sonar ace's ears to verify the absence of unwanted submarines.

Remy betrayed his inability to obey Jake. "The *Wraith* is slowing and rising. I hear hull popping."

"I told you to listen for surprises, not to the *Wraith*."

"I hear everything. Would you prefer I didn't?"

"Fine."

"Now the *Wraith* is deploying a drone and raising a mast. I expect you'll have radio contact with Dmitry soon."

Moments later, Volkov's face appeared on the screen, with his translator, who spoke for him. "We just deployed our drone and are broadcasting secure active transmissions from the bow sonar. We'll have the dolphins in the water soon, too."

Renard was enthusiastic. "Excellent. We'll have a group meeting once the dolphins are deployed, and I'll share my plan."

Jake recognized the time to shift the geometry of the team's listening devices. "Antoine, steer our drone right thirty degrees."

Remy's fingers danced over his screen. "Our drone is steered right thirty degrees."

While waiting for Volkov and his crew to load the cetaceans into a torpedo tube for their swim, Jake sought a casual conversation. He considered speaking in French to escape the Australian's ears, but he thought better of alienating Cahill. "Any news from Olivia?"

"Nothing useful. She's checking what she can, and so far she's demonstrated that we're free from interference by merchant vessels and surface combatants."

"She still has no idea who's behind this?"

"No, unfortunately not."

"Not even anything connected to Iran?"

"No. Neither she nor I see any evidence for Iranian involvement. It's quite possible the hijackers are making for their waters just because they know we'll hesitate to follow."

"Well, we are hesitating, aren't we?"

There was slight delay in the Frenchman's response. "Of course."

"Then we're running out of time. I can't wait to hear your plan."

"Patience. Dmitry will be back soon."

Volkov's voice rang in the background of the *Wraith's* control room, and the translator snapped back in Russian. He then turned his face to the monitor as his translator shared his update. "Our drone detected a submerged contact. Possibly two. We're holding the dolphins back while we're analyzing. We're sending information over the data feed."

Jake looked to Remy. "Antoine?"

"I see the data feed. I'm already listening."

Jake let his ace listen during a deathly silence.

"Nothing, Jake. There's nothing making noise in that direction."

"You're sure?"

The toad-head turned, and its face shot an angry look.

"Sorry, Antoine. I had to ask."

Volkov's translator offered an update. "Dmitry's confirmed it. There are two submerged contacts. They're at zero speed. The drone is now silent and stopped."

Jake darted to a console, leaned into the screen, and glared at his boss' face. "The only question is who shoots which weapons."

The red lighting aboard the Omani patrol boat painted an eerie aura around the Frenchman. Seeming reluctant, Renard paused before answering. "Agreed. Two slow-kills from Dmitry, since he's closer."

The translator confirmed. "Dmitry understands two slow-kills."

"Launch now. I'll inform the Omanis."

Jake questioned an omission. "What about the yield?"

"Full yield. Twenty-four bomblets each."

"You're not afraid it's a friendly submarine?"

Renard sounded confident. "No friendlies would be drifting as a pair in that location."

"That's what confirmed it for me, too. Wrong place, wrong time, and operating as a team. That's nobody's standard procedure except–just guessing–a local Persian country with a bunch of small submarines who hates everyone else's submarines who might show up near their homeland." Anger rose within Jake, and he clenched his jaw to remain silent while analyzing his thoughts. After a few calming breaths, he realized his frustration.

He'd been right. Cahill and Renard had been wrong.

They should've stopped the *Goliath* hours ago with a slow-kill weapon, ignoring the danger of sinking it. Now, twenty miles from Iranian waters, they walked into at least one ambush from a navy with two dozen submarines, countless mines, anti-submarine helicopters, and super-cavitating torpedoes.

Unsure if he should share his inner angst, he welcomed Volkov's return to his screen along with his translator. "Dmitry's launched two slow-kill weapons. To minimize alerting the adversaries, he won't turn on their active seekers until a mile from the nearer target. He'll steer the weapons as they acquire one or the other target."

Renard sounded eager. "Very well. Was there any sign of a counter-detection of the drone?"

"Dmitry says no, but there's a good chance the targets heard the drone anyway. They're probably hoping we didn't get returns off their hulls."

Jake pushed his agenda. "But this forces the question. They obviously know we're here, and we're within their weapons range. Do we evade, or do we hope they have too much vested in the *Goliath's* survival to risk it?"

"Evasion is impossible. You can't abandon the *Goliath*."

The comment irked Jake. "Now's a good time to explain your plan, then."

"Indeed. Given the discovery of the submerged targets, I want Dmitry to steer left to course three-zero-zero and slow down to listen for counterfire. That leaves you, Jake, to do exactly what you want to do and shoot the *Goliath*."

Feeling mixed emotions, he looked to the Australian, who remained plastic. So, Jake kept talking. "Well, it's not that I want to shoot the *Goliath*. I just don't see any other choice."

"But you do have a choice. You can choose the amount of damage you inflict, and I've made that decision for you. You're going to use one modified slow-kill weapon."

"Just one? I've made two of them, and I've got a team modifying a third."

"One bomblet will be sufficient."

Jake saw the Australian creep up beside him. Resigned to the outcome, the *Goliath's* commander appeared calm. "How can you be so sure to hit the port engine room with just one bomblet?"

"Our Taiwanese support team verified you can take manual control of the torpedo's detonator while keeping its influence field energized. That means you can guide it in from behind the port propeller and detonate it with some certainty under the engine room."

Jake envisioned the tactic with a mix of hope and doubt. "Did you explain our predicament to our Taiwanese buddies?"

"I did. I trust them with everything, including my shame."

Jake was encouraged but wanted to hear confirmation from the brilliant minds who developed his weapons. "And they said it'll work?"

"It will be difficult, but yes. Maybe. Well, it's like I said. There will be some certainty."

In the screen beside Renard's face, Volkov turned and exchanged words in Russian. As the Russian commander stood to walk away and join his team, Remy announced his findings. "The submerged contacts are moving."

Volkov's translator confirmed it. "I think I just heard you say the submerged contacts are moving. We notice it here on the *Wraith*, too."

Keeping his eyes on his sonar ace, Jake watched thick hands press a headphone into the toad-head.

Remy's torso curled while his mind filtered reality from sonic hallucinations. "*Ghadir*-class submarines."

Behind Jake's shoulder, the translator agreed. "We've classified the submerged contacts as Iranian littoral combat submarines."

Jake aimed his chin at the translator. "So have we. *Ghadir*-class. They're small, but they're maneuverable and carry two full-size torpedoes each."

Remy's update was reassuring. "Not to worry, Jake. They're turning and running. I hear no incoming weapons."

"We, too, hear no incoming weapons on the *Wraith*. Dmitry says the drone would certainly have heard such weapons if they had been launched."

Jake agreed but needed to vent his frustration. "Dmitry's right. His drone just saved our lives. The Iranians were looking for bearing separation between us and the *Goliath*, and as close as they were to our track, they would've had it. If Dmitry's drone hadn't been in the right spot, we would've stumbled by the ambush and been vaporized."

Renard attempted a positive spin. "But now we know that Iran's involved. You've gathered valuable information."

"Okay, but that leaves a bunch of submarines out there to ambush us. Not to mention mines, which can be turned on or off depending on the Iranians' whims. We need to act now."

"Agreed. Move into position half a nautical mile behind the *Goliath's* port hull, and then I'll explain the details about your final shot to end this nightmare."

CHAPTER 17

Olivia rested her elbows on her desk and dropped her head into her palms. "How many enemies can one man have?"

Without evidence of an Iranian connection, she'd released Matthew Williams an hour ago, agreeing with Renard's theory of desperation driving the *Goliath's* flight for Persian waters.

Her last update placed the stolen ship twenty miles from the dangerous navy's coastal region, and the Frenchman's assurance of ending the nightmare before allowing a boundary crossing faded into fiction with time's passage.

For the first time in a decade, she believed Pierre Renard faced eminent and unqualified defeat.

Although wanting to believe in him, she needed to begin the damage control phase of a problem she had to define no longer as theirs but as the Frenchman's alone to bear.

Her inner monster demanded a clean break from the mercenary fleet, and one request to the commander of the U.S. Fifth Fleet would suffice.

One call stating the Frenchman had turned on her would doom the *Goliath*. She knew she could pressure the Omanis to get out of the way and free an American anti-submarine aircraft or a submarine hidden nearby to bring swift closure.

But while she stared at her phone, she hesitated to call the vice admiral.

She wondered if she owed Renard his last chance, and she admitted that down deep, the inner girl still cared for Jake. The romantic love had vanished, but they shared an unforgettable past, and she wanted him to be okay.

She wavered. "Damn you, Pierre."

Changing direction, she sought friendly help. She stood and

walked to the window to gaze at the thick, dark foliage marking the tree line beside her building.

She drew a deep breath and called her mentor, who waited several rings to answer.

Rickets was hard to hear. "Hold on a second, Olivia. I'm walking outside."

"Thanks, Gerry."

"I had to excuse myself from the dinner crowd."

"Sorry about that."

"It's no big deal. Are you okay?"

"Not really. Are you alone?"

"Yeah. Nobody can hear me, and my cell phone's secure."

"I think I screwed up."

"How bad?"

She let the inner girl express fatigue and fear in her voice. "Real bad. I screwed up real bad."

"Okay. The first thing you have to do is calm down. You sound spun up. Explain it to me slowly."

She scoffed and mocked herself with cynicism. "Sure, Gerry. Real slow. You ready? Here we go. Someone... hijacked... the *Goliath*."

"Good God, Olivia! I don't know where to begin with that."

"I told you it was bad."

"This is catastrophic, but we deal with the catastrophic in our line of work. So stay calm and fill me in."

Although she doubted he'd give her any political support, she expected his sincere concern. That was enough, for now. "Someone took the *Goliath* from its anchorage in Muscat last night, and Pierre's got his submarines chasing it with a small chunk of the Omani Navy. He flooded the *Goliath's* starboard engine room and is keeping it submerged and slow."

"Who's doing this?"

As an ace in the intelligence community, she felt sickened to give her weak answer. "No clue. Iran is the top candidate, but had my Iranian expert here tonight, and he turned up nothing."

"Nothing? There's nothing?"

"Someone's covering their tracks, or they never created tracks."

"Okay. You don't know who did this. Absent that knowledge, what's the risk?"

"The *Goliath's* about fifteen miles from Iranian waters, and I don't know what Pierre can do to stop it without sinking it."

"Then he needs to sink it. That's the worst-case end to this. It has to be."

"I'm not sure I have total control of him. He's trying to get it back without destroying it."

His voice became icy. "Olivia, listen to me carefully. I can't do anything to protect you if the *Goliath* ends up in hostile hands. You need to do whatever you can to make sure that doesn't happen."

"The commander of the Fifth Fleet doesn't yet know about the hijacking, but he's watching. He called me and said he'd destroy the *Goliath* before it gets to Hormuz. I think he'd be willing to help destroy it sooner if I asked."

"Not in Iranian waters, he won't. You're running out of time if he's going to help you."

"I know. I need to decide fast."

"Does he think you still control the *Goliath*?"

"Maybe. Probably. Do you think I should come clean and ask for help?"

"Yes. You're in damage control mode. Taking a definitive step to sink the *Goliath* may be necessary for you to survive this."

"Thanks, Gerry. I didn't want to make this decision alone."

"Make the call. Good luck."

With the phone silent, she gazed out the window mustering courage, but then fate jolted her with her phone's ringer.

The U.S. Fifth Fleet's commander was calling her directly. As she scrabbled to answer, a competing call arrived from Renard.

"Shit." After a moment of indecision, she answered the vice admiral's call. She struggled to find the breath to speak and fumbled through an inappropriate greeting. "This is Olivia."

"Miss McDonald, this is Vice Admiral Schmidt. You'll excuse my directness, but blunt action requires blunt speech. I'm afraid I need to tighten the noose around your task force."

"I... I don't understand."

"I don't have time for political positioning."

"No, really. I don't understand." Her tone sounded desperate as her words circled her head. Her inner beast hated such weakness but judged it appropriate for her pending request for help.

"No matter. Your task force just forced two Iranian *Ghadir*-class submarines to the surface. Normally, I'd applaud your sailors for harassing the Iranians, but these subs were two of nearly a dozen we're tracking near your task force."

"A dozen?"

The vice admiral assumed a pensive tone. "I see. You really don't know. Come to think of it, you can't know. This is naval intelligence, and you have no access to it unless your task force is on an approved mission."

The protective monster's instinct was to launch a counterattack, challenging why the vice admiral was spying on a CIA mission. Then the beast recognized the vapidity of the argument and judged compliance as the proper tactic. "You're right, sir. I don't have such access."

"Well, now you know. The recent Iranian activity suggests their involvement, and that changes everything. I can't risk the *Goliath* falling into Iranian hands."

"Of course not, sir. I understand."

"Do you? Do you know what its railguns can do to my fleet from the safety of Iranian waters? They could cripple the engine room of every ship I have. They could make every building on my base inhabitable."

She knew everything the *Goliath* could do. It had been her asset just half a day earlier. "I fully agree, sir."

"Good. Then you'll understand if I give the order to sink it."

Her mentor's advice aside, her world crumbled, and the inner girl groped for something to hold. The best she could find was a cry for clemency. "I'd like one last appeal to Renard. He tried to call me during our conversation."

"I'll give you fifteen minutes. If I don't hear from you by then, I'm sending the *Goliath* to the bottom."

"Thank you." The line went silent, and she called the Frenchman.

Renard sounded enthusiastic. "Great news. Jake is beginning his final approach on the *Goliath*."

"Really? Well I have shitty news. I did some math in my head after talking to the commander of the U.S. Fifth Fleet."

"You informed him of our predicament?"

The Frenchman's audacity angered her. "No, jackass, he informed me! Hours ago! Don't you think the big boys watch you?"

"And you didn't tell me?"

The beast let the inner girl vent at volume. "When he told me, it didn't matter. He only cared about you reaching Hormuz. Now he sees that the damned Iranians are involved! He's afraid they're trying to steal the *Goliath*, and he's right. He says a dozen submarines are out there waiting for you."

"Damn. That many."

"And my Iranian expert just told me there's absolutely no sign of an Iranian operation against you. Nothing's making sense. This is an unqualified disaster without a shred of insight. You got blindsided bad." Silent moments passed, and her temper receded.

"Yes, I agree."

"How do you get yourself into a mess like this?"

"I will share with you whatever insight I find as I learn it. However, we must keep our wits about us. You mentioned doing the math. What math did you perform?"

"Yeah, right. I have fifteen minutes, twelve now, to get back to the vice admiral, or he'll sink the *Goliath*. I assume that means he has a submarine watching you, right? What else could he mean?"

"No, that's logical. It's a submarine. Based upon the intelligence you've shared with me, no surface combatant or anti-submarine aircraft is close enough to attack the *Goliath* within that timeframe. Nor do the Omanis see anything close enough."

"That's bad, Pierre. An American submarine can take down your entire fleet in a snap."

"I know that. But its presence is also not unexpected."

She found his enduring confidence arrogant. "So what? You act like you're in total control, but you're not. You're about to be hunted down and destroyed by the U.S. Navy. What are you going to do about it?"

"I'm putting an end to it."

"How?"

"Jake's in position now. He'll launch weapons at the port stern until this ends properly with the *Goliath* on the surface, or until it ends sadly with the *Goliath* on the bottom."

She needed to confirm his sincerity. "That's a huge decision. Are you committed to it?"

"Damn it, yes. But I am hedging my bet. Jake will be using slow-kill weapons modified to deploy just one bomblet each."

She knew of the slow-kill weapons that served as Renard's calling card, but the details of their behavior eluded her. "What's the significance of that?"

"I'm trying to hit the engine room without hitting the adjacent MESMA plant. Flooding both compartments might overwhelm and sink the *Goliath*."

"Might or will?"

"With Terry and his crew, I'd expect him to manage the damage control and fight to the surface. With these rogues running my ship, I fear the worst."

"Alright then. How much time do you need?"

"Half an hour."

"I'll call the vice admiral and see what I can do." She hung up and analyzed her position. Seeing no way to portray Renard's attack against his own ship as anything but a response to a hijacking, she resigned herself to candor as she called the waiting naval officer.

"Miss McDonald?"

"Yes, sir. I talked to Renard. He's confided in me that someone hijacked the *Goliath*. He's going to cripple it with one of his submarines."

His tone became accusatory and belittling. "I assumed as much. The *Specter* just moved half a mile behind the *Goliath* and opened three of its outer doors. Is there anything you can tell me that I don't already know?"

She offered what little she could for her dying dignity. "Yes, sir. You're aware of his slow-kill weapons?"

"If you mean his modified Black Shark torpedoes that attach small charges to targeted hulls, then yes."

"That's what I mean. He's found a way to reduce the yield to one charge per torpedo, and he's going to try to force the *Goliath* to surface by flooding the port engine room. He already flooded one engine room, and taking out the port room would cripple the ship."

He grunted. "That explains why one propeller is idle."

"Yes, sir. Can you give Renard thirty minutes?"

"He'll need to better than that. He has twenty-three minutes from right now. I had to draw the line, and I drew it. A heavy-weight weapon will hit the *Goliath* if it reaches exactly ten miles from Iranian waters. I've already given the order."

"Can't you give him time to finish this?"

"You're in no position to negotiate. I know where the Iranian submarines are right now, and you don't. I can't risk any complexities beyond my present order. My decision is final."

The monster knew to stop negotiating time and to focus elsewhere to give Jake a chance. "I understand. But will you rescind your order if Pierre's ship forces the *Goliath* to surface?"

"Yes. But don't look to me for help in extracting the *Goliath* from the Iranians if they decide to attack it. And God help you if they try to commandeer it if you make it surface. I'll have it destroyed before I let that happen."

"Of course, sir. I appreciate your candor."

"Good luck, Miss McDonald."

The line went silent, and she dialed the Frenchman.

"Yes? What news?"

"The vice admiral says he'll sink the *Goliath* with a heavyweight weapon ten miles from Iranian waters."

"That's twenty-two minutes from now. That's a challenge, but Jake may be able to succeed."

"He has to, Pierre."

She saw her career crashing in a fire of shame followed by a desperate effort to avoid imprisonment during the ensuing witch hunt. Nobody stood out as a possible sacrifice in her place. It was her private fleet for her private use, and she derided herself for overcommitting to it.

In contrast, the Frenchman remained confident. "If anyone can do it, he can."

"How can you be so calm? Weren't you rattled when this started?"

"Rattled? Of course. It's only human nature. But I've felt calmer as this morning has unfolded. Indeed, the sun is already rising here in the Gulf of Oman."

His optimism inspired a nervous laugh, which escaped through her nose. "The world's ending for both of us, and still, you're so damned sure of yourself."

"Sure of myself? No. Sure of Jake? Yes. Remember, young lady, that I recruited him, and I only recruit those who are charmed."

"I hope you're right. Get it right, Pierre." After hanging up on the Frenchman, she called her mentor.

Rickets skipped the pleasantries. "Yes. Go ahead."

"Stand by, Gerry. One of two things is going to happen in the next half hour. Either Renard gets the *Goliath* back, or the U.S. Navy blows it up."

"I know how to handle the former outcome. But if it's the latter, this is going to hurt your chances of seeing that appointment to your next position. A lot."

CHAPTER 18

Jake's heart raced. "How long do I have?"

Renard sounded neutral, like he recognized the enormity of the task but considered his team capable. "Eighteen minutes."

"Couldn't you buy me more time?"

"It wasn't my negotiation, and Olivia had no leverage. I'm afraid there's a swarm of Iranian submarines dead ahead of you."

The news flustered Jake. If he magically detected every threat, and if he launched a perfect torpedo shot at each one, he'd still face an impasse of Persian firepower. "And there's an American submarine watching them, watching the *Goliath*, watching me, Dmitry, you... watching everything. And it's ready to shoot."

"Indeed."

"Then I need to tighten my launch window. I'll send all three weapons out a minute apart."

"Agreed. You must make haste."

Jake thought of his Russian colleague on the *Wraith* who had raced ahead of him and scouted the perilous forward waters. "Is Dmitry in danger?"

"Yes, unfortunately. I don't know where the Iranian submarines are, but he'll be close enough to be heard at eight knots. So, I've mitigated his risk by ordering him to six knots and having him launch a second drone to bolster his search."

Looking at the tactical display, Jake estimated the *Wraith's* new speed meant the *Goliath* would overrun it in eighteen minutes. He realized his French boss had perfected Volkov's logistics. "What about the dolphins?"

"I'm letting Dmitry decide. He knows better than I how to use them. I trust him to protect himself."

"He went deep before you knew that half the Iranian fleet was lying in wait, though."

"Mind your own battle, Jake. Trust Dmitry and the information I've shared with him."

"Right. Got it."

"Back to your haste. You have seventeen minutes."

Jake turned his attention towards his own submarine and looked at his mechanic. "Henri, what's the status of tubes one through three?"

"Tubes one through three are loaded with modified slow-kill weapons, mated to the Subtics system, and flooded. Ready to shoot tubes one through three."

"Antoine, who controls weapons one through three?"

The toad-head twisted. "I have weapon one. Julien has weapon two. Noah has weapon three. All weapons are ready to launch."

"Presets?"

"Floor of one hundred meters. No ceiling. Torpedo speeds will remain at twenty knots throughout their runs."

Remembering his tight time constraints and discounting his torpedoes' fuel economy and range, Jake altered a tactic. "Change the initial speed to sixty knots for the first five hundred yards for each weapon. Then set them to slow to twenty knots automatically."

Three technicians seated side by side updated their screens in unison and then shared their statuses with Remy, who relayed the confirmation to Jake. "We've set the weapons to run at sixty knots for five hundred yards and then slow to twenty knots."

"Very well, Antoine. Shoot tube one."

The pneumatic impulsion system beyond sight in the forward compartment thrust a weapon into the sea while sucking air into its piping. The rapid pressure change popped Jake's ears.

"Tube one indicates normal launch. I have wire control. I hear its propeller."

"Henri, start a forty-second countdown to the next weapon's launch. Notify me at ten seconds."

The Frenchman grabbed his personal phone and tapped its screen. "A forty-second countdown's in progress."

Thankful to have a commanding officer's talent working the central table, Jake stayed standing above his team and watched Cahill zoom the chart to a one-mile-square resolution.

With the huge zoom, a large torpedo icon appeared, flashed, and settled into its trek with a speed vector extending beyond the chart.

Lines of bearing to the noises from the limpets dotting the *Goliath's* hull formed from the icon of the *Specter's* torpedo. Crossed with lines from the submarine's bow array, hull array, and towed array, the geometric intersections modeled a legion of limpets clamped against the transport ship.

Sonic acuity separated the port noisemakers from the starboard, but ambiguity of limpet placement over the long ship's length complicated placing the torpedo under the engine room.

As informational overload created a tangled sonic web, the Australian wiggled furious fingers over pixelated buttons to tame the tactical representation. Colored pixels receded into darkness, yielding a calmer view. When finished, Cahill looked up at Jake. "I picked the four limpets closest to the *Goliath's* four corners to track our weapon."

"Not bad, Terry. Good thinking."

Remy shared his update. "The first weapon has reached five hundred yards and is slowing."

"Got it, Antoine."

Henri updated the countdown. "Ten seconds left of your forty-seconds, Jake."

"Got it, Henri. Status of our second weapon, Julien?"

"The second weapon is ready, Jake."

Jake counted the final seconds silently. "Shoot tube two." The impulsion system whined and popped his ears.

Julien gave his update. "Tube two indicates normal launch. I have wire control and hear the propeller."

"Henri, start another forty-second countdown and notify me at ten seconds."

"The second countdown's in progress."

Jake watched the Australian repeat his artistry on the display, cleaning the view of the second weapon, and he heard Julien's report about the second weapon slowing to twenty knots, followed by another ten-second countdown reminder from his mechanic. "Got it, Henri. Status of our third weapon, Noah?"

"It's ready."

Jake counted silently again. "Shoot tube three."

The *Specter's* barometric pressure fell a third time as the third technician launched the third weapon, giving birth to a third icon behind the first torpedoes that became the vertex of a sonic web.

Again, the Australian cleaned the view. "The first weapon has pulled even with the *Goliath's* stern."

"Got it, Terry. Antoine, give me an eighty-degree steer to the right."

"My weapon's turning right eighty degrees."

"Energize the influence field."

"The influence field is energized."

The Australian commander's participation became vital as he announced his observation of the overhead visual scene. "The first weapon's passing behind the *Goliath*."

Hoping the weapon's upward-looking magnetic influence field sensed the disturbance by the port hull's ferrous metal, Jake watched his sonar ace's body language.

Remy's shoulders slumped and the toad-head shook. "No detection."

"Very well, Antoine. Steer the first weapon left eighty degrees."

"My weapon's turning left eighty degrees."

Cahill shared the visual perspective. "It's passing behind again."

Again, the toad-head shook. "Nothing. No detection."

"Steer weapon one right eighty degrees."

"My weapon's turning right eighty degrees."

More from the Australian. "The second weapon's even with

the *Goliath*."

"Steer weapon two right eighty degrees."

Julien nodded. "Weapon two is turning right eighty degrees."

Remy raised his hand. "Influence field detection!"

Fearing sensory overload if he tried to micromanage two torpedoes, Jake took his first shot. "Detonate weapon one!"

"Detonating!"

"Did it attach?"

The toad-head nodded. "Yes! Waiting... and, yes! Explosion. Flooding... That was too fast. That was the railgun magazine. We hit too far aft."

"Shit. Terry, can I still flood the engine room without sinking the ship?"

"Yes. I think so. I mean, yes."

From the computer screen, Renard broke his silence. "I concur. The burden of this decision rests upon me. Continue your attack."

Jake glanced at the chart and noticed the second torpedo farther right than he'd wanted. "Steer weapon two left seventy degrees."

Tapping icons, Julien obeyed. "Weapon two is turning left seventy degrees." As the weapon veered back on target, the young sonar technician half-stood in his seat. "Influence field detection!"

"Wait, Julien! Let it pass through."

Cahill shared the final torpedo's status. "The third weapon is even with the *Goliath*."

"Got it, Terry. Noah, steer weapon three right eighty degrees."

"Weapon three is turning right eighty degrees."

Amid the controlled chaos, Remy curled forward with thick fingers pressing speakers against his ears. The toad-head swiveled, allowing the sonar ace to aim his voice towards his commander. "Torpedo in the water. American ADCAP Mod Seven."

The announcement stung Jake. "Shit. Terry, you're playing defense for me. Make sure the ADCAP isn't coming for us. If it is, find a way to make it hit the *Goliath* and not us."

"I'm on it, mate."

"Julien, steer weapon two right eighty degrees. Noah, steer weapon three left eighty degrees."

The young Frenchmen obeyed, and Julien lifted his buttocks from his seat while curling forward into his console. "Influence field detection!"

"Detonate weapon two!"

"Detonating!"

"What's going on, Julien? Talk to me."

"Nothing. It's a miss! My bomblet missed!"

To avoid dismay, Jake reminded himself each bomblet had a historical sixty-five percent chance of attaching. Odds favored the third weapon bailing him out. "Let's make the last one count. It's up to you, Noah."

"Understood, Jake. I have influence field detection!"

"Let it pass through."

Cahill stood from Remy's side. "The American torpedo is aimed at the *Goliath*. At least that's the educated guess. We're too close to the *Goliath* to tell if the Americans are aiming at us or them, with the margin of error in the tracking."

"Any idea of range?"

"It's still at least a few miles off."

Recalling his boss telling him about the U.S. Fifth Fleet's ultimatum, Jake checked a timer ticking in the tactical chart's corner coinciding with the ten-mile buffer from Iranian waters. "Solve the American weapon's range to coincide with detonation under the *Goliath* in eight minutes."

As the dejected Julien sank into his seat, the same eagerness that had lifted him towards his console shifted to Noah. "Jake? The steer?"

"Noah, steer weapon three right eighty degrees."

As he glared at shifting pixels, Jake realized the American torpedo nullified his chances of recapturing the *Goliath*. The unwelcomed weapon would destroy the flagship unless he found an opportunity to stop it.

Noah's announcement provided that opportunity. "Influence

field detection!"

"Detonate! Detonate!"

"Detonating!"

"Come on. Attach to the damned engine room."

"Yes! My bomblet is attached! Explosion! Flooding!"

"Is it the engine room?"

"I don't know, but I hit a big compartment. Weapons bay, engine room, or MESMA six. It should be the engine room. We timed it correctly. I know we did."

Jake wanted his expert's opinion, but with the American weapon and submarine nearby, he let Remy focus on them.

Cahill reminded him of his need to play defense. "The American torpedo is four miles away."

"Show it on the chart."

The Australian returned to the central table and zoomed it out, causing a red icon to appear to the east. "This can't end with an American torpedo. Me ship can't go down like this. They'll have to shut down their weapon when they see the *Goliath* surfacing."

"If they see it surface, you mean. We don't know which compartment we hit." Jake assumed his expert heard the flagship, in addition to listening for the Americans. "Antoine?"

"I'm already listening. I hear everything."

"Well?"

"Noah's right. It's a major compartment, but it's impossible to tell which one. All machinery on the *Goliath's* still running."

At his control station, the French mechanic stood. "Jake, you must consider opening range from the *Goliath* to avoid damage from the American torpedo."

"Damn it, you're right, Henri. Come left to course two-six-zero."

As the deck angled and rocked harder in the swells, Renard's voice came from a loudspeaker. "Jake, contact Dmitry and have him retreat. There's nothing left for him to do except avoid harm, and I have no low-bandwidth communications at my disposal."

"Right, Pierre. Will do. Henri, use the underwater sonar communications suite to order Dmitry to course…" Jake looked at the chart and estimated the *Wraith's* position before continuing. "… course two-four-zero. And tell him to make ten knots."

The silver-haired Frenchman spoke into a microphone and then waited.

Moments later, the Russian translator's accent passed through the room's loudspeakers acknowledging the *Wraith's* new course.

Then Noah stood and yelled. "The engine room is shutting down!"

The toad-head nodded. "Agreed. The *Goliath* is slowing! The propeller has stopped!"

A weight lifted from Jake's shoulders. "Sweet! What about the American torpedo?"

"I still hear it running three miles away."

"Why don't they shut it down? Can't they hear the *Goliath* stopping?"

Renard added the qualifier. "That wasn't the agreement. The *Goliath* must also surface."

"That's only because we assumed it would surface. Apparently, they're staying underwater and having a hard time debating amongst themselves how badly we've just beaten them."

"I'll make the phone call. Don't do anything rash while I do."

Jake looked to Henri. "Rash like what?"

"He knows you well, Jake. Perhaps he considers you capable of threatening the American submarine."

"I don't even have a shred of evidence where it is, other than its torpedo, do I Antoine?"

The toad-head shook. "I can hear everything, but that applies only to things that make sounds, which excludes a drifting *Virginia*-class submarine."

Henri continued his psychological analysis. "But Pierre knows you'd risk a salvo and hope to get lucky enough to have a weapon acquire."

"Am I really that reckless?"

"You have been in the past."

"You make me sound like a monster. I invented the damned slow-kill weapon to save lives."

The silver-haired Frenchman shrugged. "Maybe you were a monster. I believe your inspiration for your slow-kill design was you compensating for the guilt of hurting people in the past with your uncontrolled anger."

Cahill refocused Jake's attention. "I hate to break up this therapy session, but we need to extricate ourselves from the kill zone of a possible heavyweight torpedo blast."

"Henri, increase speed to ten knots."

Eager for an update, Jake welcomed his boss' voice.

Renard was enthusiastic. "Great news. The commander of the U.S. Fifth Fleet agreed to have the incoming weapon shut down. Please listen for it and let me know when it's done."

Nobody spoke for thirty seconds until Jake broke the silence. "It's getting close and still running, Pierre."

"The man assured me. All I can do is trust him."

"Too damned close, Pierre. I'm going deep and sprinting the last minute, just to be sure."

The toad-head spun. "Don't bother, Jake. The American torpedo has just shut down."

Inhaling a deep breath, Jake tried to let himself accept and enjoy the moment of victory, but something irked him. "That's great, Antoine, but what's going on with the *Goliath*? Going up? Staying on depth? Or God help us if it's sinking."

"Trim and drain pumps are working nonstop on both hulls. No sign of a depth change yet."

"Then our damage was perfect. Its propulsion is gone, and the ship is completely salvageable."

Cahill clarified a technicality. "Not all propulsion's gone. Remember the outboards. That gives it a little over a knot. The local current runs west, which means it could still make Iranian waters while getting dragged towards Hormuz."

Jake sought a way to stop the crippled giant from crawling, but his focus had been punching holes in its hull. Fearing another flooded compartment would destroy his prize, he changed his mode of thinking. "We need to find a way to tow it. And I mean grab hold of it tight and pull it wherever we want, whether it's surfaced, submerged, or stuck somewhere in between. The Omani patrol craft can only handle the surfaced work. So that means we need to think about what we can do from the *Specter*."

The room became quiet as men entertained thoughts, but the Australian appeared uncomfortable. As Jake wondered if Cahill struggled to generate a coherent concept or if he wrestled through his final internal objections to a clever idea, the *Goliath's* proper commanding officer straightened his back and spoke confidently. "I've got it."

"You're sure?"

The Australian smiled. "Yeah, mate. I'm sure I've got it."

"Okay, then. Go ahead."

"We've got a big anchor and a strong chain. If the *Goliath* stays on depth, there's just enough room for us to climb over it and lower the anchor a few meters below and next to the cargo bed. Then we drive away, and I'm sure the anchor would grab one of the crossbeams."

Jake envisioned the maneuver and offered it silent applause. "I like it—a lot. It's brilliant. Any objections?"

In the control room, heads shook and shoulders shrugged.

The American offered his boss a veto. "What's your opinion, Pierre?"

"It's cruder than I might have hoped, but I can see no better options. I agree."

"That's a plan, then. Terry, do us the honors and draw up the details."

CHAPTER 19

Under the dome, the colonel's world crumbled. "The Iranians won't help us."

The sergeant's pained face revealed betrayal. "They're out there, some of them only ten miles away, and they won't help?"

"They can't be implicated. That was part of the bargain."

"Two of their submarines were already hit and forced to surface."

"But that doesn't prove their involvement, nor does it force their retaliation."

The sergeant shook his head. "I don't understand. Where's the loyalty?"

"There is none. This was a transaction. If I can't sell them the *Goliath*, there's nothing to transact. All they could do now is blow up Renard's fleet at great risk to their own safety for no gain."

"How can they stand by idly?"

The colonel grew weary of his partner's commentary. "They have no obligation to help us, written, verbal, implicit or otherwise."

"Then I question their courage."

"You're also forgetting the American submarine. How many Iranian weapons do you think its captain needs to hear before he would launch a counterattack?"

"I expected more from the Iranians."

Consoling his colleague helped the colonel address his own sense of distress. "Do you think anyone's more disappointed than I am about this mission's possible failure?"

"You're giving up?"

The loss of the second propeller hurt, but the colonel blocked failure from his mind. "By no means. I have more options than just running, but I do want to continue moving north, however slow it may be." He tapped an icon to open the private conversation to his submarine commander. "Control room, bridge. Over."

"Bridge, control room. Over."

"Deploy the outboard motors and give me your best speed."

The commander hesitated.

"Did you hear me?"

"Yes, colonel. It's just… that's desperate."

"I see that you fully grasp the situation. It's indeed dire. Now make yourself useful and follow my order."

"I'm deploying the outboards."

The colonel watched pixelated numbers showing the *Goliath's* speed creeping upwards.

"Colonel, I should also mention that we hear the *Specter* getting closer to us."

"How close, and what does that mean?"

"Very close. Unless we're about to be rammed, there's no tactical advantage the *Specter's* crew gains by being any closer."

"So be it. We have graver issues to consider."

The bulldog looked at his display and grunted. "One point two knots. This will take forever."

"It will take us all day, literally, to reach Iranian waters. But what can Renard do about it?"

"He can send divers again, sir. This time, we won't have the speed to shake them off."

"But we can surface and shoot them."

"And then the patrol craft will shoot us."

"At least we're moving in the right direction again, and the next move is Renard's. If he does nothing, we'll salvage this mission."

A technician's voice rang from the overhead speakers. "Bridge, MESMA plant two. Over."

The colonel tapped an icon to respond. "Go ahead MESMA plant two."

"I'm going to shut down MESMA plant two along with plant four. With the port engine room lost, we're just dumping steam into the condensers. I'll keep plant six up to run electrical loads. I suggest you keep a plant running on your side, too."

"I thought we were sharing electrical loads between port and starboard?"

"We are. The insulation around our cables through the tunnel is holding, but I want one plant running in each hull for redundancy."

"Very well. We'll run on two MESMA plants, one per side. I'll trust you to coordinate it." The colonel found his technician's focus admirable while facing the grave reality of mission failure, and he realized he needed to keep his men occupied. Purpose would keep them sane, and he risked a new idea with his sergeant. "Can you get a man into the starboard engine room to repair the hull breach from the inside?"

"The welding equipment supports underwater welding. And we have enough rebreather oxygen sources to last me. I'd have to cut off some jagged edges, but there's a lot of flat pieces of metal I can choose from to plug the hole."

"It doesn't have to be perfect. The pumps can almost keep pace now, if dedicated to the engine room. And I've been assured that power can be rerouted to the propulsion motor."

"But the hard part's getting into the compartment."

The colonel realized he was plotting beyond his naval knowledge and aimed his voice upward to the submarine commander. "Control room, bridge. Over."

"Bridge, control room. Over."

"I'm considering entry into the starboard engine room for repairs. Is such entry possible while remaining submerged?"

"It's too dangerous. It would be suicide. You'd be unable to close the door against the water pressure, and you'd flood the adjacent MESMA plant. The ship would sink, guaranteed, and we'd be caught in a tomb."

A pit formed in the colonel's stomach, cautioning him to honor the submarine commander's pessimism. His technician's driving focus on the MESMA plants contrasted the stubborn tone of his undersea tactics master, who oozed futility. Though withholding overt judgment, the colonel sensed his commander had given up. "Counting myself, you have three soldiers in this half of the ship. Are you saying it's impossible for us to manhandle the door?"

"Yes, that's what I'm saying."

"Based upon what?"

"Based upon my desire to stay alive."

"That's hardly scientific."

"I could estimate the sea pressure and the area of the door and then tell you how much force you need to cycle the door open and shut again. But what of it? It would be a battle of wills against you and the sea, and I already know you're the type of man to accept the challenge. So why bother asking me?"

Agreeing with the submarine commander's assessment, the colonel shifted his approach. "Let me rephrase the question. How can I optimize my odds of success to access the engine room?"

"You shouldn't try it. You'll kill us all."

"I am going to try it, whether you advise me or not. So, I suggest that you advise me."

The commander's extended sigh hung in the air as he responded. "You'd want to be as shallow as possible and pumping from the compartment to minimize backpressure. If you really want to do this, you could also bleed high-pressure air into MESMA plant five to attempt to equalize pressure with the engine room, but I fear the high-pressure banks on this ship are inadequate to bring plant five equal to sea pressure."

The colonel looked to his bulldog for feedback. The sergeant nodded and seemed upbeat about tackling the problem, adding confidence to his leader's voice. "That all sounds plausible."

"You may want to consider accessing the port engine room instead. Your technical experts are there to give us the best chance of a speedy recovery of propulsion."

Inhaling deeply, the colonel sought to clear his mind. He

trusted himself to handle the challenge personally on the starboard side with his bulldog as his champion, but he saw merit with the submarine commander's suggestion. "True, but the extent of the damage on the port side is unknown."

"I estimate it would be a cleaner cut than bullets. And the sizes of the holes the mercenary bomblets create are comparable to that of the starboard engine room."

"But the hole's located on the bottom of the compartment."

"That only matters if you plan on surfacing, although it will have an effect on sea pressure when cycling the door for entry."

As the decision weighed on him, the colonel sensed time ticking against his mission. Renard had to be plotting his next move.

The sergeant added needed encouragement. "We've all trusted you this far, sir. The men will follow whatever you choose."

The colonel laughed at himself as he remembered a nearly forgotten impasse. "Did you ever move any of our rebreathers to the port side?"

The sergeant scoffed. "No, sir. I guess you have your answer."

"We enter the starboard engine room. Make the preparations and contact me before entry."

A terrible metallic bang, like Thor's hammer tolling a colossal gong, rang with impossible power. Losing his sense of time and space, the deafened colonel cringed and covered his ears while the ringing fury resonated through water and steel before receding. Regaining his awareness, he stood and heard an annoying, rumbling, grinding clamor. "What the hell's going on?"

Even the stalwart sergeant seemed disoriented. "I don't know."

"Lights! Lights!"

Whiteness bathed the back of the submerged beast, and the colonel disbelieved his eyes.

Halfway down the port hull, an anchor chain hung from the back of an oblong shape suspended above the *Goliath*. The large links grated the steel cylinder and fell behind its outer side.

The colonel watched in anxious wonder until he recognized the *Specter*, backlit by the rising sun's rays, and surmised the adversary crew's intent. "They're trying to grab us with their anchor."

"Maybe. But if they are, they missed."

The chain tilted forward and scraped the port hull's outer curves, competing with the bridge's overhead speakers in carrying the commander's voice to the colonel's ear. "Bridge, control room. I'm watching through the cameras. The *Specter* just hit us with its anchor chain."

"And its anchor, too. What sort of madmen are driving that thing?"

"Bold ones."

The scraping stopped, and the chain floated forward, blending into the bluish blackness ahead of the drifting *Goliath*.

The colonel aimed his voice upward. "If this isn't an attempt to snag us, what else might it have been?"

"I can only speculate."

"Might that have been a call to surrender?"

The commander's tone was dismissive. "One of the vessels surrounding us would have instead called us on a sonar phone, like the *Specter* and *Wraith* have been using."

"They wouldn't know what language to use."

"That may be true. But it wasn't a warning. We hear the *Specter* circling around to try it again."

The colonel realized he'd become a prized marlin to the adversary submarine's oversized fishing hook. "Damn. Can this be stopped if we come shallower?"

"No, we'd expose our railguns, and the patrol boats would blow them off. We'd then be prevented from submerging again."

"What of the outboards? Can't they be used to rotate us and make us uncatchable?"

"Perhaps, but what of it? If you try that, you lose what little progress we're making towards Iran and bind us to an endless game caught in a stalemate. You may as well accept being towed."

As the submarine commander's opinions wearied him, the colonel groped for something positive. "Can you not think of anything we can do?"

"We can contact them. Instead of silly games, we've reached a point where a proper line of communication could serve us."

"I hope you don't mean to use the radio?"

"Perhaps in later discussions I'd risk the mast, but to start a conversation, we can use the unencrypted underwater telephone."

"Like the *Specter* and the *Wraith* used, only using my voice instead of encrypted tones?"

"Correct."

"Very well, then. Line me up so I can talk from here."

"Give me a moment, while I work the menus."

The bulldog pointed towards the after port-side windows. "If you have something to say, sir, you'd better hurry."

Again, the colonel disbelieved his eyes. The sharp edges of the *Specter's* anchor avulsed a hydraulic arm while tolling the bell of the port hull a second time. Despite his bulldog's warning, he cringed with the rasping ringing and watched the plummeting bulk topple towards the cargo bed. "They had better luck with their aim this time."

The sergeant's nod was stoic acceptance. "Agreed, sir. That's going to catch."

Loud links grating over steel snapped taut under the *Specter*, turning the anchor into a pendulum that swung its chain forward to destroy a second hydraulic arm.

The commander updated the colonel with an option. "The underwater telephone's ready now. If you want to negotiate, now's a good time."

The colonel sought something suitable to say to the mercenary fleet but found nothing. He instead aimed his voice upward to query his submarine commander. "I have nothing to say to them, and I have no intention of flinching and requesting a negotiation. Tell me, how do you expect Renard to retrieve this ship without sinking it?"

His angst clear over the loudspeaker, the commander became defiant. "We have no propulsion, and we're a whisker away from losing our depth control. Don't you understand that you're one flooded compartment away from dying? If the shoring gives in MESMA plant five, that alone may be enough to kill us."

"That's not an answer."

"You're a pompous ass."

The colonel touched an icon to mute his microphone and spoke in privacy to his bulldog. "Can you think of a reason why I shouldn't walk downstairs and snap his neck?"

"When I get into the engine room and give you back your propulsion, he'll be useful again. And you're not the type of man to kill a loyal colleague."

"I've given him too much leeway already."

"You've coaxed a competent performance out of him."

With thoughts buzzing about his submarine commander's insubordination, the colonel watched the *Specter* accelerate forward and drag its anchor chain against the *Goliath's* port hull. Links skidded across steel, snapping a series of hydraulic rams from their mounts.

Then the chain reached a crossbeam, jerked it, and then released it as its lengths ran up and over the metal bar.

The anchor rose into view and snagged the beam. Then, with excessive scraping and groaning, the *Goliath* accelerated under the *Specter's* power.

The sergeant remained stoic. "And now we're being towed."

"I might have hoped the anchor chain would interfere with the *Specter's* propeller, but apparently not."

"This situation appears helpless, but somehow I know it's not. It just makes me want to fight back harder. Let me enter the engine room and give us the propulsion we need to snap this anchor chain."

The colonel found his colleague's optimism inspiring. "Yes. Make the preparations and contact me when you're ready. When it's time, I'll help you get in."

The sergeant darted down the stairs, leaving his leader alone.

Screeching a ferrous cacophony, the anchor scraped across the beam and dragged two entangling nets into the central cargo bed. The *Goliath* rolled into a right turn, and the colonel turned from the metallic tether to watch digital dials.

Compass numbers swung upward, ticking to a southeasterly heading while his speed gauge walked to five knots. Patiently watching for minutes, he noticed the giant ship maintain its depth and stability while the submarine dragged it.

Accepting his passenger role, the colonel descended the stairs and entered the control room, where he offered his commander a gruff greeting in passing.

He then continued his sternward trek, passing multiple watertight boundaries, until he reached his bulldog and the starboard hull's third commando. The younger warrior helped strap the sergeant into his rebreather, and a stuffed canvas bag of welding gear lay beside spare oxygen sources.

"Good timing, sir. I was just getting ready to call you."

"What's the status, sergeant?"

"All that's left is to pressurize this compartment and come as shallow as we can to minimize the pressure difference across the door. The water's going to push it open hard, but we can give ourselves good odds of closing it again."

"Hold on."

"What's wrong?"

"If the three of us can't close this door, we'll all drown."

"Do you want more hands back here?"

"No. There's only enough space here for two of us to have good footing on the outside, and you'll have to pull from the inside."

"I can block the water flow a bit with my body."

The colonel drove himself crazy trying to quantify the odds of killing himself if he opened the door. Then a new idea struck him. "What if we all just swam out?"

The bulldog stared blankly.

"You're looking at me like I'm mad. I mean if we open a hatch and swim out of this ship."

"We'd fail in our mission."

The truth stung, but the colonel wanted to assess the option. "I know that. Just humor me."

"We don't have enough rebreathers for everyone."

"We have enough for everyone on this side of the ship. We'd need only to flood a compartment with a hatch and open it when we're ready to swim out."

"You would abandon the others?"

"Never. Those on the other side could breathe forced air from the submarine while they flood a compartment that has a hatch. Then they could make for the surface while holding their breath."

"Those with proper training could do that. But it's doubtful for our technicians, and our unconscious man would die."

As another truthful statement stung him, he updated his plan. "I'll carry a rebreather to that side."

"Just one?"

"For the unconscious man only, meaning I'll give him mine when I get there. The rest can show some courage and survivability and follow me out the hatch while holding their breath."

"How will you get in?"

"Through the hole in the starboard engine room."

"You'd flood MESMA plant six on your way in."

"MESMA plant four and forward would be fine. That would leave us enough time to escape from the forward hatch."

The bulldog frowned while reflecting. "It could work, but it sounds like a last option. I'd rather enter this engine room now and regain propulsion."

Like an epiphany rising from the confluence of seemingly random factors, a scintillating idea sprung into the colonel's mind. He inhaled deeply while processing it. "Would you be willing to wait if I told you the *Specter's* taking us somewhere favorable for our chances of survival, no matter which plan we follow?"

"Sure. I guess that depends where we're going."

Hungry after avoiding eating all night, the colonel decided to allow his team food. "Let's make breakfast and have the port side eat as well. We need our strength, and I'm in the mood for eggs and bacon."

"I'm always willing to eat. Just as long as I know I'm not letting myself get killed for lack of doing something else more important."

"I need to verify my assumptions over the next several hours, but if I'm correct, time's now working in our favor."

"How so? What changed?"

"I just figured out Renard's next move. He isn't taking us back to Muscat. That arrogant bastard doesn't know it yet, but he's taking us straight home."

CHAPTER 20

Terry Cahill required a conscious effort to walk without wincing. As he slid closer to Jake, the Australian hid the pain behind his face. His abdomen and loins ablaze with acid from his combat swim, he'd hate himself if he missed his second chance.

The American's question was a fair one. "You up for this again?"

"Bloody well right, I am."

Having expected the anchor grab to end the escape, the Australian battled disappointment. Though the grab had averted the Iranian threat, it had failed to surface the *Goliath*, compelling him and his colleagues to debate their next move.

The consensus–a final, unstoppable plan in which they'd continue dragging the *Goliath* to shallow waters to prevent its irrecoverable sinking. Settled on eight knots at snorkel depth as the optimum towing parameters, Jake had the *Specter* pulling the transport vessel towards the closest non-Persian shore.

Beyond that, the debate continued about how to force the hijackers from the ship, but sending swimmers played into all the top options, and Cahill vowed to be ready.

"I figured you'd want to get back to your ship. But let's finalize the plan before you even think about suiting up. We're talking ourselves in circles. We need to pick an idea and run with it."

"I know. But we've got eight hours before we're in shallow enough water to act. This is our first chance to plan something without having to race a clock."

"We already have a good plan. If we place small explosives on every compartment, we can selectively set them off one at a time until they figure out they need to either give up or drown."

The American's default destruction mode chafed Cahill.

"There's no reason to risk more damage to me ship."

"It's just water damage. Half the equipment is waterproof, and there's a French shipbuilder pumping out spare parts for anything we'd need to replace."

Cahill welcomed his boss' retort from the loudspeaker. "I appreciate your desire to end this Jake, but I am concerned with your enthusiasm to spend my money so liberally."

"It's spending pennies to save dollars when you consider the risk of anything worse happening to the *Goliath*."

Across the table, the eldest legionnaire spoke with a thick French accent. "My plan to enter the engine room is best. I don't have to flood things. No more damage. Not much anyway."

Cahill saw a flaw. "Except bullets and grenades, and I don't see how you'll stop the flooding. My plan's the only one that guarantees no further damage. We block the seawater intakes for each MESMA plant, and they become unusable. No more electricity, and eventually the air becomes unbreathable."

Jake scowled. "That'll take days to force them out."

"We've got days, mate. What's the hurry now?"

"Common sense. You give them days to think about how to escape, and they'll find a way to escape."

The legionnaire sounded frustrated. "No, you don't understand. Nobody lets me explain." The security leader then rattled off phrases in French.

Beside him, Henri listened in patient silence.

Next to Cahill, the American tapped a stylus on a dark section of pixels to vent his apparent annoyance. "Fine. Terry, he's going to explode if he doesn't explain himself in gory detail in French."

"It's okay, mate. You'd better let him talk. I'll stretch me legs a bit and come back."

Cahill strolled to the toilet and then relieved himself. After a detour to the crew's mess, he sat at a dining table and massaged his aching muscles. Careful to avoid exacerbating his soreness, he released his legs, stood, and headed back to the control room, reminding himself to hide the persistent pain from his peers.

Around the central table, he sensed a renewed vigor, especially in Jake. "You won't believe it."

"Go on, Jake. Try me."

"After hearing all the details, his idea's brilliant."

"Brilliant? Really?"

"Well, it's better than ours, and I had to give it a lofty label to protect our egos."

"If it's that good, I can't wait to suit up."

After hearing the elder legionnaire's plan, Cahill agreed in its viability. Before dusk, he would swim to his ship again. Eager to join the boarding team, he hated waiting, but he welcomed the time for a refreshing nap.

He retreated to his rack to rest. Fatigue overpowered his anxiety, and sleep came faster than he expected.

When he awoke five hours later, he dangled his legs over the side of his mattress. He lowered his bare feet and stifled a grunt while straining his abdomen. His toes touched the deck, and then he shifted his weight to his heels and stood to assess himself.

His stomach and loins had stiffened, and he struggled with his first step towards his sink. Sharing the stateroom with the *Specter's* usual executive officer, he crept to avoid waking Henri from his slumber in the lower rack. The deliberate movement required careful muscle control and worsened his suffering.

After brushing his teeth, he grabbed his slacks from a hook on the door and then stepped into them. He lifted his white shirt from the hook, passed through the doorway with care to avoid disturbing the sleeping Frenchman, and then slipped his arms into his sleeves in the passageway.

Aromas of fennel and saffron mingled with diesel particulates, and he stuck his head through the galley door to examine the cook's effort. Famished, Cahill salivated upon seeing pots of bouillabaisse, but he delayed satisfying his hunger by continuing to the control room.

The staffing seemed sparse, with Jake as the lone man he'd known prior to last evening's outing. With his efforts to recapture the *Goliath* behind him, the American appeared satisfied in his exhaustion. "Good afternoon, sleepyhead."

"You look ready for a nap of your own."

"I'll pass out after lunch."

"I'm starved, but I can bog in to that fish stew real quick and be back here fast."

"Sure. You won't have much to do. The Omanis took over the towing honors while you were racked out." Needing to find the obscure status icon, Jake tapped through several menus to arrive at the anchor.

"Stowed nice and neat."

"Our anchor's right back where it belongs, at least until we reach Jiwani. Renard called his buddy, Admiral Khan, and he verified there's nowhere to tie up. So, I'll be dropping anchor again right inside Gwatar Bay."

With the day's original destination being Karachi for repairs, Cahill found the decision logical to drag his ship into Pakistani waters. "That's the most anchor usage any submarine's ever had in any given day in years. I guarantee you that, mate."

"Yeah. At least I don't need it on the *Goliath* anymore. The Omani patrol boat sent divers to tie onto its cleats with nylon ropes. It's being towed the right way now."

Shaking off sleep, Cahill recalled the planned actions that had occurred during his rest.

To avoid stranding the *Specter's* anchor on the transport vessel upon grounding it, Jake had transferred its towing to the patrol boat. When the seafloor had risen enough to disallow the *Goliath's* pulling the Omani craft under water, Renard had permitted the exchange. And, as a precaution against the unwanted resuscitation of the huge ship's propulsion, divers had mounted to each engine room explosives which either submarine could trigger with a sequence from its bow-mounted sonar.

"That's why we're moving so slow." Cahill glanced at the speed gauge showing four knots, mirroring the struggle the small Omani craft faced in pulling the *Goliath*.

"We've still got about three hours before we ground the *Goli-*

ath. So you'll have a few hours on watch before I send Henri and Julien up here to handle things. Get some food inside you and get back up here."

"Did the Omani dive team weld the *Goliath's* hatches shut?"

"Yeah. Just enough to prevent them from opening. They said it was quick and dirty work, but the hijackers won't be escaping unless they blow their way out."

"Don't jinx it, mate. God knows what they'll be willing to do when they finally realize the game's over."

Cahill returned to the mess deck where he grabbed a bowl of stew and sat at an empty table. With a couple of engineering sailors as the room's only other occupants, he assumed the rest of the crew had eaten and was resting.

He powered through his late lunch, satiating his hunger more than enjoying the tastes of Marseille. After depositing his empty bowl by the scullery, he went back to Jake and relieved him.

With a lone technician at the sonar consoles and Henri's backup at the control panel, the room felt sparse. Cahill checked in with both sailors and verified the quietness of the *Specter's* situation.

He then stepped to the central chart to visualize the scene.

The Omani patrol boat leading the formation towards the western Pakistani wrestled the submerged *Goliath* forward, and the surfaced submarines trailed them. A second Omani craft mirrored the transport ship's undersea trek, guns aimed towards its submerged position to prevent the unlikely use of its railgun. From the distant east, a Pakistani corvette approached to represent its country's interests.

Time moved slowly as the task force approached the coast. After a couple of hours, Cahill's moment to suit up for his final swim approached, and the legionnaire came for him. "Half an hour to go in the water."

"That's true if the grounding happens on time."

"How close are they?"

"Twenty minutes. In fact, we should watch it. Let me raise

the periscope." Cahill stepped to a console and sat, and then he tapped icons to raise the optics. The Omani patrol boats came into view driving towards the sandy Pakistani beach. Farthest from Cahill, the towing ship pulled two nylon lines that lowered its churning stern, and then the ropes became rigid and yanked the vessel to a stop.

With a thick French accent, the lone seated sonar operator, Noah, confirmed Cahill's suspicions. "The *Goliath* just hit the bottom. It was a smooth landing on the sand."

"That's great news. Can you hear any activity on the *Goliath*?"

"Nothing. It's been quiet inside for many hours. Just a little noise here and there. Nothing important."

Cahill tried to recall the present tide but remembered its irrelevance. The one-foot variance between tidal extremes in Gwatar Bay simplified the grounding. The *Goliath* might rise and fall, but with its bows buried in the sand, it was stuck.

He tapped another sequence of pixels to unmute his microphone. He then aimed his voice upward, frequent use of the radio allowing his informality.

"Pierre? This is Terry. Are you there, boss?"

"I'm here. I'm recovering from my abrupt stop from four knots to zero. That's harder on the body than you might expect."

"Sure. Can I drop anchor now?"

"Yes, we all can. I'll get the skiff ready and send it to you."

Thirty minutes later, Cahill stood on the back of the anchored *Specter*, the sun heating his face. A gangway offered him a path to the mated Omani skiff, which the armed security force had already boarded. The elder legionnaire waved him over, and the warm puddles on the wooden planks tantalized his bare feet.

He stepped into his fins while the skiff took him the short distance to the dive point, and as he looked over the boat's edge, he saw the *Goliath's* black form through the blue water.

The elder legionnaire slapped his back. "You're with me again. We go last."

Carrying weapons, explosives, and welding gear, the first four divers rolled backwards into the water.

As they kicked downward, the legionnaire lowered an underwater phone over the boat's side and then energized its console. Over several minutes, he exchanged words in French with his team and then warned Cahill. "Here it comes." A crack rippled through the water followed by watery words in French.

"What'd he say? He sounded a bit excited."

"Excited? A little, I guess. They blew open a bigger hole through the existing damage. They're going in."

"Can we go now?"

"No. First, they secure the room."

Hearing no signs of resistance, the *Goliath's* commander remained optimistic. Minutes later, the report came in French, which the legionnaire summarized in English. "Yes, it's clear, now. You go. I follow."

Cahill slid his facemask over his chin, tested his air, and then rolled himself backwards over the skiff's stern. Warm water enveloped him, and he turned towards his ship. Excited to board the *Goliath*, he kicked downward.

As he swam into the port hull's shadow, he questioned the wisdom of continuing underneath a vessel a hostile force could bring down upon him. But the steel cylinder remained stationary above him, and he pulled himself through the gap that plastic explosives had widened for human entrance.

Lights atop four facemasks greeted him, and one warrior spoke in French. Cahill nodded his ignorant response and raised his thumb. After hand gestures, more French words, and a gentle nudge, the Australian understood the order to swim out of the way.

When the legionnaire emerged from the hole, he issued an order, and his team lowered a thin piece of metal an Omani crew had shaped. As it reached the hull, it offered a flawed covering of the breach, but Cahill believed his powerful ship's pumps could outpace the overlay's imperfections.

As the men lit a welding torch and applied it to the metals and filler material, the legionnaire swam by Cahill. Watching the swimmer's shadow traverse the silent gas turbine gave the Australian a chill.

At the engine room's door, the legionnaire stopped, popped his head towards the porthole, and retreated. Reporting in French, he shook his head to indicate the lack of visible hijacker resistance in MESMA plant six.

The arcing behind Cahill reminded him he'd volunteered to breathe limited air while sealed within a flooded steel tank. While he waited for his French teammates to bar his escape, his imagination taunted him with his adversary's having blocked the door into MESMA plant six.

Before he could think himself into anxiety, the legionnaire spoke the dive's first words in English. "Terry, please move. Hold something strong."

Two warriors faced the door, their rifles pointed forward, while two other commandos transformed themselves into tethering lines, grabbing machinery mounts and their colleagues' belts. A pistol in hand, the legionnaire rested his fins on the deck, counted to three in French, and then lifted the handle.

The outrush rolled the door open and carried the legionnaire out. Instead of fighting for balance as Cahill expected, his companion pushed forward to his knees and then recovered himself on the adjacent compartment's deck.

As the water flowed, Cahill noticed air gurgling from the MESMA plant's space into the engine room's upper recesses.

The weld behind him had held.

One commando released his rifleman, who then surfed through the door and sought stability on his knees behind his leader.

With the forward men's heads exposed to air, communication with the immersed Cahill and his companions became impossible. But when seconds passed without gunfire, the next rifleman risked his passage forward.

Every five seconds, another swimmer moved, and then Cahill took his turn.

With his eyes wide open, he swam through the door, and a

torrent pressed his back. He welcomed hands reaching into the temporary waterfall to pull him forward.

At the entrance to the next compartment, the legionnaire yelled a command in French, and his team gathered near the door. With water rising up its length, they threw the portal open and entered, weapons readied. With four men through, the legionnaire barked in English, and his amplified voice sounded strange in the air. "Come on!"

Flapping his fins, Cahill waddled through the rising water and ducked through the door. The legionnaire followed behind him and started rolling the door shut. "Help me."

Cahill pushed against the small flow that issued into MESMA plant four, and he helped his companion muscle the door against its machined seating. He cranked the handle closed and breathed a sigh of relief.

At the dry compartment's forward end, a French commando offered a thumbs-up, indicating no resistance. He then lifted his facemask to sample the *Goliath's* air, which proved clean.

The team shifted from rebreathers to the transport ship's atmosphere, and they regrouped at the entrance to the last MESMA plant. After the legionnaire peeked through a porthole to verify his colleague's initial assessment, he shook his head and uttered a quick phrase in French.

Cahill voiced his opinion. "They may be waiting for us in the next compartment. That's where all the spare weapons are."

"You said they cannot get into the gun locker."

"I know I said it. It's true, but if they brought spare explosives, they could blow their way in."

"I wish you had said this earlier."

"Sorry, mate. I just thought of it."

"If so, we will have to win in combat." The legionnaire turned to his men and began a heated discussion in French that Cahill assumed pertained to his increased predicted probability of armed resistance. Until he'd thought of it, the hope had been that the hijackers had stashed their weapons on the starboard side prior to the tunnel's flooding.

As the voices of French commandos rose with their ire, Cahill saw movement through the porthole. He pointed. "Hey!"

The Frenchmen stopped talking and darted out of the portal's view. Sweeping his arm, the legionnaire compelled Cahill behind him.

Then, from the door's other side, the hijacker knocked.

The Frenchmen looked at each other in surprised disbelief, and then the legionnaire issued his order. Taking positions behind large pipes and pumps of the MESMA systems, they raised their weapons and waited. Cahill joined one of them and watched.

The legionnaire moved to the portal and made eye contact. He then raised his hands, and the hijacker mimicked the gesture. Then the legionnaire whirled his finger in a circle, ordering the hijacker to expose his backside. Apparently satisfied, the legionnaire gestured the man into the room while stepping back with his pistol raised.

The hijacker clicked open the handle and crouched through the door.

The legionnaire gave his order in French and pointed to the deck. The man obeyed, dropping to his knees, but the legionnaire repeated his demands until the arrival's chest flattened against the walkway.

The elder legionnaire crept around the hijacker, examined the room beyond the doorway, and then pulled the door shut. He snapped an order, and one of his men tossed handcuffs from his bag. The legionnaire bound the hijacker's wrists behind his back.

After searching the man for weapons and explosives, the legionnaire ordered his men from their hidden positions and attempted to talk to the hijacker. A few of his men tried varied languages, including English, but they gave up.

Then the man looked at Cahill and pointed with his nose.

The legionnaire raised his eyebrows. "I think he wants you, Terry."

"Me? What the heck?" Cahill stepped towards the man, but he

frowned and shook his head.

"Maybe not."

The man pointed his nose where Cahill had been. The Australian turned and noticed a sound-powered phone. "I think he wants to talk to someone."

"Maybe. Let's see." The legionnaire lifted the man to his feet and shoved him towards the phone. He grabbed the receiver and placed it to the man's face. The man spoke, but nobody answered.

Cahill shared his idea. "Wait. This is set to the bridge. Let me put him through to the control room." He flipped a dial, and the man spoke again.

A response burst from the loudspeakers, startling Cahill. The Frenchmen cringed as well, but, shrugging their shoulders and sharing a nervous laugh, they seemed to understand the message.

Cahill felt left out. "Was that French? What did he say?"

The elder legionnaire snorted. "My English will be a bad translation."

"Do your best."

"He thanked us for being nice to his colleague, and he hopes we'll be nice to all of them. They wish to negotiate a surrender."

CHAPTER 21

The colonel gathered six men around the control room's central table. "We're going to escape. Unfortunately, the men on the port side had no chance. No explosives, no weapons, no rebreathers. And with our wounded colleague, surrender was the only merciful option."

The sergeant was stoic. "Nobody's blaming you, sir. You did the right thing letting them surrender."

"It's good to hear it."

"They'll be fine. It's not like we broke any laws."

"Piracy."

The bulldog shrugged. "Okay. So, we stole from a pirate. Who's going to enforce any sentence? The Omanis? They're just hired policemen."

Although the wording left an opening to an ongoing dialogue about surrendering the rest of his team, the colonel trusted his bulldog's loyalty.

Nine years ago, as a young officer on a counter-terrorism operation for the Pakistani Special Service Group, he'd rescued the bulldog from death. Skilled militants had taken forty-two hostages at the nation's military headquarters, and the colonel's platoon had rescued them.

But the resistance had been brutal.

Nine soldiers and three hostages had died, and the bleeding bulldog had been minutes from adding his corpse to that tally when the colonel had taken two bullets pulling him to safety. Medics had patched the victim's belly, and surgeons had repaired the soldier enough to continue his career and retire.

The bulldog would die for him.

"Our adversaries are just pirates and policemen. That's a good summary, sergeant. Then I shouldn't expect much resistance when we swim away."

"We saw them weld our hatches shut, sir."

"Did you forget that we have exactly enough plastic explosives to blow through a hatch? We were prepared to blow our way in. I see no reason we can't blow our way out."

"Then there's no reason to bother with a hatch. We can blow a hole anywhere you want."

A distant whir caught the colonel's ear. Standing beside the bulldog at the table's far side, the submarine commander looked over his shoulder at the ship's control panel. "That's the trim pump. It shouldn't be running."

"I thought it was automatic."

"Not when we're stuck in the sand. There's no change in depth for the pump to compensate for."

"Then what's happening?"

The submarine commander stepped to the panel. "We're surfacing."

"That's Cahill. Stop him!"

Tapping buttons, the commander assumed a defeated expression. "I can't. He's locked me out."

"Damn him!" Brushing by the submarine commander, the colonel darted up the stairs. On the bridge, he looked up and watched darkness become translucent water and then open to the clear sky. Though exposed to his captors by standing behind the glass, he needed to see them.

Behind him, the catamaran hulls surfaced next to drifting Omani patrol craft, one on each side. Farther aft, a Pakistani corvette pointed at his stern, and in deeper waters, the twin submarines floated at anchor.

Skiffs tied to the patrol boats carried boarding parties wearing the combat fatigues of soldiers trained for the task, as opposed to sailors forced to wield small arms as a collateral duty.

The colonel sensed his options fading as the heavy, rapid steps of his loyal bulldog jogging up the stairs echoed. "What do we do now, sir?"

"Get the French translator up here."

The bulldog darted halfway down the steps and yelled for the interpreter. When he clamored back up, the thin translator joined him. The noncombatant appeared terrified.

"Announce to the entire ship in French that our surrender is unconditional."

"Sir?"

"Trust me. Do it."

The translator obeyed, and after time elapsed to allow for an expected second translation for Cahill's benefit, the French response rang from the loudspeakers.

"What did he say?"

"Teams will board both sides of the ship, and they have a medic to deal with our injured man. They'll cut through their welds and use the forward hatches."

"Thank him for taking care of our injured man. Then tell him we await his further instructions."

A brief acknowledgement followed the translated message, and then the bridge became silent.

Omani skiffs motored to the *Goliath* and mated to it, and soldiers mounted the ship's backs.

Loyal to the death, the sergeant remained stoic. "So, this is how it ends."

Portraying a feigned confidence, the colonel assumed his final role of the mission–actor. "Not quite. Follow me downstairs, and I'll explain everything." The translator went first, and the colonel grabbed his bulldog by the shoulder to whisper in his ear. "Play along with my ruse." After reaching the bottom of the stairs and walking to the central table, he tried to appear smug. "It's been an honor, gentlemen. But it's time to end this."

Somber faces nodded, and some men appeared scared.

"These men who are apprehending us will give us humane treatment. You have nothing to fear."

The submarine commander challenged him. "Who's going to claim us?"

The colonel speculated. "The Omanis, the CIA, or perhaps

even Renard himself–if I don't negotiate our freedom within the hour."

"How could you?"

"I personally will hide explosives in every compartment in this hull, and I will set them to detonate in one hour."

As the bulldog raised his eyebrow, the colonel sharpened his gaze on him, demanding silence. They had plastic explosives but hardly enough to flood one compartment, and the implication of a timer was a complete lie.

But if his men believed him, the chances improved that Renard would believe him.

As he heard the cutting sounds attacking the weld in the hatch above him, he gave his mission's final order. "Wait here and obey our captors. I will set the charges and return before the last of you is up." He then ventured sternward, leaving his men to their jailers. As he heard them climbing to their captors, he maintained his spirits by hoping in his final gambit.

When he heard his last man's ascending steps, he walked forward, climbed into the sunlight, and surrendered.

*

Olivia gulped from her latte and then plopped the cup onto her desk. Although the *Specter's* latching of the *Goliath* had allowed her a modest night of sleep, nightmares of indictments, imprisonment, and public ridicule had tormented her.

But with the new day, her nightmare evaporated.

"Thank God." She reread Renard's text stating that the Omanis had grounded the stolen ship in Pakistan, ending her anguish.

Her ordeal's terminus quieted the inner girl, but her inner beast pondered ways to profit. An unknown team of hijackers had brokered some sort of backdoor deal with the Iranians, and she wanted to exploit this new lead.

She stood and paced in front of her desk, sorting thoughts and quelling emotions in hopes of clearing her mind. Stopping at her window, she closed the blinds to prevent the low December sun from hurting her eyes. Having indulged in Ciroc vodka to unwind from yesterday's terror, she endured a mild hangover.

Recommencing her walk, she pursed her lips and tasted the disappointment of failed potential. For a moment, she wished Renard had transformed the *Goliath* into a Trojan Horse, somehow staffing it with an assault force to surprise the Persian players that appeared to be helping the hijackers.

But she recalled the crippling fear of having watched the powerful vessel slipping away, and she judged using the *Goliath* as bait unacceptable. Knowing she couldn't catch the Persians off their guard, she committed to following her new leads.

It started with the prisoners.

Renard had conveyed their Pakistani origins, but she suspected they operated outside official channels.

The Frenchman's longtime friend and retired naval officer, Admiral Khan, had arranged for his country's support of the *Goliath's* retrieval. Khan also networked with enough flag officers to know if anyone had authorized the theft, but he assured Renard that the Pakistani military was uninvolved.

Olivia decided to explore angles of a covert military operation or an independent group.

She needed more information and called the Frenchman.

When he answered, he sounded angry. "Yes, hello."

"What's wrong?"

"I've just been threatened."

"By the prisoners?"

"The apparent leader says he placed small explosives throughout the *Goliath* that will detonate within the hour. He insists that I let his team go free in exchange for telling me the explosives' locations."

The prisoners were her only link to an unknown Persian plot. "You can't do that."

"Easy for you to say. It's not your ship."

"You're in shallow waters. What's the worst that can happen?"

"I would incur hefty expenses of raising the *Goliath*, welding it tight again, and replacing every piece of exposed electronics."

"It's just money, and it could be a bluff. Don't let them go."

"If it's not a bluff, would you incur the costs for me, in exchange for delivering you the prisoners for questioning?"

"Who said they're my prisoners? Don't you want them, too?"

"Hold please."

The line went silent, but the call remained connected. "That French jackass just put me on hold."

When she heard his voice again, he sounded enthusiastic. "I do hire brilliant men. Terry's solved the problem."

"He found the explosives?"

"No, that's impossible with an acre of hull insulation to search. But he's going to run the *Goliath* aground on the beach to prevent its flooding. If the prisoner's threat proves true, my costs of repairs will be small."

"Okay, that's great. To be clear, you're not letting my prisoners go?"

"Your prisoners? Now we come it. No, I will make sure they remain in Omani custody until you say otherwise. Half of them are on one patrol craft, half on the other."

Since she'd never caught him lying to her, she trusted him. "Thank you, Pierre."

"Yes, of course. My pleasure. And now that I know which hijacker was in charge, I'll get you a photograph for facial recognition. I'll send you photographs of the rest, but I assumed you'd start with the leader."

"Yeah, send it. Get me fingerprints, too, but send me the photo first."

"Of course."

Minutes later, a picture appeared on her phone. She found the man handsome with sharp features and hard eyes, and he appeared to be forty years old.

She scanned her contacts for the in-house laboratory and dialed. A technician answered.

"Hello, forensic lab."

"This is Olivia McDonald. Can I get a facial match on a subject, pronto?"

"Miss McDonald? Yes, of course. Do you know our email address?"

"Yes."

"Send it, and I'll stay on the line and confirm receipt if you'd like."

"Hold on."

She lowered her phone and forwarded the picture. "Sent. If it helps your search, I think he's Pakistani."

"I got it. Give me a few minutes, ma'am."

After returning to her seat, she watched photographs of the hijackers and their fingerprints arrive. As the last image arrived, she forwarded them to the lab, and then the Frenchman called her. "Yeah, Pierre?"

"Did you receive the photographs and fingerprints?"

"I just got them. I've sent them to the lab."

"May I assume you wish to transfer these prisoners?"

"I do. I want them sent to the Pakistani CIA station chief."

"Is he ready to receive them?"

Olivia knew the chief would agree when she had the chance to contact him. "He will be. Get them ready for transporting to Islamabad, and I'll have a team ready to take them into custody."

"That's a lot of ground to cover in their home country. What if they have local supporters who might attempt a rescue?"

"That's a chance I'm willing to take." Her phone chimed, and she extended it to inspect the caller's identity. When she saw it was the lab, she took pleasure in pausing her conversation with the Frenchman. "Your turn to hold." She answered the lab.

"Miss McDonald?"

"Go ahead."

"Your guy is Lieutenant Colonel Imtiaz Raja, Pakistani Army, Special Service Group. Active duty. He's stationed with–"

"You're sure?"

"Yes. It was an easy match. I'll verify with fingerprints, but it's just a formality."

"Verify it, and get started on the identities of the others." She switched back to the Frenchman. "The leader's a Pakistani lieutenant colonel in their army's special forces."

"*Merde!* I will speak to Admiral Khan immediately."

"How immediately? This effects who's taking custody of the prisoners."

"He's here on the ship with me, in the brig at the moment, helping the Omanis with the questioning."

"Get him!"

"Please forward me the information, and I will have him investigate through his channels who might be behind this."

His confidence calmed her. His decades' long relationship with the Pakistani admiral would bring her information faster than her channels. "Okay, Pierre. Hurry." After hanging up and sending the hijacker's identity to Renard, she passed the minutes pondering speculative scenarios, latching onto the possibility of taking credit for her fleet having ferreted out Pakistani traitors. Perhaps she could create an unseen benefit from the crisis.

Renard called her.

"Yeah, Pierre. What did he find?"

"There's nothing authorized that Admiral Khan's channels could uncover. In fact, the local general is furious and wants to take custody of the men and place them on trial for treason."

The concept flushed the final vestiges of worry from her. A local and official imprisonment would relieve her of all responsibility but give her access to the information. After her next phone call, she expected the Pakistan CIA station chief would use backchannels to negotiate leniency for some of the prisoners, in exchange for their providing intelligence about their intent with the *Goliath* and their involvement with the Iranians. "Perfect."

"I thought you might appreciate the outcome, young lady. It looks like we've averted disaster and found a positive outcome."

"Yeah. But what about the *Goliath*? Isn't it supposed to get a bunch of nasty holes in it soon?"

"I trust not, if Terry can prove that he's still charmed."

*

Terry Cahill felt his steel child's pain as he peered over his stocky engineer's shoulder at the starboard motor. "Can you get it working?"

"I'll know in a minute. The entire compartment except the motor is disconnected from the main battery."

The drained engine room smelled like brine, and Cahill was concerned about electrocuting his crew with shorted wires and puddles. "But you're optimistic?"

"I'm never optimistic until it works." The man removed a test meter from the replacement motor controller he'd installed, and then he labored to his feet.

"Well?"

"According to the diagnostics, it works. If the control panel controller works, you should have use of the motor."

"You've checked grounds?"

The man rubbed his sleeve over his sweaty brow. "We connected the battery to the motor, and the grounds are high but in-spec."

"Give it a spin, then." Cahill followed his waddling engineer to the engine room's control panel where a technician stepped aside.

The engineer waved a thick hand. "Go watch the motor." As the technician darted away, the engineer moved stubby fingers over a touchscreen, making colored needles jump from their leftmost stops as current flowed. "Rolling forward!"

From the room's far end, the technician responded. "Confirmed, rolling forward!"

The engineer tapped icons, stopping the engine. "All stop!"

"Confirmed, all stop!"

A final tapping sequence. "Rolling aft!"

"Confirmed, rolling aft!"

"Your starboard motor's ready, Terry. If the port team's having equal luck, we can give you propulsion to the limits of five

MESMA plants."

Cahill hurried forward through the starboard hull, the still-shrieking limpets sounding like slow smoke detectors on steroids. He climbed to the bridge where his executive officer, Liam Walker, investigated the status of the *Goliath's* systems. "What do you have, Liam?"

"We're ready on both main engines. All MESMA plants are up except six because the team was too busy in the engine room to repair it."

"Good. We should reach at least eleven knots, I'd guess."

Walker pointed out the windows at four sailors on the cargo bed. Using knives and bolt cutters, they slashed through the lingering parasitic nets. "They've cleared one of them and are halfway through the second."

"Bring them in. It's not safe out there. I'm not going to trust the hijacker's honesty or accuracy about the timing of his bombs, and I'm beaching us ASAP."

"Got it, Terry. I'll get them in." Walker tapped an icon and aimed his nose to a microphone that sent his voice outside the ship. "Come in on the double, gents. Your work is done."

The men gathered their tools and crossed a temporary gangway from the bed to the ship's starboard hull. They then lowered the walkway into the open hatch and returned inside the ship.

"It's now or never. Contact Pierre and make sure the Pakistanis have secured our landing area."

Renard responded over the loudspeaker. "I'm listening, Terry. Your landing area is secure. I assure you, you won't be killing any civilians. You're free to beach yourself."

"I understand I'm free to beach the *Goliath*. I'm going to back up and get a running start. I've got control. Coming to all back one third."

The patrolling Pakistani sailors became smaller as the transport ship slipped backwards a quarter mile from its starting point. Eyeballing the distance to the breaking waves, Cahill estimated a full nautical mile. "Good enough?"

Walker shrugged. "Go for it."

"Coming to all ahead standard."

Cahill tapped the *Goliath* to life, and wakes formed at its bows.

Walker announced the forward progress. "Five knots."

"Hold on to your knickers."

The executive officer laughed. "Seven knots."

"Me hair's practically on fire."

"Enough, Terry. Nine knots."

"Would you like to do a crossword puzzle while waiting?" Inwardly Cahill laughed at himself for his accelerated adrenaline rush. On land, he could outsprint his crippled ship, but the mass and momentum of his beautiful beast hitting hard sand caused concern.

The Pakistani sailors who formed a wide perimeter grew larger, and the breaking waves became clearer.

Cahill sank into his console's chair and strapped his seat belt. He grabbed a railing with both hands and watched Walker do the same. He aimed his voice upward to his crew. "Brace for collision."

"Eleven and a half knots."

Before reaching twelve knots, the ship grazed submerged sand, and Cahill tapped a rudder command. "Left hard rudder."

The beachscape rolled right across his dome windows as the *Goliath* rode onto the sand. Slowing hard under grinding friction, the starboard hull slid to a stop, and momentum angled the deck right ten degrees.

For a frightening moment, the port hull rose a meter into the air, but then it recovered and splashed into the waves.

His heart pounding, Cahill declared his success. "That's a fine parking job, if I don't say so meself. Get the boys far away from the ship, and let's watch the explosions from a safe distance."

CHAPTER 22

Three days later in a Karachi submarine base officer club, Jake gobbled skewered mincemeat while he scanned the table's other faces to gauge his colleagues' moods.

Each man showed outward appearances of processing the hijacking differently.

On his right, Henri appeared stoic, having endured the crisis with a quiet wisdom. Beside him, Cahill appeared animated and engaged, valuing his moments with the team that represented his connection to the *Goliath*.

He sensed a renewed connection between the Australian and his ship. He also noticed an enhanced relationship between the *Goliath's* commander and the *Specter's* crew, and he expected that Cahill was willing to volunteer for many future missions.

Skipping to Volkov, Jake saw a happy man who'd enjoyed the crisis as a spirited challenge. Having solidified his position within the fleet as the hero of Israel, the Russian commander was a welcomed sight at the table.

Renard, however, appeared pensive as he nibbled on a stuffed grape leaf. Reaching for a glass of sparkling water, he generated the energy to speak. "Gentlemen, I see that most of you are finishing your main courses."

Having lifted weights before dinner, Jake remained hungry, but he lowered his fork and listened as his boss continued.

"I believe we've spent enough time in Karachi. Given what has happened to us, it's taken me time to admit that our ships can survive without us again, but it's time for us to head home."

Watching the dry dock repairs to the *Goliath* had been interesting for the first couple of days, but Jake missed his wife and welcomed the freedom. "You're sure?"

"No, I'm not. But I can't keep you here forever, and I need to trust my hired technical and security teams again. So, as of tomorrow, I recommend you all get as far from here as possible and forget about your ships until our next mission."

"I don't suppose you'll say where or when that is."

"Have I ever? But you can be assured it will be at least a month. The *Goliath's* new bow section's two weeks late, and I don't see the ship being ready until late January."

Cahill sounded upbeat. "This is great news. Ariella wants to meet in Mumbai for some holiday time."

Renard frowned. "I suggested getting farther away. That's practically around the corner."

The Australian shrugged. "A ship needs its father. I'm planning on checking in on it every so often."

"Pride of ownership, I see, even when I technically own your ship."

"Guilty as charged."

"It is indeed your ship, too, Terry. I don't suppose I can stop you."

"No, sir. I'm already starting to miss it."

The Frenchman placed his elbows on the table. "I'd like to share news I received earlier today. Apparently, Lieutenant Colonel Raja reached his breaking point at a very early hour this morning."

Jake snorted. "The poor bastard probably hasn't slept in days."

"That poor bastard is getting no less than he deserves. He stole my ship, killed my security personnel, and on top of it, he tried to bluff his way out of my grasp by lying about planting explosives."

"At least I got to have fun beaching me ship."

"And I needed to request one more favor from the Omanis to pull you back into the sea. These favors aren't free."

Jake believed his boss would repay his debt to the Omanis with a mix of cash and armaments the Frenchman could broker through his connections to military suppliers. "It's not going to set you back, too bad, is it?"

"No, it's never that bad, especially compared to the cost of losing the *Goliath*. I hate spending money, but I remind myself that every dollar I spend on relationships with local navies is an investment."

"I sent us on a tangent, mates. Let's get back to the news."

"Yes, of course. Raja finally confessed his plan, and I find it disturbing." The Frenchman leaned back, arranging his thoughts. "There was a powerful financial motivation for each man who joined Raja, but I believe that was only half their rationale to participate. More interestingly, Raja compelled fifteen men to join him in what amounts to an act of vengeance targeted at me, personally."

Jake recalled the hijacking team roster, which photographs and fingerprints had identified days ago. Raja was the only active duty military man, and one special forces retiree had joined him. Six younger commando veterans had participated, two of whom had perished while taking the *Goliath*. A retired *Agosta* submarine commander had helped, as had a veteran sonar operator. Six military veterans with specific technical skills, including two translators, had rounded out the team. "We knew it was a decent sized conspiracy. I just figured it was for money."

"Let's address that angle. The obvious connection turns out to be true. Raja was planning to sell the *Goliath* to the Iranians. Rather, that's what he's admitting to under duress."

"Not a surprise, but it still stings. The idea of me ship in their hands is terrifying."

Speaking through his translator, the Russian interjected. "Dmitry says he trained the Iranians earlier in his career during the *Kilo*-class exchange. He respected their eagerness to learn and found them capable students."

Cahill raised a palm. "Wow, and here I was getting ready to keep rambling on about how evil they all were."

"They aren't all crazy men."

"Dmitry didn't say that, did he?"

The translator shook his head. "No, that was my personal

opinion. I thought you could tell the difference by now between Dmitry and myself. I've dealt with the Iranians, as well. Their submarine warriors are capable men."

Jake tried to play the peacemaker. "But the point stands. We can't let anyone hostile to the United States take the *Goliath*." As the lone American, he realized his unshared patriotism. "I mean hostile to any nation we'd all agree is worthy of protection."

Renard recommenced his update. "You were right, Jake. The target was the United States. Raja admitted the Iranians stated their intent was to hide the *Goliath* in Iranian waters and use its railguns against the Fifth Fleet."

Cahill shook his head. "Again, not a surprise, but it stings to think how close we were to screwing up."

Jake found the explanation suspicious. "Isn't that too obvious? Isn't it possible that Raja spewed that story to make people stop torturing him?"

"I thought that as well. But Olivia has corroborating evidence."

"But you said Olivia couldn't find anything suspicious about Iran."

"That changed when she received the hijackers' names. It took some digging, but she discovered that each man on Raja's team received payments from Iranian shell companies in crude oil futures. The payments are all but worthless without a jump in oil prices, but if prices had gone up in the days after their attack, each man would be a multi-millionaire."

Jake missed a connection. "I'm not following."

The Frenchman became animated, slicing the air with his hand while talking. "Olivia's discovery aligns with the next piece of Raja's confession. He was going to demonstrate the *Goliath's* abilities by destroying the Saudi Aramco oil-processing facilities at Abqaiq from deep within Iranian waters. That's a vital facility for the world's largest oil producer. Hitting vulnerable targets at that facility would have crippled it, driven up oil prices, and pushed demand to Iran."

The explanation became complete per Jake's reckoning. "Raja

gets rich, his minions get rich, and the Iranians make enough money to cover the cost of the *Goliath*."

"And then some. The financial implications would have been global. And, of course, the absolute brilliance of it is that the chain of evidence behind the whole affair would have started with us. We'd be in the ugly position of defending ourselves from an outraged world, and I know it would have ruined us."

The news helped Jake understand the enormity of the *Goliath's* true reach. "But there's more to the story. You mentioned vengeance."

"Indeed, I did. Raja holds me responsible for killing his brother."

During a cold silence, Jake stared at his boss and then probed deeper. "That's a serious accusation. Do you know why he's holding you responsible?"

"Yes. Because I killed him."

"Shit, Pierre. Seriously? Did you at least have a good reason for it?"

"Indeed, I did. And so did you. You helped me."

The accusation became a clue in Jake's mind, and he recalled his first mission a decade earlier with Renard's French veterans. "The *Hamza*."

"Yes."

"I knew you blokes had a sordid past, but bloody hell. The *Hamza's* submarine lore. It's a case study on avoiding underwater mountains."

Skipping his translator, Volkov protested. "*Da*. Impossible."

"The *Hamza's* true demise is quite a different story than the public case study. Its commanding officer had armed it with nuclear weapons from China and had taken it rogue. He was going to take out an American aircraft carrier outside of Honolulu. Hundreds of thousands would have died from the fallout."

After the Russian translation, Volkov tested his English. "Why do that?"

"He was dying, and he reverted to a fundamental ideology in his terminal status."

While Renard paused to let the Russian translator engage Volkov, Jake recalled how Olivia had scoured the dying man's dossier to uncover his hidden motivation. It was the first and last time a psychologist's acumen had helped him pursue a submerged adversary, but her advice had allowed him and Renard to predict the crazed captain's location.

Cahill snorted. "I'm on a team of superheroes."

Renard withdrew a Marlboro from his blazer and lighted it while a steward cleared plates. A second server placed a large bowl of dried fruits in the table's center and lowered dessert plates beside each patron.

When the waiters left, Renard continued. "Lieutenant Commander Faisel Raja was the executive officer of the *Hamza*. According to Admiral Khan, whom I trust implicitly, only Raja and the commanding officer knew of the submarine's true mission. But it's doubtful that Lieutenant Colonel Raja knew of his brother's culpability. The cover story that became submarine lore was fed to all but a select few, and I'd wager everything that Raja thought his brother was an innocent victim."

Jake felt a modicum of guilt for the Pakistani deaths. Though ten years old, the memory occupied a spot within a large carousel of ghosts that rotated through his nightmares. "Raja's brother deserved what he got, but that leaves a crew of thirty-six innocent men we killed."

"We've killed hundreds of innocent men. This is our unavoidable fate."

"I'm not defending Raja. I'm just saying I see why he could talk fifteen guys into joining him. Money–yeah. But money plus a chance to crush the guys who killed their innocent countrymen? No wonder they were motivated."

"But that was forever ago, long before I even knew you blokes. How'd they know it was you? I mean us? We are a team now, after all, and this was an attack on all of us."

"That's the nastiest part. Someone told him the truth about the *Hamza*."

Jake corrected his boss. "You mean a partial truth. The part about us sinking it, but not the part about his brother support-ing the captain's going rogue."

"Indeed. And I can only assume the purpose was to fuel this mission against us. The sum of skills required to storm the *Go-liath* is easy to find, but to gather a group of confidants for a private attack takes months, even years of recruiting. This took planning, and that leaves a puppet master unaccounted for."

Jake questioned the gap. "I thought Raja was broken. Didn't the interrogators get the puppet master's name out of him?"

"He claims to have been contacted by an anonymous source, and I've been assured all appropriate techniques were used to compel him to give a name. He said he called his contact his 'dis-tant friend' but never saw him in person." Renard inhaled from his Marlboro and then blew smoke. "This is a lead for Olivia to follow, and I'll trust her skill and hunger to uncover hid-den truths. I am frustrated, though, that the number of enemies working against me continues to rise."

"You mean working against us, mate."

"*Da*. Against us."

"Count me in, too, Pierre. You've known me long enough that I don't have to say it. All three of your commanders are loyal."

"I feel like King Arthur. You all honor me."

The conversation became subdued while the patrons ate the dried fruits. Jake ate dates and figs, filling the gap left over from his incomplete devouring of meats.

While the servers brought coffee and tea, Renard lit a new cigarette. "I believe this news ends our ordeal. I suggest you all make travel plans tonight and that we meet for breakfast to-morrow. After that, we part ways and forget about each other for weeks."

After finishing their beverages, the men stood and began to bid each other farewell. As Jake turned to say goodnight to Henri, he saw the Frenchman's back. The mechanic faced Cahill, who extended his grip.

As Henri reached outward to accept the gesture, the Austra-lian kicked the Frenchman's hand.

"Damn it, Terry! You whore! Why would you do such a thing?"

The *Goliath's* commander smiled broadly, and Jake could tell that his ace mechanic was surprised but not angry. The joviality between the formal loose acquaintances signaled a new foundation for a tighter team–a growing family.

"You offered me money back on the submarine if I could do that. And since you never specified a time limit, I want me hundred Euro."

THE END

About the Author

After graduating from the Naval Academy in 1991, John Monteith served on a nuclear ballistic missile submarine and as a top-rated instructor of combat tactics at the U.S. Naval Submarine School. He now works as an engineer when not writing.

Join the Rogue Submarine fleet to get news, freebies, discounts, and your FREE Rogue Avenger bonus chapter!

ROGUE SUBMARINE SERIES:

ROGUE AVENGER (2005)
ROGUE BETRAYER (2007)
ROGUE CRUSADER (2010)
ROGUE DEFENDER (2013)
ROGUE ENFORCER (2014)
ROGUE FORTRESS (2015)
ROGUE GOLIATH (2015)
ROGUE HUNTER (2016)
ROGUE INVADER (2017)
ROGUE JUSTICE (2017)
ROGUE KINGDOM (2018)

WRAITH HUNTER CHRONICLES:

PROPHECY OF ASHES (2018)
PROPHECY OF BLOOD (2018)

<u>John Monteith recommends his talented colleagues:</u>

Graham Brown, author of The Gods of War.

Jeff Edwards, author of Sword of Shiva.

Thomas Mays, author of A Sword into Darkness.

Kevin Miller, author of Raven One.

Ted Nulty, author of Gone Feral.

ROGUE KINGDOM

Braveship Books

www.braveshipbooks.com

The tactics described in this book do not represent actual U.S. Navy or NATO tactics past or present. Also, many of the code words and some of the equipment have been altered to prevent unauthorized disclosure of classified material.

ISBN-13: 978-1-6406203-2-2
Published in the United States of America